# The Old Gilt Clock

## A Novel

# Paulette Mahurin

Cover Design: Aspire Book Covers - https://aspirebookcovers.com/

Cover photo: Willem Arondéus, Public Domain

OTHER BOOKS BY PAULETTE MAHURIN

THE PERSECUTION OF MILDRED DUNLAP

HIS NAME WAS BEN

THE SEVEN YEAR DRESS

TO LIVE OUT LOUD

THE DAY I SAW THE HUMMINGBIRD

A DIFFERENT KIND OF ANGEL

IRMA'S ENDGAME

# DEDICATION

Dedicated to Ellen

# DISCLAIMER

The Old Gilt Clock is a work of fiction. All incidents, dialogue, and all characters, with the exception of some well-known historical figures and incidents, are products of the author's imagination and are not to be construed as real. Where real-life historical figures appear, the situations, incidents, and dialogues concerning those persons, while attempting to adhere to the historically researched facts, are fictional and are not intended to depict actual events or to change the entirely fictional nature of the work. In all other respects, any resemblance to actual persons, living or dead, events, or locales is entirely coincidental. It is of note that very little research was found regarding Willem Arondéus' earlier years up through his involvement with the Dutch resistance movement. Documentation that does exist after this time period, circa 1942, has been incorporated into the storyline. Any misrepresentations or errors from reality are the author's alone.

# INTRODUCTION

The history of World War II is replete with stories of heroism and courage. Some of the individuals who resisted the Nazis' efforts to create a new society were from historically persecuted groups, such as Jewish people and homosexuals. Willem Arondéus was one such individual who sacrificed his life to help save the lives of thousands of Jewish people. Arondéus' courage is largely forgotten by history but not by the Dutch and Jewish people.

# PROLOGUE

The day was sultry, the weather in the mid-seventies. The languid trees had celebrated a full spring of bloom, but now, well into the summer days, the rays of an August sun beat down upon them. A misty breeze floated through the humid air as men, home from work, sat on their porches with their wives, sipping cooled tea, herbal mixed liquids, and heavier more intoxicating drinks. Perspiring children ran and played, fumbling to catch a ball, wrestling a playmate or sibling, daring a friend to a race, and sharing stories, among the giggles. As the fiery sun drifted to the edge of the earth bringing on night, evening-meal dishes were cleaned and put on drying racks in kitchens, waiting to be put away. The yellowish-red colors infusing the horizon dripped down, like a watercolor painting, leaving a faint glow of shimmering purple, as day met night. It was time to ease off activities and get ready for bed.

It had been an ordinary day for most in Naarden. Quiet for all, except Catharina Arondéus who was restless, silently cursing the difficulty she'd had in the last several months, which started with extended morning sickness and night sweats. When exhaustion had given way to uterine cramping she was sent to bed by her doctor. Rest didn't ease the debilitation she felt in her heavy legs, like anchors weighing down a ship. Battered by constant physical aches and pains and the relentless commanding sounds emanating from her spouse, Catharina was at her wit's end; a taut chain ready to snap.

The inside of her head pounded, vibrating her temples and adding to an already tender scalp. Fixing two fingers to each side of her head, she rubbed to relieve the tension headache. Why was this one so hard? The earlier pregnancies had flowed like melted butter, each succeeding the prior with ease and joy. Not this one, her fifth. When the false contractions finally gave way to the cumulation of sleepless nights and fitful days and her water finally broke, she was ready for it to be over with. "They all lied," she muttered under her breath but not soft enough for her husband to not take notice.

Puffing out his proud virile chest, Hendrik Cornelis Arondéus impatiently replied to his wife's moans, "they could not have known this one would be other than the rest." He shook his head, a habit he had when disapproving.

Catharina parted her lips to speak but before another protest erupted, she was silenced.

"Be still woman and bear our child!" He stomped a foot, anger etched on his face, knuckles bent with tension. "I have a meeting to go to." He went out the hospital room door.

Bristling mad at his arrogance, his insensitive carrying-on, and bluster, to his friends through the months, about how his seed could fill all of the Netherlands, Catharina seethed that now, after nine long months, he was silencing her. Once again! Proud and loud, he boasted endlessly while his daunted wife remained sullen. She was filled with remorse and hatred toward the man who ruled her and their children. The man who took her to bed when she was tired, not in the mood, not ready, disgusted. And now, to aggravate matters, even more, the outcome of all Hendrik's carnal enforcement was stirring in her abdomen. Causing misery.

Yes, they lied. The doctors had told her it would go fast. Like the days that shorten in August, "the labor span will not be a problem," they said. They were wrong. When eight hours progressed into nine, Catharina started to panic. Finally, as the daylight hours moved to dusk and the nightlights in Naarden slowly replaced the sun's rays, her cervix opened. It had been a warm, sunny day, typical of August weather for that time of year. Catharina was relieved that the warmth of the day had dissipated and appreciated the refreshing breeze floating through a cracked window, cooling the sweat rippling down her arms. It was a short-lived respite.

"Oooooh," Catharina moaned, as the contractions increased. "Noooo, please—"

A nurse in a starchy white uniform, at Catharina's bedside, seeing her bear down, lifted her hospital gown to see how far along she was. "Don't push. It's too soon. Take a deep breath," she demandingly prickled, her lips as taut as her stiff dress. She quickly grabbed a cool compress from a bowl on a small table within her reach. Above Catharina's next scream, the nurse raised her voice to be heard as she firmly wiped the cool cloth across Catharina's brow. "It's too soon," she repeated. "Do... Not... Push!"

It was no use. Catharina's momentarily soft abdomen and relaxed uterus gave way to a rock-hard distension from the pressure building. "My back!"

Hearing the screams, a second nurse who had entered the room rushed to Catharina's side. One look at her coworker, shaking her head and she knew there was no stopping the labor from progressing way too fast to avoid ripping the patient's perineum. The new nurse's demeanor was soft and kind, in complete contrast to the snippy one at Catharina's side. "Breathe, my dear. Breathe," she entreated.

"Ooooooh, my Lord," was the last outburst from Catharina before her cervix had a chance to fully shorten, thin, adequately stretch, and dilate. Before the opening was sufficient for the baby to pass through the cervical opening and into the vaginal canal, Catharina's rock-hard pelvic muscles contracted moving the baby's head to the unopened door. Another tightening gave way to a burning, cutting, perineum tear. "Ohhhhh, God!"

Seeing the blood soak through the sheet, the pallor on Catharina's face and the fearful, pain-laden pupils that increased with each howl of pain, the congenial nurse feared the degree of the tear was serious and Catharina would need suturing. Ignoring the comments from her coworker she left to get a doctor. By the time he arrived, gloved and gowned, the head of the baby was out and Catharina was delirious.

The doctor, a tall thin man with long fingers, took a quick look. "The right shoulder…" It was not moving through the gaping laceration. "Move that over here!" he ordered, indicating a tray with surgical equipment kept in the room for emergencies, in the event a patient could not make it to the operating room.

Catharina saw the man lift what looked like a knife and saw him whisper something in a hushed tone to the nurse beside him. She tried to make out what his moving lips were saying, as his eyes became redirected from the white-starchy-uniformed woman beside him, to focus on Catharina's private area, where the painful pressure was demanding attention.

As the scalpel in his hand dug into her flesh, the doctor widened the area where the baby's head met the mother's tissue, where the baby's torso was blocked from moving. There had been no time for anesthesia. The baby needed to be removed. Fast. The bleeding needed to stop or the mother would die. When another forceful incision was made, thankfully Catharina passed out. Through rips, leaking fluid, and a mother's bloody screams turning silent, the baby entered the world.

\* \* \*

Hendrik was out having a glass of gin with Gerard, a merchant he had been negotiating a fuel deal with. "Yes, sir," he lifted his glass, spilling liquid on his pants, "that's what they're good for." Emphasizing his last statement, he nodded his head forward displacing a few strands of dampened kinky-brown hair before his attention shifted to a mildly-attractive, middle-aged waitress wearing a blue dress. Upon noticing that her ample bosom stretched the material by the top buttons, revealing a slight amount of cleavage, Hendrik disdainfully shook his head. Yet he failed to immediately avert his lingering glance off of the activity she was involved in, serving drinks to other customers. No doubt he was concentrating on her hefty bosom.

Watching Hendrik's focused eyes shift to the waitress, the hypocrisy was not lost on Gerard. It was a sentiment he understood. A wife in bed was one thing but flaunting your body in public was quite another. The latter generated a pejorative label, albeit an innuendo, while the other, entered into commonly accepted jargon. A clear delineation of a woman's role, what was acceptable and what was not.

"Don't waste the good stuff," Gerard winked, referring to the booze his business partner was wiping from the spill on his trousers.

Hendrik responded in kind, with laughter, as he swiped the loose hair from his receding hairline. Slurring, "yes, two good things. A woman in bed and a drink," he responded. "They just need to keep their mouths shut and—"

Shifting positions and leaning in, Gerard had more

important matters on his mind. "When will the contract be ready?" referring to the negotiation he was working on with Hendrik.

The two men had arranged the business meeting to discuss a project that needed to be completed but when Catharina went into labor, he had earlier said to his client, "the wife is having number five. How about a little celebration first?" Hendrik couldn't resist the opportunity to grandstand his triumphant, virile manhood.

Gerard, wanting to get a good deal, agreed to the diversion. After social chit-chat and Hendrik imbibing way too much, Gerard was frustrated with the lack of attention to business and progress with the contract at hand.

Further distractions from the busty waitress continued to grab Hendrik's concentration.

Gerard knew Hendrik was preoccupied with more than that woman and the patrons in the bar. Frustration mounting and bent on wanting to settle the negotiation details, he squirmed anxiously in his seat. Seeing Hendrik take another swallow of drink and begin to incoherently slur his words, he gave up hopes of achieving anything, today.

A few more minutes passed, in wasted silence, until Hendrik raised his glass, puckered his brow, and out came, "Toooo... bad... hafta... cut... disss... short."

Hendrik downed that last drink, whilst Gerard silently cursed the waste of time.

*   *   *

While one of the nurses took ahold of the newborn, from the doctor, the other assisted by handing the metal, surgical suture-forceps over to his gloved hand. Catharina, rousing from unconsciousness, moaned. The baby's first cry echoed through the room as the doctor's hands made haste suturing the wound. Catharina's wide-open, dark-brown eyes and dilated pupils screamed pain. Her pale complexion was drenched in sweat as her groans turned into loud hollering for the agony to stop. Never again! Whether it was from the long, agonizing, cramping pregnancy, with extended morning sickness, the sharp searing rip that burned with urine leakage, or the needle punctures during closure of the wound, Catharina had had enough. No more pregnancies! She thought of her husband, his face, the slobbering lips moving in on her as his naked body pressed against her helpless body, shifting her to belly down and having his way with her. Defeated and prone, her swollen abdomen could barely take the plunging pressure he subjected her to. His whispering something crude, about how new positions excited him, stayed with her, repeating, like a haunting vile refrain, all adding to her unrelenting nausea.

Before the doctor left the room, he ordered a nurse to place a protective pad over the wound and an antimicrobial cream to prevent infection. As he left, he commented, "a big boy," referring to the nine-pound, red-faced baby. He furrowed his brow, "there's the problem," lifting his chin to the baby, indicating his size was the reason for the long labor, delivery, and torn external genitalia.

Hours later a sobering Hendrik arrived to meet his new son. Hoisting the bundled, hefty, boy above his head, like a raised trophy, his father proudly smiled. "He's bigger than all the rest." Hendrik lowered the wrapped child and handed him to his wife.

There was no eye-contact between mother and son. Nor was there any between wife and husband. A cold chill ran through the room as Catharina heard her husband say, "my big strong boy will take after me. Willem." He wiped perspiration from his upper lip. "We will name him Willem."

Catharina, swiping a few loose strands of her long brown hair back over an ear to meet the loosened chignon at the back of her head, looked past her husband through an open window to where noises of life were vitally present. Horses carrying riders. Chatter. Laughter. Footsteps. Dainty feminine voices. Life moving through another day. A wistful tear rolled down her cheek. In the past, she had often wondered what the next day would bring. Now she didn't care.

And so, baby Willem, with light-brown hair, hazel eyes, high cheekbones, and a long thin nose atop well-defined lips entered the world. All nine pounds of his wailing and shrieking filled the room. A voice that demanded to be heard. And not forgotten.

# CHAPTER ONE

Willem's life, like all other newborns, began with the impact of his family. Also affecting Willem's life were environmental circumstances. Circumstances that would continue to influence his existence, as he grew. They went beyond his home in Naarden, way outside the boundaries of the Netherlands, in particular to Austria. To one specific youth, Adolphus Hitler, who was born on April 20, 1889 and was five-years-old when Willem was born. To understand Willem's development is to see how Hitler's years shadowed him.

Similar to conflicts Willem would have with his father, a father-son conflict existed between young Hitler and his father over the boy's refusal to adhere to strict discipline in school, resulting in beatings by his father. It is here the similar, familial, antagonistic relationships diverged for the two boys. But it is not here where their preferences differed, for both would go on to have an affinity for art and a strong desire to become an artist. Had Hitler not been overruled by his dominant father, when he wanted to attend a classical high-school and become an artist, had his father not insisted on his son attending Realschule, which taught an organized state structure, the impact on the lives of both boys would have been dramatically different. Perhaps lifepaths not filled with treacherous cliffs and valleys and certainly ones offering longer lives.

By the time Willem was four and could pick up a pencil and doodle, the distance between him and his family was as cold and wide as the North Sea. As a result, Willem sought refuge in his early scribbles of nature and animals; it was safe to relate with his verdant surroundings where bluethroats, with their brightly colored blue throat-patches, floated freely in flowering meadows of juniper filled with berries. Circular squiggles transferred from Willem's forming brain onto scraps of paper. Images of the outdoors took an early artistic form. Observations, from rare outings, substance that left calm impressions on his forming creative nature, motivated a deep-rooted, awe-inspired expression.

Squealing at his first sight of a badger drove his father to irritation; he had no patience for Willem's distractions from what Hendrik considered important for a young boy to learn. The louder the protest from his father, the more Willem sought out refuge in nature and plants, etching them in his head to transfer to paper to be put in secret places where he kept his artwork. He refused to be robbed of his fundamental essence that had a gentle leaning and expression.

It wasn't just Hendrik who forced Willem into a manner of seclusion, an inward drive, it was also the rest of the family. By the time Willem was walking and talking, the bond between his mother and other siblings and himself was irrevocably broken. Catharina's cold-shoulder treatment and worsening controlling manner, since Willem's birth, gave rise to a bitter existence for them all. The blame cast on Willem.

Despite his father's early protection of his large-bodied, baby boy, the lack of Willem meeting Hendrik's robust expectations, as the years moved on, caused Hendrik's rejection of Willem. In defiance of the rejection, Willem adhered to his passion for drawing and maintained his reflective creativity. What made Willem strong enough to adhere to his passion did not also manifest in Hitler. While Willem was steadfast, despite parental lack of support, his mother's neglect and his father's resistance to his son's less-manly conventional way, Hitler succumbed to his father's forceful attitude. The oppression Hitler received from his father's dictatorial manner would go on to mold his life. Hitler became a heartless man who would oppress and vilify those he felt were unworthy human beings. Whether the seeds of evil can be exclusively attributed to Hitler's father's suppressive nature or whether Hitler was born genetically evil can never be known. What would become undeniably evident were the tidal waves of atrocities he committed on millions upon millions of innocents. Floods of destruction that would reach all the way to the Netherlands. And Willem.

The years while Hitler's rise was incubating, when threatening storm clouds loomed over the horizons of Germany and Europe, had not been easy times for young Willem. It started with his birth and his mother's painful resolution to push away from the rest of the family and especially her newborn who had caused her so much pain. Ignoring him through the years, when Willem sought her attention and ran to her, as a toddler, for a hug, he was met with Catharina's outstretched stiff arms.

Then there was Hendrik's smothering attitude that "my boy, Willem, will grow to be virile and strong, like my other boys." Willem's brothers did not share in Hendrik's view of reality, that they should obey his every command. When they were of age, they left home for Canada. That gave rise to Hendrik's attention shifting to his last remaining son. Willem also would go on to disappoint his father by being anything but a firm, masculine presence, as he grew.

Days shifted to months and months to years. Their sub-oceanic, humid, and rainy climate, influenced by the North Sea and the Atlantic Ocean, brought cold winters and cool summers to Naarden. Frequent intense freezing winds from November to March kept a dawdling Willem indoors most of the time, improving on and expanding his artistic talents. On one particularly chilly autumn, in 1903, the young artist added words to his visual arts, composing a poem. Unrhyming, and beyond his years, it was clear to an educated eye that a serious talent lived in the body of the nine-year-old-boy. Pleased with his words; he had written what he imagined a famous painter thought of, while putting brush to canvas. He loved imagining what the minds of brilliant artists envisioned. On that particular drizzly day, as droplets pelted his bedroom window, his pleasure was interrupted by a recurring disturbing event.

"Willem," Hendrik yelled to his son, "down here now!" He had taken up arguing with his son on a regular basis, whether provoked or not. Years of frustration, from his two older sons' leaving, to his daughters following after his wife and ignoring him and a mammoth disappointment in his youngest son, his last hope, Hendrik took out his dissatisfaction on Willem. Annoying his father further, a mellow Willem puffed out his chest and took it on the chin. Courage reigned in the small, yet growing, body of the young Willem.

Standing in the open doorway, his clearly disturbed father yelled for him and waited while Willem came from his room. Looking curiously at his father, Willem raised an eyebrow. When his father elevated his voice even louder, to what clanged like a discordant piano out of tune, Willem swallowed hard. What now? He tensed but he knew what was coming.

Hendrik slammed the door behind him as he tromped into the living room. He waited a moment to be sure they were alone and that his son didn't happen to have an after-school friend visiting. Hearing a quiet house, "what have you been doing all day?" he accusatorily waved a finger in his son's face, as he moved in on him. "What!"

Willem stepped back. His chest anxiously squeezed tight around his airway as he gently squeaked out, "etching."

"Did you go to school?"

"Ye…Yes," stuttered Willem.

"Speak up. Talk like a man!"

Talk like a man. Act like a man. Be a man. Those words, a mantra, erupted from his father daily. Hammering into his son, when Willem failed to respond adequately to his commands, Hendrik's face turned red.

Willem cleared his dry throat, attempting to draw some saliva onto his tongue so it would work. Words failing him, he nodded.

Without any further comment, Hendrik smacked his lips and moved in. A quick open palm to the side of Willem's head brought a dizzying response. Hendrik stood before his stumbling boy taking no action to help him stay erect.

Willem fell backward over the arm of a couch hitting his back on the wooden side. "Ouch," he moaned, as he scrambled to come to a sitting position.

Without further words or actions, his father went to the liquor cabinet and poured himself a drink. Nothing further was said between the two of them, as the air of disgust, from father to son, permeated through the air. Watching his father quickly down a shot, Willem slithered back to his room. Pooled tears dripped from his face onto the sketches he had been working on, blurring the few words written on them. Hearing banging footsteps head to the front door and leave, he was relieved to be alone.

Eventually, his mother and sisters returned and, as if by some silent command, the girls made dinner for the family while his mother busied herself with unknown chores. The mood was like a monastery minus any uplifting religious ambiance until way beyond nightfall, when a slurring Hendrik returned demanding food and attention. He was met with a mortuary-like muteness.

To escape, Willem found ways to occupy not only his hands but his mind. Ways that would develop and guide his preferences. Ways that put him in touch with his body's longings. Ways that afforded him an escape to momentary pleasure.

# THE OLD GILT CLOCK

# CHAPTER TWO

The years moved on without much change, the divisions within the family widening, leaving Willem an island in the privacy of his bedroom. He spent the majority of his time drawing. Most of his socialization occurred at school. Also, on occasion, when he went out and ran into a neighborhood kid, he'd be invited to play catch with a ball, or engage in superficial chit-chat. On the other hand, there was virtually no social interaction between Willem and his parents or sisters. When the family did come into proximity of each other, comingling was usually done without conversation, perfunctory head nods and hand gestures for a plate to be passed at mealtime or a sweeping finger point indicating dismissal from the table were the ways the family related. Close to zero interchanges were more to Willem's liking than the caustic words his father indiscriminately spewed at him; denigrating syllables running one into the other. Indiscernible utterances from his father had increased in frequency during the years, in direct proportion to the cold chill his mother manifested when Hendrik attempted to touch her in the simplest way. A finger swept across her hand was rapidly pushed away, her body grew rigid when he approached her and so many other physical expressions added to the arctic climate the family dynamic generated, from wife to husband and spread down to the children. All had long given up on any attempts to thaw the frost.

In 1904, Willem's uneventful tenth birthday was celebrated with the same meal they had every Tuesday, Hollandse Nieuwe, with one difference being that the herring was caught a few days before by Boris, a merchant friend of Hendrik's. Due to the gift of the fish, Boris had been invited to dinner, creating a rare occasion when the family sat together at the table with another person. The herring had been prepared in the traditional Dutch manner: First, it was cleaned then de-headed followed by conserving it in salt. Served with mashed potatoes and gherkins, Willem watched the guest lift his piece of fish by its tail into the air then take a bite upwards; a tradition that turned his stomach. Give me my food on a fork in bite-size pieces! Looking askance, acid rose in Willem's mouth at the sight of saliva dripping from the sides of Boris' lips, his puffy azure eyes beaming satisfaction.

Hendrik broke through the hushed tones, offering Boris a drink. "Gin?"

Boris wiped the sides of his mouth with the back of his hand. "Sure, let's have something to wash down the meal."

Willem squeezed hold of the napkin in his lap as if attempting to stop what he knew was sure to come, another night of slurred, loud talking. Berating. Disgusting, abusive diatribe. Helpless, he moved the mashed potatoes around on his plate until a look from his mother stopped him. A look that Willem took to mean, don't aggravate your father. Eat your food. Willem wished the meal was over, as his father handed a glass of booze to the pudgy guest. The next several minutes continued quietly, without invitation to comment.

One last course. Dishes clanked in the kitchen. Catharina readied a modest dessert, a token birthday gift to the son she barely acknowledged. When she returned with a plate containing stroopwafel that she had purchased in a store on her way home from work with the girls, Hendrik was back at the liquor cabinet. The dish and smaller plates were placed on the table but before anyone could have a serving, Hendrik handed a hefty sized drink to Boris. Slurping from his own, he motioned to the pastry, "have as many as you like," he said to Boris.

Willem counted the number of cookies on the plate. Six. One for each. Not wanting to intercede between his father and Boris, he looked at his mother, whose neck muscles were visibly knotted. Having none of it, she shot her husband a look, grabbed hold of the plate and passed one each to everyone at the table.

The only pleasure, for Willem, was the cookie; waffles made from baked batter, sweet syrup oozing out the sides of the filling. Willem's mouth watered as he tasted the combination of butter, flour, yeast, milk, brown sugar, and eggs. Another couple of drinks were poured and tongues loosened. The men chatted while Willem and the rest finished in silence, excused themselves and left.

Gulping down his third drink, Boris commented, "the fishing was good." He swiped a hand across his rounded cheek, wiping away rivulets of perspiration streaming from his forehead.

"Too bad it's not for many months during the year," replied Hendrik, who knew that May through July was the best time to catch herring with the other months being slim pickings.

"So," Boris lowered his voice. "Any news on the contract negotiations with Japan?" He sipped his fourth gin, the sting now gone from his numb tongue. An indication that he'd had enough. It wasn't enough, however, to loosen his vocal cords and be heard outside of the room.

Willem lingered just outside the door to the dining room, straining to hear the mumbling but to no avail, finally giving up and going to his room. What Willem missed hearing was a conversation about his father and Boris negotiating a fuel deal with Japan.

Imperialistic conflict had been building between Japan and Russia over their rival goals concerning Manchuria and Korea. While Japan was attempting to negotiate a distribution of the area, an inflexible Russia failed to withdraw from Manchuria and moved into North Korea. Russia was betting against Japan reacting. It felt that were Japan to engage in armed conflict it would be defeated. To Russia's surprised humiliation, Japan severed diplomatic relationships with Russia and very shortly after, without a declaration of war, attacked a Russian port, restraining the Russian fleet. Boris, in consort with Hendrik, wanted in on the action.

"Good relations exist with Japan and I've no issue with helping them." Hendrik cleared his throat. "We've no diplomatic restrictions with them."

"True," responded Boris. "Japan, much to the chagrin of the Russians, has been victorious."

Their conversation continued into the night as Willem took to sketching and Catharina and the girls went to bed. Replaying the looks passed around earlier at the dinner table, Willem thought of the silent hostility in his mother's eyes intentionally averted from Hendrik. The continued trouble between them was something that Willem never fully understood. So much bitterness. He hated confrontation, arguments, whether overt like the escalating controlling manner of his father or covert like the quiet hostility and rejection levied by his mother. Willem abhorred war of any kind, subtle and domestic, in the home or outright nation to nation, in battle. In the past, the mere mention of the Russo-Japanese War, or any fighting, sickened him. Bloodshed, bodily harm, lost lives went against Willem's gentle nature.

Willem slept fitfully that night awakening before sunrise in a cold sweat. Something was troubling him that he couldn't quite put his finger on. It had started with his father demanding he do more manly activities. Why his father protested Willem's interest in his art was a mystery to Willem. Why can't he accept what I want to do? I don't want to do sports, he reflected back on his father's urgings. Hendrik wanted Willem to mirror his concept of male virility; that a boy should be involved in sports and rugged outdoor activities, not things girls do, like art. What Willem could not fully articulate at this early age was that he was okay with who he was and that he felt there was nothing wrong with the incipient male virility stirring in his body. In fact, Willem liked the dawning of his sex drive and that on the edge of becoming a teenager, a man, much excited him. Much also stirred in his subconscious that came in nighttime dreaming, adventures spurring exploration.

The next morning, feeling unrested, Willem readied himself for school. The distance to where his schooling took place was a few blocks from his house; it was a stretch of time when he enjoyed being outside and communing with nature. Not always appreciating the destination, the education system didn't appeal to him. It had been hammered into him by his father and the teachers who taught him, that attending school was compulsory until he turned twelve years old. "You get your education and you succeed," demanded his father along, with other commanding tirades Hendrik projected onto his son. Willem paid no mind to the forceful admonitions, for even though he didn't like school, he was a sharp, bright student who did very well. He wouldn't be accused of dropping out because of poor grades or being a failure. No, when he was ready to move onto his own path, it would be from a position of success. Do what you can, do your best whether you like it or not, was an attitude he cultivated at a young age. At times, entertaining a positive attitude was all he could do to combat his father and to control what came at him, the things he had no control over, from domineering adults. Not wanting to be like his father or other forceful friends his father brought home, he ruminated on who he wanted to emulate. Plant your own acorns and grow into a fortified English oak tree, be yourself. Lead yourself, he had read in a book. It spoke to him. While he was yet to grow to capacity and fully realize who that self was, he excelled in his curriculum.

While he did well in his studies, Willem was slow to make friends, his first two, Daan and Birgit, happened by chance. It was a school day like all others until on his walk up the school entrance, Willem noticed a three-pawed limping dog. A mere thirty-pounds fit tightly on its skeletal body, as it sniffed around for what must have been dropped scraps of food. A thumping pang in his chest, an empathy Willem felt with wounded creatures, seeing the tangled, matted, long-haired dog with bald, mange-encrusted patches, he reached into his lunch bag and took out half of the herring sandwich he had made for himself the night before. Clicking his tongue to his teeth, he made a sound to draw the dog's attention to the dangling food in his hand. The part-keeshond appearing canine was very hesitant. Frozen, with its tail-down, wide-eyed, a black and silver furry face with small triangulated pointed ears stared at the offering.

Sensing it was afraid, Willem moved closer to the scared animal and in a soft tone said, "it's okay." A closer look discerned the dog was a male. "It's okay, boy." Willem gently lowered the half-sandwich to the ground and stood back. "Go on, boy... I won't hurt you." He stepped back further but stayed put to ensure the meal went to the hungry dog.

As other students headed into the building, a few glances passed Willem's way. He slowly turned and maneuvered himself onto the ground with his back to the dog. He'd read that eye contact with a dog can appear intimidating, frightening them away. Waiting, Willem ignored a few giggles directed at him. Leaves crunched on the ground as the dog approached. More stillness from behind and finally Willem felt the body heat of the dog on his back. One quick swallow and he was gone.

That day in class Willem doodled a sketch of the dog. Its eyes. Its wedge-shaped face, a medium muzzle with a definite abrupt halt to it. Its whole body, with attention to detail – a tightly curled tail, the protruding ribcage and dense, knotted coat thinned on its legs. As the teacher lectured on the subject of a book the class was to be assigned to read, all eyes faced forward. Except Willem's and one other student. Lars, the gruff, overweight, blond sitting beside him looked at what Willem had etched and smirked. The conceited, smug look needed no words. A glance at the boy with the shifty, almond-shaped eyes, Willem put his pencil down and shifted his attention to the front of the class. He took a deep breath to release the distressing muscle-tightening in the back of his neck.

At lunch break, the play-yard was cluttered with students grabbing seats on benches, sitting on the ground under a tree, for shade from the sun and standing, looking around, mulling over where to sit for their lunch. The few missing had headed for the indoor dining hall, used during winter months. Today was warm, the sun was high in the clear, cloudless sky and Willem wanted to breathe fresh air away from the stuffy interior. As he approached the outside and looked around, he headed back to the area where earlier he had fed the dog, hoping to see it again.

The shade of a tree had kept the ground cool where Willem sat to have his lunch, near pawprints where the dog had dug into the spongy dirt. He liked the feel of the earth beneath him, the firmness of the ground; next to a tree felt safe. Away from brittle comments with finger-pointing undertones, outside he felt free. He took out what remained of his lunch; half a sandwich and a pear. Interrupted by the sound of something hitting a bush behind him, Willem saw Lars and another kid named Thomas throwing stones.

"Looky here, Thomas," snickered Lars, his teeth showing and eyes lit up like a hissing cat.

Thomas, cast a curious, narrow-eyed look at his friend. "Huh?"

Lars motioned with an upturned chin for Thomas to look at Willem.

"I see him, Lars."

Lars moved closer and stood before Willem with clenched fists.

An anxious flush drew claws over Willem's back, the trouble before him was obvious. Refusing to be intimidated, he stood.

"Little sissy artist here, doesn't like to pay attention in

class," poked Lars. "Too bad we missed hitting that crippled mutt."

A stabbing pain moved to Willem's gut. The dog must have returned for food and the two pompous asses saw him first. Throwing rocks at a dog! Willem stood up straighter, making himself appear taller than his five-foot-nine-inch height. He knew that Lars saw his drawing and that the smug-teasing-superior grin on his face let Willem know he didn't approve. He must have joked about it to Thomas. The brow-beaters weren't satisfied picking on other students, they took it further with the handicapped dog. And that was one step way too far for Willem. "Strong boys have to pick on an innocent, crippled dog?" challenged Willem, as he held his position, now mere inches from the rotund, overpowering Lars and the medium, muscularly-built Thomas.

"A wise guy," Lars said to Thomas. Before anyone responded, Lars, rounded a fist onto Willem's left cheek.

Willem, stumbling to the boys' laughter, reached out for the tree behind him to right himself. Before he could say or do another thing the two bullies walked off, with Lars mumbling, "no one messes with me."

"Yah, especially not a sissy!"

Off in a far corner, two other kids – Daan and Birgit – watched the whole incident, with keen attention.

## CHAPTER THREE

A three-inch, pink, circular welt had formed on Willem's cheek, the imprint from where the bully's punch had landed. His high cheekbone felt as hard as dried oil paint. Rubbing the tender area, Willem saw two students from his class moving toward him. The looks on both of their faces, their soft, concerned eyes, told Willem they meant no harm. Just then, rustling leaves drew Willem's attention to a motion in the bush where patches of silvery and black hair peeked through a few bare branches. Not wanting to scare off the dog, Willem held up his palm to stop Daan and Birgit.

Daan nodded an understanding, as he took hold of Birgit's arm for her to stay put. They watched Willem reach for a partially eaten sandwich.

The dog's brown eyes, wide and fixated on the motion of Willem's hand, were distracted by a cough from Birgit. Up went its hackles. Its tail lowered, backing up. Willem's outstretched arm held the dangling food and, hoping he could coax it back, he slowly stepped forward but to no avail. He threw the herring and bread into a cloud of dust. Foliage swayed, as Willem dug a frustrated foot into the ground. "Blazes!" All he wanted to do was show a little kindness to a hungry animal and what did it get him? A smack to his face and name-calling; being referred to as sissy was an accusation that made his skin crawl. None of it, the unwarranted and uninvited wrath of hatred directed at him and the innocent animal, was new to him.

Daan and Birgit cautiously approached, moving slowly toward Willem, whose posture was now as stiff as a tree trunk.

Wanting to offer support, Daan lifted a hand to Willem's back. A sorrowful heavy heat permeated through the connection. "Don't let them get to you."

"Yes, don't…" Birgit's expressive, brown, pleading eyes shimmered with wetness. The round-faced blond leaned in toward Willem, her breaths shallow, her soft posture matched her speech. "They're not worth it."

Shaking his head, Willem was at a loss for words.

"That was nice what you did for that dog," she said.

A deep sigh, followed by another, then, "I just don't understand why some people have to be so mean," said Willem. "Me, I can take it. But, to…" he looked back toward the bush, where moments before the dog stood drooling in anticipation of a meal, too crestfallen to finish. But it wasn't just about the dog. No, it went way deeper than one incident. It was the latest in a long chain of moments that played out in Willem's mind. Mean spirited words. Hateful hand slaps. No one to talk with.

"Yes," she paused. Birgit knew that this strange boy, an obvious loner, was in a bad way. An empathetic girl, she had to do something, just like Willem had to do something about the dog. "Yes, it's awful what some kids do. Really awful. Then they grow up to be mean adults! It never ends."

Again, it was something in her voice, an inherent resonance of understanding that rang through Willem's body and in that communion, she got through to him, again. "True," he half-smiled.

A sweet sound of silvery intonation, a gentle pat on his back, plus an offer from Daan of some of his leftover lunch and the ambiance shifted. The cave of isolation had cracked open allowing in the sun, a hundred rays of sunlight and with this change, Willem relaxed.

Tall, lanky Daan, with stiff-short-cropped black hair, and inset, cat-like, amber eyes, the right one drifting in toward his nose, moved closer to Willem. "I have extra food… my mom," he laughed, "thinks I'm undernourished." Just about to say something more his attention was caught by Willem's staring.

Willem's face flushed, darkening the forming bruise. Feeling caught in an uncomfortable situation, he stepped back.

Familiar with people reacting to his eye defect, Daan pointed to his lazy eye. "This—"

Embarrassed, and not understanding what Daan was about to communicate, Willem lowered his head and turned to leave, to avoid what he perceived would be something unpleasant. Avoidance was how he coped. Learned from his mother, the acquired-reflex response was automatic.

"Wait, don't go," Daan reached for Willem's arm. "My

eye… what I was about to say to you a minute ago, it doesn't bother me if someone notices it. I'm used to that."

Once again, in the short time the three had been together, Willem had been put at ease. No sharp edge in the utterances, no unspoken, dismissive, insulting insinuations, no tongue-wagging disapprovals, none of that came from this encounter. Nothing morose. He was used to morose, expected morose, and to those living in a morose household, even the taste of honey was bitter. Today there was a sweet sense of nectar in the air. He relaxed, to the background description of what Daan described as lazy-eye and something about the eye and brain not working together. When he's home, he uses a patch so he's forced to use the weaker eye and eventually it should get better. "I won't wear a patch during school, though," he smiled. "Can you imagine how Lars would treat me if I looked like a pirate."

Birgit laughed, inciting Daan and Willem to join in.

Daan, still holding his leftover lunch, repeated, "do you want any?"

Still grinning, "thank you but I'm not hungry." Plus, Willem signaled to his lunch bag, "I still have my pear."

"Are you going to eat that," joked Birgit.

"If you want it," Willem held out the pear.

"That's sweet of you but I was just kidding."

A lightness had eased into the conversation inviting Daan to take a liberty. "That was really something, what you did to them. Stood up for yourself and—"

"Daan," Birgit elbowed him, "how about asking him how he is?" Instinctively, she reached for the darker-red, broken-blood-vessels mark on Willem's face, just below his left eye, a couple of millimeters from dangerously damaging his vision. Willem's head jerked back causing Birgit to lower her outstretched arm. "I'm sorry—"

Willem, used to being quiet, accustomed to being alone, not having any friends to speak to, not wanting to bring anyone home to his unfriendly family, broke from his usual reticence when he saw the hurt on Birgit's face. "It wasn't anything, really," referring to what Daan originated. "Those guys... I just automatically responded. Nothing to take credit for. And this," he pointed to his bruised cheek, "it doesn't hurt."

"Well, we beg to differ. Other kids just don't stand up to Lars and his crowd," replied Daan.

"That's true," added in Birgit. "You know they rule the school. Pick on whoever they choose to and it's usually kids like us," she motioned to Daan.

"We're targeted because we have intellectual and academic pursuits." Disgusted, Daan shook his head and continued, "but then isn't that what school is for? The upside, the teachers like us."

Birgit nodded agreement. "Enough of that," she held out her hand, "We haven't been formally introduced, I'm Birgit. And this here genius is Daan."

In the few moments he had already shared with Daan and

Birgit, he began to learn what it was to make friends. "Willem," he smiled, loosening knotted ropes of tightened muscles in his back. The way Birgit's eyes lit up when she thoughtfully introduced them, as if an invitation to a friendship, brightened the day.

The last to return to class, the three were smiling and laughing. It felt good. It was a buffer from oppressive Lars. The power of three yielded a good result, for Lars left them alone. Seeing him, Willem reflected back on the incident with Lars and his sycophant follower, Thomas. Predators, he thought, no different than any other beast of prey, their victim a lone student, someone they must have thought was vulnerable, who they could overpower. They were wrong in hunting down Willem, thinking they could attack him and get away with it. Seeking superiority over Willem had fallen flat. Lars may have hurt Willem's flesh but he didn't impact his spirit, for he was not someone easily intimidated. Immune from his father's abuse and mother's neglect, instead of pushing him down several rungs on the self-confidence ladder, to cowering enslavement, Lar's abuse proofed Willem up. No, it didn't turn out as well for the two tormenters as they anticipated, for standing in the middle of the classroom joking about the queer loner they took care of, Willem had walked in, with his chest puffed out, cozy with the class intellectuals who had the teacher's protection.

A few minutes after the teacher started to explain the lesson for the afternoon, Willem noticed a stain on his pants. He recognized it was from the herring in his sandwich which dripped when he threw it for the dog. He thought of that skinny pup with protruding ribs, malnourishment evident by its wobbly bowed legs. He fought an urge to find an excuse to leave the room, to go back out and look for it. To ease his own misplaced guilt that he didn't do more for it but what more could he have done. Maybe tomorrow?

When the lesson was over and school was out for the day, the three new friends walked home together. "I'm glad we live close to each other," said Willem referring to an earlier mention at lunch about where their homes were. A block, in silence, to gain distance from the schoolhouse, Willem asked, "you're not bothered by Lars and Thomas? I mean, not bullied?"

"Oh, it bothers us," Daan side-looked at Birgit then put his attention back to Willem, "I just don't show it. Right, Birgit?"

"Um-hum."

"What's the good of trying anything with them?" replied Daan.

That made sense to non-confrontational Willem. Matured early by necessity, having to fend for himself, he was emotionally advanced for his age. It also seemed that he'd just met two similarly rational, mature kids.

The next morning when the three returned to school together, Willem stayed back while Daan and Birgit went ahead into the building. He went to look for the dog in hopes of giving it another meal. Not finding it, or any traces it had returned, Willem went to class. He never saw that dog again.

*   *   *

A couple of years passed, during which bullying Lars and his clan of hoodlums moved on to other victims to torture, leaving Willem, Daan, and Birgit to continue to cultivate their deepening relationship. As they got to know each other, close bonds were formed and when not in school they enjoyed their time together in Naarden.

On one summer's day, walking past stone and brick homes and businesses spiral-tower architecture, they came to the towering Grote Kerk where Daan attended Sunday service with his parents.

"The Great Church," Daan craned his neck to look up to the top of the massive structure. "Have you ever been in it, Willem? Look at that spire. How did they do that back so long ago?"

They'd never discussed religion or religious buildings even with having passed by Grote Kerk before. It was odd, that now, after all this time, Daan stopped to talk about the structure. Willem was reluctant to bring up anything about religion, the fact that in consort with his family barely spending any time together they were not religious nor did they attend church.

Daan looked at Birgit.

"Being Jewish, I've never been inside, so no thank you," Birgit smiled.

Willem let out a sigh, refreshing and calming. "Oh, I see," he smiled. Now feeling more at ease, he continued, "my family... I don't go to church. Religion just isn't…"

Sealing their bond, Birgit picked up the slack in the conversation. "We're not religious either. Not practicing, I mean. My father works too much, that's what he's dedicated to—"

"A banker," piped in Daan. "Owns and runs one of our largest—"

"Enough," interrupted Birgit, not wanting to boast directly or indirectly about her father's position. Growing up, it had been a no-discussion topic in front of the children. When her father shared his business privately with his wife, Birgit's younger brother took to snooping and shared what he had learned with her. What Birgit knew from clandestine communications between her parents, as relayed through a nosy, prying nine-year-old, surprised her. Somehow, his being a wealthy bank owner was tied to their religion. What made this an even greater oddity was the word anti-Semitism kept coming up, which made absolutely no sense to her. Birgit's confusion intensified when her brother returned one night with a wild fable-like story that she was sure was his fanciful imagination incited through sleepy ears. Seeing Daan open his mouth to respond, his words fell on mute ears and she drifted back.

"That's enough of your nonsense," she protested.

"It's true," he demanded. "I swear to you, it's what I heard."

Sounding so convincing, it made her flesh tingle. "Okay, slow down. Tell me again exactly what you heard."

"Something about auntie seemitzm spreading through

Europe." The smell of perspiration rose from his pajamas.

"Go on."

"I remembered that the auntie person is Jewish. But she doesn't like Jews. Oh yeah, and some soldier who is Jewish just got out of prison. In France that happened. Even though he was freed, a lot of people don't like him just 'cause he's Jewish."

"This is too bizarre to believe. You've never lied to me before—"

"I'm not lying!" he spat back at her. His arms waved like a bird trying to escape danger. Loudly slamming a foot down on the carpeted floor, "I'm not, I tell you, I'm not!"

The commotion was interrupted by their father bounding through Birgit's bedroom door. "What's all this noise about," questioned Ernst Levin. A five-foot-seven-inch, slimly built man, he had a commanding matter-of-fact voice, even when pointing a finger, with his neck veins pulsating from annoyance. Controlled, he was a learned man who knew how to deal with people, including his family.

Ben, anticipating what was to come - punishment for snooping, turned pale. Trepidation covered his face, bleached of all color. Holding his lips tight, he waited for his sister to answer.

Birgit gave Ben a look; she was annoyed that it was up to her to explain. There would be no protecting her big-mouth brother now. "Father..." Struggling to find the right words to gain clarification, conflict arose over how to soften it to lessen her brother's punishment, for she was sure discipline would be following.

"Speak," Ernst unfolded his bent arms from his chest to invite a response.

"He," she nudged her brother's shoulder, "accidentally overheard you and mother talking."

"Overheard?" Ernst's eyebrows came together suspiciously. "Where?"

"Does it matter, father?"

"Yes, Birgit. Now out with it."

Without any further filter on her thoughts, words, or concern for her brother, "who's auntie seemitzm," she phonetically replicated what she'd earlier heard.

"Auntie who?" Ernst wasn't quite sure he'd heard what he thought he had.

"Some auntie through Europe that doesn't like Jews."

"Anti-Semitism?"

"Yes, that's it. Something about a French soldier—"

Ernst's attention turned to his son, now standing behind Birgit. "Ben, step out from your sister's shadow." Before explaining to his children what he'd been talking about with his wife, about the Dreyfus exoneration in France, the spreading of anti-Semitism in Europe, and why it's a topic for adults to be whispered behind closed doors, he admonished his son for eavesdropping. "No more! Do you hear and understand me!"

Ben, facing his father, nodded yes.

"Your young mouth can bring danger to our doors! No

more, Ben! I mean it!"

Birgit would later learn from her father about the conversation that transpired between her father and mother after he left her and Ben.

Back in his bedroom with his wife, a distressed Ernst rubbed the nape of his neck. "Gabriel, Ben overheard us talking about the Dreyfus exoneration. He most likely also listened in when I told you about the new anti-Semitism wave sweeping across Europe," he said, referring to racial anti-Semitism, which started as an expansive Weltanschauung and conviction of the superiority of the white race over other races. In this rapidly spreading belief, Jews were considered an inferior race, with emphasis on non-European ancestry and culture. The most alarming part was the "conspiracy theory," he called it when mentioning, "a crazy connivance from ignorant factions promoting a malicious deception that the Jewish people want world economic domination."

"How it is possible, these falsehoods?" Fogged with worry, she removed her eyeglasses to wipe them clear. Beads of sweat ran down her forehead. "It is all too frightening. Way too close to home that they are targeting the Rothschilds."

Fresh in their memory, it had only been a year since the tidal wave of persecution during the 1905 Russian Revolution sent thousands of Jews to their early graves and millions fleeing to America and other countries. The ripple effect racing across Europe lived on, threating to ignite another tsunami of devastating pogroms. Yes, the Rothschilds were a target of the dangerous rumors, which brought it too close to another major European banking family, namely the Levins of the Netherlands, Ernst Levin, more precisely.

"…a storekeeper, carpentry tools," said Daan, talking about his father's work.

Daan's words came back into focus, the swirling memory remaining in Birgit's coiled stomach. Religion was not a topic to be loosely discussed.

# THE OLD GILT CLOCK

## CHAPTER FOUR

While incipient hostilities, against Jews, in Europe were fomenting, another year passed. And three more. By 1910 when Willem turned sixteen, much had changed in the world. Built for ordinary people, the masses, the Ford Model-T made headlines. Also impacting a vast number of people, the worst earthquake in European history, the Messina earthquake and tsunami, took place in Italy killing over 80,000 people. Another influencing factor that would change the lives of millions was a twenty-one-year-old Adolf Hitler being exposed to racist rhetoric in Vienna. Populists exploiting virulent anti-Semitism, to forward German nationalism absorbed Hitler's attention. Rumors spread of covert atrocities, one Jew at a time. Before long, a harmful event hurled against one Jewish man, woman, or child would escalate to include many others.

While the impact of the spreading animus wove its cancerous fingers into clusters of populist cults, fearful Jews limited their talk to bedrooms and secret parlors, not to be overheard as what had occurred earlier with Ben. Children were to be protected by all means possible, to not terrorize the peaceful-minded innocents. Additionally, their innocent mouths could not be trusted. "Why stir up trouble when this too shall pass," proclaimed Ernst to Gabriel. Despite clandestine adult discussions out of earshot from Birgit, her ears were not immune from the spreading rumors. A horrific thunderous blackness on the distant horizon was brewing a storm, indiscriminate winds were circling and building a force. Would it pass, as Ernst had proclaimed?

Birgit's source of information, regarding the scourge racing through Europe, came from Daan and Willem, who weren't protected from news to the same degree. Not aware of the whirlwind ahead, yet several years from touching down, piecemeal sharing occurred along with other activities between them. Birgit's response to the hearsay being spread about in newspapers, what she was sure was trashy folklore – just as she had earlier dismissed what her brother told her that he'd overheard a few years back – was that it was silly, ridiculous blather. It reminded her of Lars and how he mouthed off nonsense to frighten kids. "It's just some mean-spirited rumormongers with nothing better to do than pick on someone else," she'd dismissively profess, with a swift back-fling of her hand. With that, her interest would instantly shift to what any normal sixteen-year-old would find interesting. "How about a hike today?"

"Where do you want to go?" replied Daan.

Knowing Willem had been involved in developing his art through the years and now loved to paint, she suggested, "let's find a nice spot for Willem to capture in paint."

Willem appreciated that his friends expressed a liking for his proclivity toward anything artistic – drawing, painting, and of late, jotting a few poetic words down on paper. "I know just the spot. Gooyergracht." He indicated a place that was dug in the mid-1300s to demarcate the border with the adjacent province and the river Vecht. Willem loved the higher, sandy, lavishly-green forested area, with flowing estuaries, tributaries, and rivers. He loved sketching water landscapes, interpreting them into a hybrid of conventional and symbolic forms. From his early years, he was impressed by the design of furniture – curves, surfaces, geometric configurations, differing textures, and colors. He loved colorful textiles with designs typical of the art during that time period, a blending of Art Deco with some hangover from Art Nouveau. During his mid-teen years, Willem's work matured like a dragonfly, from a crusty-humped, dull-brown pest into an iridescently-brilliant, flying adult. He loved to sit in nature and transform what he saw into writhing figures and clustered architecture. With his friends, he was able to fly free like the dragonfly, letting his passion blossom.

A long walk to the destination, a stopover for an hour or two and by end of the return walk back it ensured they were all exhausted. It lent to a peaceful night's sleep. The days continued like that, with modifications added to the routine, a bicycle ride, a visit to a museum, and on one particular day, Daan decided he wanted to go to the Spaanse Huis. The Spanish House was situated at Turfpoortstraat 27, not a long walk from their collective homes.

None of them having ever been there, Daan read up on its history and came ready, a wealth of information. "It was originally a church," he strode by Willem's side as a disinterested Birgit fell behind. Ignoring her diverted attention, Daan continued, "it was converted to a home for migrants…"

When Birgit heard the word massacre, she quickened her step, "What'd you just say?"

"Hundreds were gathered to hear a peace proposal from the Spanish but the place was surrounded by Spanish troops… you know, during the Eighty Years War—"

"The Eighty Years what!" Astonished by what she had heard, she couldn't believe her ears.

Daan doubled back on the commentary he had just explained. "The Dutch War of Independence… multiple provinces against Spain. Spain played dirty," he went on to tell her, repeating himself to Willem, "that's when 700 inhabitants assembled to hear a peace proposal, that the Spanish fired on them. In a converted church no less!" Tight-fisted, drawn-back rigid shoulders, his flesh ached when he added, "after they fired on the citizens and then killed every remaining man, woman, and child in Naarden, the despicable soldiers went and burned down the town."

Suddenly the air smelled like a thousand spent bullets. "That's horrible," moaned Birgit. She sniffed in the mucus running from her nose and as if she was having an allergic reaction to the topic of discussion, her eyes itched. "I hate hearing things like that. How could anyone… innocent people—"

Willem, being averse to war and mindful of what he'd read and heard about horrible things happening to Jews, thought he should say something. Side glancing at Birgit and then to Daan, he asked, "do you really think that'd be the best place for us to visit?"

"I think you just took us on a mental journey there. That's enough for me," said Birgit, rubbing her right eye until it was bloodshot.

Feeling the mild backlash, a chagrined Daan pulled at his ear, a habit he had when he had said something he'd wished he hadn't. When absorbed in a new topic he had learned about, he liked to share, whether his information was invited or not. Once he started, it was difficult to shut him up. Not easily making and holding friends, he often wondered if one of the reasons was his proclivity for didactic messaging.

To Daan's pull back and averted eyes, Birgit responded with an understanding light in hers. "I still love you."

Love. Not a word Willem often heard. In fact, he was hard-pressed to recall any time it was said in his home. He wondered what it meant, not just the word but the fact. He'd pondered it in simple poetry. Jotted notes. Daydreams. But he couldn't find a definition that came organically – from the depths of his body, where love resides. A squeezing confinement usually felt around his heart, felt less so with Daan and Birgit, which generated the notion that perhaps he was beginning to love them. Entertaining the thought, their friendship is loosening my heart, expanded his chest even more. Caught up in his reverie, he considered the possibility that intuition was the door he needed to walk through, to discover who to trust and take a chance with. It wasn't a new concept but up until now it had existed in reverse, instinct had told him who to close himself off from when protective emotional boundaries were needed to allow him to breathe. Hearing Daan clear his throat, a sensation moved through Willem. Suddenly, his body no longer felt like a forgotten loaf of bread, hard to penetrate.

"So then, a hike?" smiled Daan.

Willem looked at his friend, the vibrancy of sun reflecting in his short black hair, sparkling-jeweled, shining amber eyes and the way the right eye turned inward like it was talking to the left. What Willem saw, not just in Daan's face but Birgit's as well, was life, rhythmically pulsating, right to his heart. He saw them not only through his dilated, black pupils surrounding his hazel irises but with his skin, his arms, his legs, abdomen, every inch of his organism. Looking around, he also saw buildings. The fractures on stonework. Tiny details. Trees with cracked, lined limbs, minute grooves from footprints of aging. Flowering plants spreading perfume as petals of magenta, gold, and crimson floated to earth. Experiencing an awesome amazement, he felt his asleep senses, which had been numbed since his birth, beginning to wake up.

Through the streets, into the verdant wooded area, they strolled and the day moved on. Three friends sharing a grand day.

Not all days would be so grand.

*　　*　　*

Through the years, as Willem's friendship with Birgit and Daan grew, he risked it and invited them to his home to study. It was the fact of being friends with them that Willem decided to stay in school, that he could continue his art and enjoy his studies. This was to his father's liking. Also, to Hendrik's liking, was the fact that his son was now friends with the daughter of Ernst Levin, the Jewish banker.

Willem never understood the change in his father, which started shortly after he brought his friends home. It was after one of their first visits when Hendrik stopped hovering over his son, giving him space to do his art. On that day his father was home and Willem had introduced his friends to him. What Willem didn't know, was that it was also on that day that things changed. Hendrik overheard Birgit mention who her father was. Willem would never find out that his father's altered behavior was a self-serving agenda.

Hendrik was sly in his covert manner; his modus operandi to ingratiate himself to anyone who could benefit him. Salesmanship and currying favors got him loans, contracts, and status. Ernst Levin had the money-power Hendrik needed, the backing for a business he sought to succeed in, with higher productivity. The fuel industry didn't come cheaply. He set an appointment to meet with Levin.

The bank was busy and Levin was in a hurry when Hendrik entered the large, simply-done, but-elegant-to-a-discerning-eye office, it was not what Hendrik anticipated. He expected a conspicuous display of wealth. "Very nice office you have," he murmured as he held out a hand to Levin, sure he hadn't overdone the syrupy tone.

A handshake and motion for Hendrik to have a seat brought a one-sided conversation on the need for a loan. It remained one-sided until Hendrik mentioned, "you have a lovely daughter, Mr. Levin." Mr. Levin! Kowtowing to that man turned his stomach.

Surprised by the mention of Birgit, Ernst Levin sat up straighter. Leaning into his desk, the bored, dull glint left his eyes. "You know my daughter?"

"She's friends with my son," Hendrik gladly revealed, "Willem."

The shift in Levin's demeanor was instantaneous, relaxing back into his chair. The sound of leather beneath him quieted as he now spoke with a lilt to his words. "Willem is your boy?" He hadn't made the connection earlier; he was too preoccupied with other business. He knew of the Arondéus family. Without waiting for an answer, he continued, "a fine lad he is. Comes around with Birgit and Daan to study. The three of them seem to have taken a fondness to each other."

Biting the side of his cheek, Hendrik had to prevent himself from outright smiling. His ploy was working. "Yes, I might add the same about your girl. A very fine young lady."

More chit-chat ensued about their children before Hendrik excused himself to look at his pocket watch, a planned moment. "I have another appointment and I know how busy you are. So—"

"Yes, yes, indeed. About that loan…"

Hendrik held his breath.

"I think we can do business, Mr. Arondéus."

Hendrik slowly exhaled through his pursed lips, shook hands with Levin, exited the building, and danced home to find Willem, Daan, and Birgit studying. Listening at the closed door for a minute, he thought twice about saying anything concerning his meeting with Levin. That Jew girl will find out soon enough.

# THE OLD GILT CLOCK

## CHAPTER FIVE

Whenever Daan and Birgit visited and Hendrik was home, he made it a point to discreetly eavesdrop. Having already established an amicable working relationship with Birgit's father, he wondered what else he would learn from overhearing the kids' conversations. Most days all Hendrik heard was uninteresting prattle about some new treatment for diabetes, or the International Peace Bureau winning the Nobel Peace Prize, and other silliness, like some powered flight taking place in Australia by a man named Houdini. Yes, to Hendrik, it was all ridiculous, meaningless babble until Birgit mentioned her father. "He'll be away for a few days," she waxed enthusiastically, her elevated, excited tone easier for Hendrik to hear.

That man has capitalized on the rise of European materialism, Hendrik antagonistically thought, fingers of jealousy crawling over his skin, for he desperately wanted in on the action. That selfish, money-grubbing Jew. Hendrik, never satisfied with his income that was more than enough, coveted the millions that he imagined Levin had gotten his hands on. Willem's new friend, the pretty, little brown-eyed, blond would come in handy once again.

When Levin returned, Hendrik, hiding his selfish motive, went to Levin to ask if it was alright for him to take the kids to a museum.

Smiling to himself, in hand-rubbing-together anticipation, he thought of all the world events he could cash in on. After all, revolutions brought war and that meant money was to be had for fuel. Specifically, in mind was a brewing uprising in Portugal. He pondered what he had heard about the restless Portuguese masses planning a coup d'état to overthrow the old monarchy. Hendrik was in on the hushed gossip; it was his business to search out ventures that would serve his wallet. On his way out of his house, he looked at the door to Willem's bedroom, glad his son had indirectly opened the path to Levin's bank vault.

Permission was gained from Ernst and an outing taken with the children. The reward, Hendrik also succeeded in obtaining another loan to satisfy a fuel demand he needed to fulfill. It was beneficial for both father and son for while Hendrik succeeded, so did Willem, in pursuing his art without further protest. The more his father left him alone, the greater the talent that stroked from his hand. Sketches, drawings, paintings, abounded. Willem shared them with his friends, gifting them with special pieces they had inspired. Unbeknownst to Willem, Birgit showed his art to her father who had a keen eye and appreciation for the arts and owned a few pieces from the old masters.

"You have quite a talent, son." Ernst encouraged Willem to continue on with his art. Support from a father figure was a great boon for Willem, one he hoped would last. Cheered and inspired he kept at his craft, balancing it with school and activities with his two best friends.

Despite the lull in the father-to-son dictatorship, Hendrik couldn't keep his prejudiced, caustic words to himself. One night he stumbled down the hallway to his bedroom spouting loud hateful words, sure to wake the entire family, triggered by loose, boozed vocal cords. "Greedy parasites," he slurred spittle.

Willem watched the spit flying, saw the white foam spewing from his father's wet mouth, witnessed his eyes livid with rage, shooting daggers, that pierced and cut deep into Willem's gut. Initially, Willem had written it off to simply being his father's demanding personality exaggerated by too much drink. But never had words of hateful, dangerous bias been directed at any class of people. That changed the night his father's screams shook his bedroom door. Willem was further startled by a loud thud on the wall and another bouncing-stumbling sound that slid downward. Willem jumped out of bed to see what had happened. The minute he opened the door, the stench of hard liquor and vomit hit his nostrils. Nauseated, he went to help his passed-out father.

"Mmmm," Hendrik moaned. "Leeeaf me—"

Swallowing the vinegar taste rising in the back of his throat, Willem blinked away the slobber from his father. "Come on, let's get you cleaned up," tugging at the sweat-soaked shirt clinging to his father's chest.

"Aaaaaargh, Immmm gonna be…" Hendrik dry-heaved and continued retching till Willem got his dirty clothes off and cleaned what he could of the putrid-smelling food particles and slime smeared on his face, arms, and that which had slid down the front of his open collar. While scrubbing him, Hendrik's words became clearer. Pushing his father to his bed, the one he slept in alone, Willem shook off the last of the sleep enveloping him.

Hendrik babbled, "money-hoarding inferiors… think you're so high and mighty."

Listening to a brain that had been softened way too much to hide an agenda, Willem heard his father castigate Jews, referring to them as "those filthy pigs, their kind of Christ-hating dirty filth don't deserve all they've gotten."

Taken aback by the barrage of hurtful accusations coming out of his father's mouth, he couldn't believe what his ears heard. Christ, thought Willem, you don't even go to church. The word, Jew, the way it forcefully ejected from his father, sounded something revolting. You're so nice to Birgit, now it didn't make sense. Why? What about the meetings with her father? His father bragged about the "productive relationship with the sweet girl's father," and how he wanted to get to know him better, even have them for dinner, although no plans ever materialized.

Hostilities about Jewish people abounded but until now they existed out there. Not in Willem's home. He loved Birgit. Her father was a kind, decent man. From all Willem knew, a good father to his children. So, who are these Jews everybody hates? And why? I just don't believe it. I refuse to believe it. Willem knew better. He knew to listen to his insides, what sat well in his bones and this searing abrasive talk from his father made them grind like chalk on a blackboard. What Willem did know was how his father treated him, his mother, and sisters. He was the mean-spirited person in the equation. Not Birgit. Not her family.

The rumors Willem had heard, the ones he and Daan shared with Birgit, the ones she refused to believe were real, were in fact true. Circular swells of terrible scenarios he had read about, horrible hearsay overheard in idle talk, too much negativity he couldn't shake off, played in his head. A deep sorrow moved through him. When do the insults turn into beatings with sticks?

After his father sobered up, his words changed back to pleasantries that now seemed disingenuous. Knowing better than to approach his father directly, to confront him in any manner, Willem wondered what was his father up to? He said nothing to him.

Months passed with more obnoxious intoxicated events filled with hateful talk about Jews controlling financial purse strings. Hendrik continued to refer to the Jews as; them, their kind, those people, on his mild drunken tirades but when he was really riled up, most likely from his drinking companions, what he said was downright scary. As if Hendrik hated to refer to them as Jewish or by a given name, out it would come; swine, wretched, animals, etc. To Hendrik, they were a collective group to be done away with.

To Willem, his father's mean words now sounded like the other detestable things he'd heard about Jewish people. His father's rantings disabused him of any notion it was nonsense, the part of him that believed it was idle chatter and would never amount to anything. No longer did Willem feel that way. Not when he saw the violent tendency his father possessed, clenching his fists and threatening action, "if ever…" The if ever was never a completed sentence. It didn't have to be. All Willem needed was to see the hatred, as deep as the North Sea, rippling in his father's eyes. The chasm between father and son was now a dangerous divide. The one benediction – Hendrik's hostile genetic seeds had not been planted in his son. Just the converse. It would be, in part, Hendrik's persecuting attitude that would serve to motivate Willem in the opposite direction.

*   *   *

Acclimated from years of living at home, learning how to cope with vacillating emotions and unwarranted actions from his parents, Willem continued to survive, finding ways to sublimate what he lacked from family. Never having shared any of his father's drunken madness with Daan and Birgit, Willem continued to invite them to his home, banking on the fact they would never be around late enough to encounter what Willem kept hidden.

More time passed with Catharina and Willem's sisters gone until nightfall and Hendrik leaving Willem alone. Then one day that changed. The fateful incident occurred on a day when Hendrik came home early, from a business meeting that went badly. Sour-puckered lips led his way into Willem's room where Hendrik saw Daan in animated conversation. Stumbling closer to them, drool ran down the sides of his mouth. "Wherzzz Breeeget?" Bending his head forward then jerking back as if catching himself from falling asleep, an acrid odor smoked forth, "wherzz sheee?"

Daan, now quiet as a kitten seen by a hawk, was frozen prey. The heat of Hendrik's breathing down on his arms, Daan's limbs repulsively contracted. He gave Willem a look, a wide-eyed, silent complaint. He didn't like being near anyone drunk with anger, intoxicated into meanness. Not to mention the nauseating stink. Before it had been his uncle, his father's abusive brother, a man who was no longer allowed in Daan's home. He was wiggling in his seat, just about ready to get up to leave, when Hendrik passed out.

Daan watched the dark-wooden door close behind them, traced the lines of the cracked surface, from top to bottom, patterns of life lived. Wondering what would come through next, a drunken rage, a calm friend, his forehead bubbled with perspiration. Trudging sounds coupled with scraping and rebounding slack feet. Daan knew Willem must be dragging his father to bed. Minutes passed before another door slammed shut and bounding footsteps brought Willem back to the room that still held his father's odorous expirations.

Willem opened a window to rid the room of the fetor. Flagging an opened palm to hasten the entry of refreshing air, he felt ashamed of the embarrassing, unfettered display from his disgraceful father. Daan's fidgeting, clammy-appearing skin caught Willem's notice. Addressing the anxiety caused to Daan, Willem's, "I'm sorry you were subjected to that," were the only words of apology he could utter. There was so much more he would have liked to verbalize but to do that might risk the friendship. Willem knew that once you put it out there, there was no taking it back. So, he made no further mention of his father's continued obnoxious behavior, the tirades that occurred several times a week. Willem didn't expect the response he was about to receive from Daan, an exposition that would open the door to more intimate sharing, a passage through shadows to arrive at daylight.

Swallowing back what felt like a lump of dry cotton, Daan said, "oh Willem, I know how it is… I don't want you to feel guilty for your father. You did nothing wrong. And you'll most likely never hear any apology from him."

Willem, facing Daan in the chair at the side of his bed, slowly sat himself on his bed, not saying a word, attentive to the seriousness showing in Daan's glossy eyes.

Rubbing his chin, Daan continued, "I had an uncle… he's still my uncle but I haven't seen him in several years. He's not allowed in our home," he said and went on to tell Willem that his father's brother used to come to their house unsteady, staggering, in a tipsy stupor. "The words that came out of his mouth…"

Willem nodded for him to continue, remaining silent. Heedful.

"His mouth was foul, not just from the smell but the

crassness. But that wasn't the worst of it." Daan crossed his legs in a protective gesture as if something was bothering him. He folded his hands over his lap and picked at a nail. "He came into my room one night when my parents weren't home, dangling our house key. How he got it no one knew." Daan brought his finger to his mouth to bite off the last of the fingernail he'd been whittling away at. "I had been asleep. He woke me with his hand... down there," Daan nodded to his groin. "In his other hand was his penis, moving up and down. Sickening moans came from deep in his throat, doglike. I jumped, fully awake, kicked him off me and reached for an object on my nightstand. I smashed it onto his head and ran out of the room, out of the house. In my pajamas, I went to the neighbors."

Willem, letting out the breath he'd been holding in, shifted back against a pillow.

"That was the last time he ever came to our house. My father tried to explain that his brother had a problem with the bottle, that's what he called it. My mother was having none of it. 'Not around my boy,' she protested. 'That man is no longer welcome in my home.' That was when I was nine."

When all the strained words had been spoken, a stillness thick with pain had filled the room. Finally, Willem broke the silence. "You were so young." Then cautiously, he continued in a slow drawl. "My father has never done any more than verbal..." forgetting the time when he was younger when his father slapped him. "He's never laid a hand on me. I don't want you to feel unsafe here."

Daan, not feeling assured with accepting that it ended with Hendrik's verbal diatribe, asked, "what did he want with Birgit?" A deep, slow breath of hesitation, then Daan lowered his tone, "you don't think…"

The pleats on Daan's forehead and dark circles under his hooded eyes reinforced Willem's concern for Daan. He feared that Daan felt that Hendrik may be just like his uncle. He desperately wanted to reassure Daan that his father was not a physical aggressor. Feeling confident that his father was not a sexual predator, nor likely to ever become one, Willem addressed Daan's question about Birgit with, "it probably has something to do with the business he's involved in with her father." Wanting to de-escalate any further concern, he strongly added, "he's never crossed that line with me or anyone in my family."

Daan relaxed his shoulders. "Ohhh, yes, their business dealings," he remembered.

Although there was tension radiating from a drunk man sleeping down the hallway, the conversation continued shifting to other things. Not wanting to offend his friend, Daan did return to Willem's. Alone and with Birgit. There were no further flareups from Hendrik. Not for a period of time.

## CHAPTER SIX

The lull from the recent thunderous storm in the Arondéus' household lasted for several weeks and during that time Willem's two friends' visits were uneventful. Superficial pleasantries had been exchanged. Hendrik's civility, albeit ostensibly phony, convinced Daan that Willem's father was okay to be around, that the verbal abuse wouldn't escalate to something physical like it had with his uncle. Birgit, after hearing about the incident and not having had any personal issues being around alcoholics, took no offense and continued to go to Willem's home. This would soon change.

The day had started out innocently enough, like most others. Birgit at home with a chest cold was absent when Willem and Daan arrived at school to encounter a boy who looked like a new student. The well-built, muscular, straight-haired blond with deeply penetrating, light, smoky-quartz colored eyes, was attentively listening to one of two girls he was standing with. Momentarily looking away from the girl who monopolized the conversation, his eyes made contact with Willem's eyes.

Embarrassed that he was staring, Willem blushed. A gush of warmth ran down his cheeks, neck, and into his belly, spreading heated excitement in his body. His penis stiffened. It ached. In bed, at night, he could cover the throbbing stiffness with a blanket to hide what he was doing. Now he was uncovered and exposed, watching the new guy he became embarrassingly harder. Feeling self-consciously uncomfortable, he lowered his lunch bag to cover his crotch and headed for the classroom to hide his lap under the desktop. Ten minutes into the lecture, struggling to focus on the teacher, his erection calmed.

No longer fidgeting, Willem comfortably stretched his legs, but his attention remained riveted on the memory of the new guy. Like a flower, a beautiful pattern on well-constructed furniture, or the silky-smooth, sun-reflecting texture of a cat's hair, made Willem want to put pencil to paper, so had the blond boy. He couldn't get the mental image of his shiny blond hair nestled around piercing eyes and lips that looked soft as pillows, out of his head. Tapping a foot on the floor, Willem was anxious for class to be over, to find out who the new guy was.

"Oh, Oliver, he's Emma's cousin." The words dulled Willem when he heard that the object of his infatuation was visiting from out-of-town and stopped by the school to say goodbye to one of a classmate of Emma's friends. Like a hot, thirsty traveler using his last ounce of energy to walk to an oasis only to discover it's nothing but a mirage and what is desired is unattainable, Willem's daydream dissipated. The disappointment settled into his arm muscles, weighing on his shoulders, dragging them down.

"What's going on," Daan caught up with Willem.

When he coughed, Willem quickly asked, "you're not getting sick also, are you?" referring to Birgit's chest cold and wanting to refocus his attention off his discouragement.

"No. I just swallowed wrong."

Willem stood up straighter, putting on an all-is-okay demeanor. "Want to come over?" It was Friday and there was no school the next day, so they didn't need to get up early. Willem's father had an afternoon business appointment so they should be safe for a few hours of hanging out together.

"Sure," replied Daan.

Since the earlier eruption with Hendrik, the boys had gotten closer, opening a space that allowed for sharing guy-talk, as they called it.

In Willem's room, a tingling sensation ignited Willem's testicles, his attention had returned to the blond boy. His concentration drifted from what Daan had been talking about, to something the teacher brought up in class, to the sensations flooding his lower extremities. Scratching his leg, he pretended it itched rather than let on the emotion causing the irritation. Daan's muted sounds became audible.

"Did I lose you?" laughed Daan. "You were far away."

Willem shifted his position. He fidgeted until he couldn't stand it any longer and stood to readjust himself, which sent Daan into fits of laughter.

"Oh that," Daan choked out a giggle. "Down boy, down," he joked, amusing himself until the reddening on Willem's face dissipated. "I hate it when that happens... when I see a girl... oh never mind."

A girl. Suddenly, the sound of that word was foreign. It meant nothing special to Willem. Birgit was a girl. His sisters, others at school, seen on the streets, were ordinary people. But they ignited no bodily response in him. Not like the boy in the schoolyard had. Something, up until today, he had only read about in novels. Now, the mere idea of that blond boy was like the sun breaking through dark rain clouds that parted, making everything bright. No longer able to contain himself, Willem asked Daan, "did you see that new guy today?" He had to risk it. If he couldn't take a risk with his best male friend, then what was the worth of their friendship? In a brief moment, nothing mattered but sharing. A gossamer of clouded illusion lifted from Willem's soul, exposing his heart and he yearned to say out loud, I like boys.

"The one you were fixated on?" Daan smiled and with a wink, crooned, "sure... I saw him."

Willem's body felt like it would float away, light as a dust mote. The conversation was easy. Much easier than he imagined and it was then, when he expressed his sexual preference, that Daan said, "I see no problem with that. Can't be helped who we like. What we like."

What Daan said expanded the buzz Willem felt.

The excitement intensified when Daan added, "Birgit is open about things like that also. I can say just about anything to her."

"Just about anything?" Willem wondered what Daan would confine to himself.

"Well, nothing's absolute," he laughed. "I didn't have anything specific in mind but… well, yeah, all that jabbering stupidity about Jews. I don't like to tell all I've… I mean, why?"

"Agreed."

The chatter continued between the two and like most normal sixteen-year-old teenagers, they talked about what they found attractive in someone. They fantasized about things they'd do if they were older with jobs. "Someday, I'd love to meet and live with someone," said Willem.

Daan looked at the slightly-ajar, bedroom door, distracting Willem.

"What?"

"I thought I heard something," said Daan. After a couple of minutes of silence, he continued. "I guess it was nothing."

Without getting up to check, Willem put a hand on Daan's back. "I really want to thank you for hearing me out today." He reiterated things he'd said earlier, including parts about masturbating and how now he had that blond guy to think of while enjoying himself.

Out in the hallway, Hendrik oozed a perspiration stain onto the wall where his forehead rested, where he had been listening in.

Home early from the meeting, he had entered the house quietly. Made himself a glass of gin and gulped it down. The meeting went well and he was in a good mood. Hearing voices upstairs piqued his curiosity; what more could he learn from Birgit about her father's financial dealings, any simple comment could put him right on the money trail. Gingerly, he made his way up the stairs trying to avoid squeaky floorboards. To his pleasure, Willem's door was left ajar but Birgit wasn't there, her voice not heard. Just as he was about to turn away, what he overheard lowered the temperature, as the chill in his relationship with his son turned to a hard frost of glacier proportions.

There was no mistaking the words pulsating into Hendrik's ears, throbbing in his temples. The unclosed door afforded him clarity as to what was being said. In the past, he'd had to strain to discern the content, pieces of a puzzle, not always making sense. Today, not a chance of misunderstanding. What he caught wind of was more than sounded syllables, there was emotional activity, flowery feelings, that turned Hendrik's stomach. Overhearing Willem effuse about a boy he saw in school, "radiance of his eyes, upturned nose that rested on full, sensual, moist lips." Hendrik wanted to rip out his son's vocal cords.

Containing his anger, Hendrik waited another couple of minutes. His jaw grew stiff and retracted, years of protesting his son's inclinations for less masculine activities like his art, all those months of protesting he wasn't manly enough, turned into disgust. The disgust quickly became violent anger as the words sank in, as

Willem's excited tone rippled out the door and into Hendrik's gut.

Not my son! He slammed a fist into the wall leaving an indentation. The fuming father had heard enough. Enough to make him strangling mad. Bounding in, with immense force, Hendrik unhinged the door.

Daan jumped out of his seat, banging his knee on the nightstand.

Hendrik, right in Willem's face, "What! Are! You! Going! On! About! Men do not belong with men! Not in my home," he screamed, so loudly Willem's ears felt like they would explode.

His father's contorted face, a dagger scowl, the bloody knuckles on his right hand, sent a terrifying electricity down Willem's backside. Hendrik's hand grabbed hold of Willem's neck squeezing the air out of his mouth making it hard for him to catch his breath. Panicked nausea permeated Willem's belly as he knee-kicked his father off him.

Hendrik stumbled. Gasped. Shook his head. Another minute of disorientation and he came to his senses.

Daan took a step back. Fearing what Hendrik would do to him, he slid back several more steps, closer to the door.

Hendrik pivoted, catching sight of Daan. In that moment of calm, Daan, quick to think on his feet, tried to defuse the scene with a prevarication. Not exactly sure what Hendrik had heard, he said, "Sir, the conversation was in a historical context. Eros, the God of love... Greek mythology..." and a few more spontaneous comments about how, in ancient times, men did love men and society accepted it." He tried to convince Hendrik it had been a discussion carried over from school earlier that day.

Willem found it completely implausible his father would accept anything Daan had just said, archaic or not. If his father overheard any part of the earlier conversation, he was sure Hendrik would know it was personal for his son. Deeply personal. But not positive his father caught all of the conversation and the fact a physical line had been crossed, he felt he needed to help Daan deactivate the explosion. Mustering up a foghorn voice. "What is it you think you heard that would warrant such a reaction, father? These things are discussed in classes… as part of history…"

A thread of doubt spun Hendrik inside out, his head in turmoil. Did he misinterpret or mistake the context? He did have a glass of gin upon returning home, a couple of drinks at the earlier business meeting he had attended and he would rather question himself than accept that his son, the last son remaining in his house, was a homosexual. I probably got it wrong, that's what he wanted to believe. That would be more palatable than believing his son preferred men. It would definitely be more acceptable than what his friends would subject him to. Hendrik's breathing calmed, the scarlet sheen blotching his facial skin melted to its normal rosy beige. Another deep inhalation and the hatred that divested Hendrik's coat of pride had eased to an embarrassed wobble. To pretend, to avoid any further discussion on a troubling topic, Hendrik, swallowed hubris when he faced Daan and said, "well then, excuse my outburst." To further rationalize his behavior, he added to the course of lies. "Perhaps, one drink too many."

To Daan, it was no longer safe to visit the Arondéus' house. Hendrik Arondéus was no longer safe to be around and was placed in the hazardous category alongside his uncle

To Willem, it was no longer okay to speak out loud, verboten subjects in his home. But also denying his nature was equally oppressive. Risking was a choice he had to make but for now, on that day, he sublimated his own inclinations, opting for peace instead of battle.

*     *     *

The next morning, Willem, still feeling the sting from the latest of his father's drunk tirades the night before, looked around his room at pieces of expensive furniture. Purchased with money the family couldn't afford. Money earned from fuel sold and used for war. How many lives bought Hendrik's solid wood-carved antique chairs, dressers, or the decorative clock on the nightstand? How much blood flowed, ripped from lives, to purchase the walnut cabinets inlaid with mother-of-pearl? It was heartless to trade on the lives of others. That's what his father had become, heartless. Any hopes Willem had for a semblance of civility with his father had dissipated with the voice of anti-Semitism and now a new hatred screamed down the halls last night, directed at homosexuals. No longer would the excuse of drink matter, like in the case with Daan's uncle. Daan's mother was right. All the drivel that came out of Hendrik's frothing mouth about rapacious Jews spending money on this, wasting money on that, was brazenly hypocritical. Willem's eyes landed on an expensive porcelain figurine, nonsense! It was all nonsense. A bunch of poppycock for show, covering the incubus.

Ernst Levin, who could afford to furnish lavishly, flaunt expensive clothing and jewelry, showed restrained humility, in contrast to Willem's boasting father, who struggled to make a deal, to get more money, never thinking he had enough. When was enough, enough, pondered Willem? His back stiffened. You are a hypocrite, father. A mean-spirited, pretentious bigot, he thought, as too many ill-spoken pejoratives from Hendrik ran through his head. The scene last night turned Willem's stomach and just as he was about to pick up something and slam it into the mirror on his wall, a sound beyond his window caught his attention.

A black-tailed godwit had mysteriously landed in Willem's yard, not far from the waterway, where it was most likely en-route to an invertebrate and aquatic, plant meal. He'd only seen one, before, when out with Daan and Birgit. Daan was familiar with the long-legged, long-billed shorebird. Picking at something in the garden below, Willem caught sight of what looked like a beetle in its bill. Its orange head, neck, and chest bobbed up and down digesting the meal. Then as quickly as it appeared it spread its fluttering wings and soared off. Animals and nature had a calming effect on Willem and this day was no exception. Parking his earlier reaction to his father, in the mental recess where he stored painful emotions, his next breath was easier as he let go of the debacle from the night before.

# THE OLD GILT CLOCK

## CHAPTER SEVEN

That night with Daan, when Hendrik listened in on an exposition of his excited son's words, he refused to face the dread he'd had about his son for years. A son he wanted to be more masculine. Men with men was out of the question, so he convinced himself that Daan was right, that it wasn't a personal conversation but a rehash of a lesson. If that was the case, he wondered, why in the hell were they discussing things like that in school! Unable to make any sense out of it, he shifted his attention to something else and drew on what the rumor mills had been spreading around Europe, about the Jewish influence. That, he could wrap his head around. That, he agreed with.

Anti-Semitism had been spreading like a slow-creeping, multi-legged, comb-footed, spider. With their thin legs and oval-shaped abdomens, those spiders looked like the bloated drunken bellies of men engorged with food and booze who thrived on hateful rumormongering. Also, like these arachnid creatures that came out of their dry, dark, rocky walls, seeking humans to sting, so had damaging lips of anti-Semites told biting lies. Multi-legged,

Jew bashing was not confined to simply complaints that they held the purse strings. No, complaints also spread that Jews were corrupting native cultures with their distinctive traditions and diacritic inflected teachings. "They are aloof, keep to themselves, and they are anti-Christ," the whispers grew, to loud roars. "They killed Christ!"

Poisonous, herd-mentality influenced the talk. Go along or the venomous snakes will empty their poison into your skin. Rational thinking be damned and the danger was when individuals were impacted by a mob mentality, their decisions were different than they would have been individually. As emotions threw rationality out the window, toxic antagonistic vocal cords vibrated louder and louder.

"They are not capable of honest labor."

"Greedy bastards!"

"Their beliefs emphasize profit for their own."

"Cheaters!"

"They don't deserve to live among us!"

The clincher would be the spread of the false notion that Jews wanted world economic dominance. It was a deception that took on speed in 1910 when Willem was sixteen, just four years before World War I. During the period from 1910 to 1914 when The Great War began, the European walls of monetary bricks went from being supportive to crumbling down. In the aftermath of the war's rubble and dust, spilled blood and guts, broken limbs and hearts, anti-Semites blamed the Jews, who they believed controlled the economy. The events that took place fueled the overt orchestration of the scapegoating of the Jewish people by Hitler. The chemicals had been put in a beaker and were pointed at the Jews. Once shaken it would explode into catastrophic events – unimaginable to humankind.

Just as European materialism began its decline into chaos so had Willem's relationship with Hendrik.

Hendrik had been out drinking and the suspicious itch under his collar had all but calmed. He did not want to concentrate on his second worse fear, the first being loss of business. No, he didn't want to think about his son's feminine inclinations. Going out drinking with friends distracted his attention.

Returning home that night, Hendrik's clothes smelled of urine and alcohol was on his stale breath. Near incoherent, tripping over himself, he climbed the stairs falling a couple of times and stumbled past Catharina's closed bedroom door to Willem's room. "Wheeeeeeze da Juuuu," he spat, banging into the wall.

One look at his father's bloodshot, red-rimmed eyes, his tongue protruding with each slur, the stink from his clothes and Willem knew this wasn't an ordinary drinking episode. He'd never seen his father this plastered before.

"Wheeeeeeze sheee, I neeeeds mooooonee," he quibbled, with a miniscule amount of lucidity referencing a business meeting gone badly earlier in the evening. Grabbing hold of the back of a chair, "Ooooouch," he quickly drew his hand back, not noticing the large splinter that broke into his palm.

Willem slammed down the book in his hand and got out of bed. A tightness squeezed his torso, his agitated stomach felt like it was eating itself. His father spat vulgar repetitions as Willem stood frozen, like a sculpted statue, arms stiff at his sides, fingers gripping his pajamas into a knotted ball.

"Wheeeeeeze the Jew bitch!" Hendrik slammed forward, falling onto his son, sending them both onto the bed. "Wiiiiidth her moooonee gruuuubing faaaather?"

After Hendrik muttered a few more antagonistic remarks into Willem's ear, Willem grabbed hold of the backside of his father to yank him off. Move the feet, and the legs will follow, was all he could think of. He wanted out, to get away from the threat his father presented. It was impossible, Hendrik's bulk had pinned down Willem's left leg. Willem kicked with his right foot to no avail. A hard smack to his father's cheek finally released him. Hendrik fell back into a lip-twitching, snoring sleep.

The miserable curse of the man before him, echoing snorts, gasping for air, was not someone for Willem to fear but rather, pity. Seeing his father like that, as he had seen him too many times before, seeking distraction in liquor, it was clear to him his father had been numbing his own misery. It was then that Willem saw that it was mostly suffering that teaches the value of things. He'd had enough of his father dictating his actions. His voice. There was no talking with that man and no way Willem would even try again. The one time he had tried to make his point, he felt like a bird pecking at a window, never making a dent. He doubted he'd ever get anywhere.

Willem left his father where he was and went downstairs to sleep on the living-room couch. Sinking into the overly worn, sunken cushions, he was too stirred up to sleep. He needed to get his mind off his father, off the prejudicial snobbery and put it on something soothing to relax his twisted muscles. Reaching around to his neck, he rubbed the tangled lumps smoother. Each stroke of his fingers and his thoughts drifted to more agreeable subjects. The painting he had been working on. The subjects he wanted to paint. Words came to him, lyrical and flowing, unrhyming poetic verse, stanzas about a bird lighting on a tree limb, a summer breeze through a tepid night, so many more untapped experiences. Imagining rhythmic sounds from Dirk Schäfer's Sonate Inagurale, Opus 9, soft music played in his head while visions of famous artists danced behind his eyes, Van Gogh's Sunflowers and Wheatfield with Crows. Willem was filled, swept away to a world he longed for. Drifting deeper, the earlier stimulation dissipated.

It wasn't just mental escape that occupied his attention. Circulating in his bodily fluids were new living cells, exciting him. His hand moved from his neck to his chest, the firm undefined slightly sunken thorax. Rubbing his nipples, he ran his tongue over his dry, parted, well-defined lips. His fingers edged lower, to his belly button, and further down. The throbbing heat in his right hand sent an arousal down his legs. At first, his hand motion was slow. Then faster until he was lost. Gone was the uncomfortable couch, the room filled with overly expensive furniture, the snoring sounds from upstairs, it all evaporated into sensation. Spasms and rhythmic contractions in his groin moved through his body until he couldn't stop the white, sticky, juice from flowing. Several more spasms and he fell over the edge into a deep relaxation. And sleep.

Willem awoke before everyone else. He went to his room to find his father gone. Despite the fetid odor on the sheets and pillow, Willem was unbothered. From all that he'd gone through in his relatively young life, all that was missing in his family relationships, he had found something more valuable. Himself. Self-reliance would continue to serve him, for the rest of the year was about to escalate into the intolerable, in the Arondéus' house.

The 1910 seasons moved from a comfortable, sunny summer to a moderate fall with leaves turning golden-orange and brown before the winter brought shedding and bare branches. It was an unseasonably cold winter, even by Naarden standards when three feet of snow was not unusual. The frigid days kept Willem inside more than he would have liked due to the escalating tensions with his father and lack of distractions from his friends' visits. When a blanketing storm kept his father home because the snow-pack was too deep, prohibitive even for walking, and Willem's mother and sisters had to spend the night before with a friend they worked with, his father was an utter nuisance.

Hendrik, finished with all the office work he could do at home was tired of the boring trampling up and down the hall and hitting the liquor cabinet, so went to Willem's room. "Where have your friends been?" he asked, really curious as to why Birgit hadn't been around in a few months. Nor Daan for that matter. "Lose your only friends?" he prodded Willem as if picking a fight for entertainment.

Willem, refusing to take notice of his father, continued with what he'd been doing.

"Stop that," Hendrik nodded at the painting Willem was working on, demanding his attention. "I'm talking to you!" his voice raised a decibel.

Willem, continuing to ignore the intrusion, finished a few strokes of the view outside his window. He wanted to capture its beauty. The crystallized flakes of brown snow perching around the ledge, jeweled, diamond-like threads of ice particles fanning out across the glass, occasionally hitting a warmer pocket of air and forming floating, cloud-like puffs. A glint of the sun's reflection, rays coming through the cracks in dark passing nebulous formations, broke into rainbow designs.

"Stop that," Hendrik's hand covered Willem's stopping his son's motion. If he couldn't verbally control him, he took to force.

Willem flipped Hendrik's hand off. "Don't do that," he protested. Refusing to give his father the attention he craved, he put down the brush, got up and went to the window. His back to Hendrik, his breath fogging up the glass sending rivers of condensation streaming down the surface. "Why do you have to be so mean?" he spoke to the pane of glass, barely loud enough for his father behind him to hear.

But Hendrik did take it in. "What!" He moved in on his

son, his breath on the back of Willem's neck and turned him around. "What... Did... You... Say... To... Me?"

"You heard me, father."

"You will not speak to me that way," as he raised a hand to slap Willem.

Willem grabbed hold of his father's arm, without hesitation, or fear. "Don't touch me! Don't ever touch me again!" He pulled back, loosening his grip.

Hendrik stood stunned. And somewhat amused. In a perverse fashion, this new way his son was acting was more to his liking. Willem's new attitude was not forceful, rather it displayed reserved confidence.

"Do you have to be so awful? You castigate Jewish people. You think men with men is wrong—"

That Hendrik wasn't going to listen to. "You defending Jews?" he scoffed.

"And homosexuals," Willem retorted. It was a risk. Worth taking.

As instantly as he had calmed down, it reversed. Hendrik's neck veins bulged. He raised his voice, "do not bring up that topic. Not in my home!"

"I will," Willem leaned forward. "There's nothing wrong with it and I will not hide in the shadows. I refuse to tiptoe around how I feel."

The bulge in Hendrik's pulsating neck looked like a balloon ready to burst. "The big defender of financial criminals, perverts… lowlifes that don't deserve the air we breathe, that's who you defend! Not in my house!"

"What are you going to do father, kick me out?" Disgust rang in Willem's tone. "Because I have a Jewish friend? A good friend. With a very decent father who has helped you. And me," the last referring to Birgit's father encouraging Willem's art. "And what is wrong with someone of the same sex… being together. Who are they hurting? You… you on the other hand… you, who care more about money, you do plenty of harm. Furthering hatred, contributing to financing wars with your fuel—"

"Enough! That… Is… Enough!"

"You asked where my friends were?" Willem pulled his sweat-soaked shirt loose from his chest and swiped a few light-brown hairs back off his perspired forehead. "They won't come around here. Not after you went for my throat—"

Having all but forgotten about the events of that night when Daan was over, Hendrik was taken aback when he interrupted, "I never…" Flummoxed, he left the room.

A day, a week, a month passed and more words went back and forth in a circular motion accomplishing nothing. Willem, repelled by his father and the years of abuse, refused to keep his words to himself, to which Hendrik, when sober, didn't quite know how to handle. Not yet. Not until he would reach the limit of his intolerance.

Willem, determined to stop stepping lightly around the quicksand of cowardice, to stop catering to his father's prejudices and to stand up for himself, spoke up and by speaking up, grew fortitude muscles. Stretching and exercising them, the stronger his courage became. With chin up, chest out, he continued to bring up the topic of homosexuality.

Arguments ensued. Hendrik, hesitant to take action because he didn't want to face the fact that his son might be doing more than voicing support, outright shied away from going to that place that would reveal Willem was, in fact, a homosexual. All Willem's life, this was something Hendrik denied as even a possibility. Not Willem! Not in my home! Ignoring indications, Hendrik's fear of being ostracized for having a homosexual son, consequently losing his reputation, customers, and livelihood, overrode any desire to face what was right before his eyes, living under his roof. Nearing a breaking point, he fumed and drank even more.

CHAPTER EIGHT

The world was a window of change for Willem, as the cold winter of 1910 defrosted into spring and ice melted into streams, becoming rivers. Inching toward his seventeenth birthday, Willem's home-life had become stifling, an existence of roller-coaster moods and altercations with Hendrik. He barely saw and interacted with his estranged mother and the sisters, not even sharing a conversation when they passed each other in the hall. It drove him to seek activities outside his home. His friendship with Daan and Birgit was trusting and comfortable. But it didn't satisfy a yearning to connect in a more intimate relationship, one in which he could explore the feelings that had been ignited in him many months before by the stranger named Oliver, in the schoolyard. Although the memory of the boy's physical appearance had faded, Willem's appetite had been whetted by the lingering sensations.

Willem loved to walk the streets to find a grassy, plant-filled area to sketch. Places where he felt included in all that was new and fresh, exciting, that he wanted to be a part of. Conversations about sports, dances, and tea parties had taken over idle, mindless gossip and he especially was fascinated by things he'd overheard from women, buzzing about changing laws to give them better rights. To Willem, it was a stimulating time. A time he relished, especially when a passerby stopped to watch him paint.

A woman with two children, a boy and a girl, sitting across the park, caught Willem's eye. The design of her dress, with a puffy chest, small waist, bright dove-colored skirt resting a few inches above her ankle, and the flower-adorned hat made her look pure and innocent to him. But what was on the surface didn't necessarily reflect the reality. He knew that from his father's immaculate appearance in his stodgy, three-piece, dark-navy, striped suit, the way his jacket with the three-inch lapel fit just right on his corpulent body but it did not hide the lack of class his manner portrayed. Covering his head with a felt derby, Hendrik was never able to hide his mean-spirited narrow-mindedness.

A quick glance across the lush grassy area, at what appeared to be cerulean colored eyes, Willem mixed a tiny amount of dark blue with green to get the shade he wanted. A giggling holler, "look, mother, he's painting," caught Willem's attention. The little girl, who was with the woman, headed toward Willem; mother instantly on her feet taking hold of her arm.

"No, Abby, don't disturb—"

The child broke loose, her bright-pink, floral-patterned, cotton dress flying with the breeze, her mother following. The boy followed suit. Right beside Willem, the little red-headed girl opened her mouth in surprise. Her rosy cheeks lifted as the Cheshire-cat grin covering her face widened. A front tooth missing, she sprayed Willem's hand when she squealed, "it's you," to her mother, now at her side.

Before the woman could offer an apology for her rude daughter, the boy in his white with blue-trimmed, sailor-collar shirt and beige knee-length knickers, said, "it is you." He took his mother's hand to have a closer look.

Willem smiled as the boy's warm breath met his cheek. The mother and two children admired the painting, which was a strong likeness to the woman. Willem put down his paintbrush, wiped his hand, and stood to greet them. "You're welcome to… perhaps, I should first apologize for intruding on your quiet day with your children." A blush of embarrassment that he'd been painting the woman, without her permission, covered his cheeks.

The woman stood speechless, eyes intent on the work, a deep sigh and smile preceded, "you have a great talent, Mr.—"

"Willem. I'm yet too young to be a Mr., Madame." Stepping back to allow the three a closer look, he added, "I thank you for the compliment, though, I am humbled."

With focused intent on the painting, she expressed, "no, Willem, it is I who is moved by your talent." She scrutinized the shapes, lines, colors, depth of shading and further said, "do you show in a gallery?"

The question surprised Willem. A gallery! His work lined the walls of his bedroom, and Birgit's and Daan's, who agreed to store things for him, lest Hendrik's rampages destroyed the pieces. "Oh no, I am only a novice. What work I've completed, sits in my bedroom."

When the woman asked if she could purchase the painting, Willem was so flattered he offered it to her at no cost. The woman insisted she could not accept such a generous benefit and assured Willem that her husband would pay amply. Flustered and not experienced in these dealings, he listened to the woman tell him to come to their home and she would give him the money to which she then asked, "how much is this piece?"

"But... it's not finished," he took a breath, and pulled on his chin, contemplating his next comment. "Perhaps, if you will allow me," a softness smoothed out the rough edge of chagrin he'd moments ago manifested, "you could sit for me to finish the few final touches?"

Now it was the woman's turn to be pleasantly surprised, amid her children's jumping up and down, anticipation mounting. "What a lovely invitation. And I thank you. But you must let me honor your work with payment."

Still feeling uncomfortable accepting money, having thus far done his craft for himself and his friends, he hadn't given any thought to what to charge. Unequipped with what to say, he chose honesty. "I've not sold anything before and no idea how to value it." He stilled himself from repeating what earlier had seemed an affront to the generous woman and felt the proper approach was to ask, "perhaps it would be best for you to offer what you can. Any small token would serve me nicely."

The woman laughed but by the light in her eyes, it was

clearly not derisive. "You, young man, are a breath of fresh air. I take it you like to paint?"

"Yes," Willem replied.

"Perhaps you'd like to paint for a living?" Her smile widened. "As most artists would like to do."

"Yes, Madame."

"Then," a stronger, forceful voice spoke, "you must ask for money in return. Do not work for a pittance and most definitely do not work for free. If life has taught me anything it's simply that the less you pay for something, the less you get, especially when there are pricier options. Payment, and the more of it the better, results in the purchaser feeling they have something of value."

Willem liked the assertive tone, intended to help. Taking it in his stride, he responded, "I see your point, Madame, but—"

"Rothstein, Mrs. Adeline Rothstein. Please feel free to address me as Addy." Her lips softened. "All my friends call me Addy."

Unaccustomed to referring to an adult, and a married woman at that, by her given name, "Mrs. Rothstein, I've no experience in such matters so how about… we start with," he hemmed and hawed, calculating what the canvas and paint cost and adding in a bit more to all in all equal the amount of two loaves of bread. He gave her the price, asking, "would that be okay?"

Suppressing a giggle and not wanting to further fluster the innocent teenager, she pressed her lips together. She calmed her amused reaction at the undercharged amount and agreed to Willem's price before they went to work. A wizard, with speed, dexterity, and finesse, the piece was finished in a little more than an hour. Concerned that the woman, needing to attend to her two children, would not be able to carry the painting to her home, he offered to deliver it.

Gazing at the canvas, she froze, the only movement tears running down her cheeks. Her attention was riveted on the portrait. A few minutes passed before she wiped the teardrops. Finally, composed, "Willem..." she shook her head, "it is rare that I am lost for words..." A few more quiet moments for the mother while the children bounced around, and, finally, "thank you," she sighed.

Soaking it in, Willem knew that no amount of money could buy him the feeling of joy radiating through his body... and soul. The amount, being less than the pocket change the woman had on hand, there was no need for her to arrange for her husband to make payment. When the measly amount of money worth two loaves of bread and a few paint supplies crossed his palm, it felt like a hundred guilder. He was as light as a soaring turtle-dove when he offered to bring the painting to her home.

"We have a carriage waiting."

She, with a child in each hand and he, delicately holding the bottom of the wet painting, walked together to a luxurious horse-drawn carriage parked on the outer perimeter of the park. A coachman sat patiently waiting, loosely holding the reigns of two well-muscled, calm, black horses. Behind the driver were two,

two-seat, upholstered, lush red-velvet, cushioned seats facing each other. The minute Willem saw it, he was reminded of Birgit's father's transportation, a representation of wealth. Thinking back to the squabbling over the price of his painting and not wanting to impose on a woman with two children who might need the money for food, he smiled to himself. "This is a beauty," he said to Adeline. "Riding in comfort, that's nice for you and your family."

"It will soon get even nicer, my dear boy."

Curious, he scrunched his head-tilted face.

"We have an automobile on order. I believe it's a Benz," she said, lifting the boy into the carriage. "My husband has his heart set on the new form of transportation. He works hard," as she proceeded to help her daughter onto the seat. "I do not begrudge him this extravagance. A little reward for all he does." A few more circumspect words nearly in an undertone, avoiding eye contact, were said as if shy about what she had just mentioned.

Willem sensed from the way her modulation and facial expression changed that she was not a rich, boastful person, unlike many of his father's friends who mouthed off about their business successes and acumen in making large sums of money. To Willem, Adeline Rothstein seemed to lack any display of superiority or showiness. No, to him, the ground beneath them was level.

Willem placed the painting on a bench behind where the passengers sat.

"Can we offer you a ride home?" she asked.

Willem wanted to walk. To appreciate the moment. The

first of many more he hoped to come. "Thank you, but no. I would like to stretch my legs."

Adeline received the gentle grip of his hand, a goodbye to the stranger whose day had changed in ways he'd never anticipated. He watched the carriage pull away, floating dust in its wake, disappearing into the vast unknown, intermingling with the hundreds of people he encountered month in and month out. The only known fact left behind, his first client's name.

*　　*　　*

When Willem later shared the news about his first sale with Daan and Birgit, he was overwhelmed to learn who the woman was, more significantly who her husband was. A man well known to Ernst Levin. Word had spread from Birgit to her father, who made it a point of contacting one of his bank's biggest clients, Oscar Rothstein. Mr. Rothstein just happened to be an international art aficionado with several masterpieces donning his walls. He also happened to be the husband of Adeline Rothstein. Ernst was keen to share with Oscar all he had learned from his daughter.

*　　*　　*

"This is quite good, my darling," said Oscar, referring to a new painting they had commissioned Willem to do for them, a surreptitious attempt on their part to help promote his work. Not only had they learned of Willem's connection to the Levin family but from the same source, they discovered all the sordid details of the trouble he'd been having at home over the last several months. It was around that time when Birgit stopped visiting the Arondéus', which was coincidentally the same time Ernst Levin told Hendrik that bank loans were tightening and regretfully cutbacks had to be made. There would be no further loans to Hendrik. Word of his anti-Semitic slurs went full circle as Oscar shook a pitiful frown from his face and told his wife, "we need to help this kid."

The Rothsteins' motivation to help wasn't solely about Willem's talent; it was also about the responses Willem had waged against his father's foul mouth, one that continued to spread dangerously vicious lies. Hendrik, in a relative position of power directly and indirectly through contacts he dealt with, had contributed to subtle mounting tensions in the Netherlands. Jewish families, way outnumbered by anti-Semites, sought friends wherever available. Willem's opposition to his father's propaganda boded well with the two Jewish families, the Levins and Rothsteins, he had befriended. The favorable view of Willem by a few prominent people would serve him when tensions at home got way out of control.

While the behind-the-scenes effort was being undertaken to promote his art, the beginning of 1911 had generated more than entrepreneurial good fortune for Willem. It also introduced him to meaningful intimacy. The first infatuation came unexpectedly when he delivered a painting to the Rothsteins' house. A nephew was visiting. Peter, with brown-wavy hair, thick-eyelashes highlighting big brown sleepy eyes, a straight nose, and full lips, had a soft voice, with a kind, gentle manner. Peter shared his uncle Oscar's appreciation for artistry and although he favored well-done paintings, he also adored ceramics and sculptures, performing arts, literature, and poetry. It was, in fact, Peter who influenced Willem to expand on his poetry and prose. Their meeting and relationship was the seed that grew and transcended Willem from a bulb to a large, showy, and brightly-colored, red, flowering tulip.

Willem had been asked to visit the Rothsteins for afternoon tea. He had not met Peter who would be present and was unaware that it was Peter who wanted to meet the relatively young, talented artist. There was something in the painting of Adeline that had inspired Peter and once seen he had to find out who owned the hands that painted with such grace. The minute Peter saw Willem come through the door to the parlor, he was on his feet. The magnetic draw was instant, the way Willem licked his lips, sensuous and inviting and the alluring way Willem moved his hand to straighten his jacket. Peter was rapt. Transported to a place that demanded to be experienced.

Introductions ensued with tea service and baked goods aplenty. Talking about Willem's paintings occupied the initial conversation until the Rothsteins excused themselves and left the two boys alone. Willem surmised that Peter must have been a few years older than him, around nineteen and was certainly more worldly in experience and appreciation of the arts. Before long, the spoken words meant nothing, they could have been talking about the texture of soil conducive for worms, for all they cared. Lost in each other, pulled by some invisible and irresistible seductive force, they discoursed until Peter asked Willem if he would like to go for a stroll.

Exiting the front door, Peter's hand on Willem's back sent an arousal to his groin. A few hours later in the sweet, succulent aftermath, when the tingling sensations that can only be physically felt and not mentally described, calmed into exhausting relaxation, they lay on a mound of moist grass far from the house they left hours before. Luxuriating in the glow, with all other worries dissipated, Willem looked at Peter, at his alluring-slightly-parted lips and deep into the space, to his moist tongue. He could almost taste the sweetness he saw. That was the first of many interludes to come.

Whenever Peter visited, from Rotterdam, arrangements were made to spend as much time with Willem as possible. The relationship lasted until one night while in a hotel room, in bed, Willem rolled over to look at Peter – the orgasm finished moments before – and wondered if it had been a mistake. The long-distance romance had failed to satisfy his need for closer, more frequent encounters. The time between visits cast doubt in Willem's mind. Something had put distance between them. Something other than the separating geography. It made Willem's hackles rise, a prickling stinging sensation he knew not to ignore.

# THE OLD GILT CLOCK

CHAPTER NINE

The niggling feeling Willem had about Peter, his skepticism, was confirmed when Daan told him that he had seen Peter with another man. Daan and Birgit had met Peter. It was by chance one afternoon that Daan ran into Peter coming out of a hotel with someone else. Willem, taken aback that he hadn't known Peter was in town, felt like a liter of acid leached onto his skin. The shock, generating disbelief, made him feel like an observer to the experience, a feeling of separation-from-his-body he liked to call it. Time distorted, ticking at a rapid pace, it moved faster by hopeful anticipation that it was all a mistake. But it was no mistake and when reality set in, time slowed; it felt like a slug could have won a race with him. Although there was a hodgepodge of ambivalent emotions, Willem was glad that his intuition hadn't let him down. Forced to grow up faster than most kids his age, without adequate parenting, Willem had learned to rely on his internal reactions.

"Yes, we can remain friends," Willem responded to Peter's chagrined plea to forgive him. At least he fessed up. Willem didn't want to alienate himself from all the contacts he'd made with and through Peter, so when Peter reached for him, for a hug, Willem extended his arms.

"I'm really sorry... but..." Peter tried to find the word to match his soft volume. "It was sweet while—"

Taking a hard swallow, feeling the heartache, Willem held the embrace. "It's okay. How about we leave it at that." Willem's arms felt like lead.

Releasing each other, Willem watched Peter walk away. It was over. The ending of his first love was painful. It was bittersweet but ended while the sweet taste was fresh in Willem's memory. He was glad there wasn't a long, drawn-out conflict filled with rationalizations, excuses, and lies. The days that followed moved painfully slowly, thoughts running rampant replayed the joy, the sharing, their first orgasm together. Over and over, images haunting Willem turned into nightmares until he wanted to hold up a palm and scream for them to stop! Stop, rang through him like an incantation, until one morning he awoke and his head was quiet. Harboring no regrets – he had been freed. He had gained his wings.

Things at home weren't flying high, though, just the opposite.

*   *   *

Before their relationship ended, Peter had introduced Willem to several locals, homosexuals who Willem befriended. Through these relationships, Willem would come to realize that some friends are stepping stones on a peaceful journey, while others are sunken concave traps, their only purpose to bring one down. Willem's direction had been uncertain until he'd met Peter. With that relationship ended, Willem's path was lit. One foot in front of the other, the walk ahead would bring lessons, about the assured reliance on the character, ability, strength, and truth of someone. It would also reveal hard, cold aspects of betrayal, what lies beneath the smiles cloaking seduction, treachery, and abandonment. Willem was growing. And gaining confidence, something he would exercise at home.

Willem's relationship with his father had sunk to filthy, mudslinging, dangerous diatribe that Willem exacerbated with talk of homosexuality. Hendrik was a time bomb ticking its last minute. No longer fearful of his father's wrath, or the consequences of speaking his mind – his truth, Willem challenged his father's mouthing off with passionate defense. Nothing was off-limits, not vigorous emotional expressions about the essential nature of homosexuality, nor defending, head-on, the innocence of the Jewish people who had done nothing to deserve the persecution leveled against them.

At an unusually early hour, just before sunrise, a loud crash was heard downstairs. Abruptly woken, a startled Catharina grabbed the first defensive object she could get her hands on, a large vase and went to see what the rumpus was. Willem, yet asleep, thought he was having a bad dream until he heard screaming. His mother, in a foghorn-shrill-piercing voice, not her normally reserved, bitter refrain, commanded, "Enough!"

Obloquies mingled with indiscernible grumbling, foot-stomping, and another shattering of glass occurred before Hendrik shouted, "not in my home!"

"I... Said... Enough!" Catharina cleared the sleepy frog from her throat. "I will get the girls and leave for work. You handle it!"

Handle it? Willem sat up in bed and wiped yellow crusts of sleep from his eyes. He had a strong suspicion what *it* meant. If his conjecture was right, it had started a little before Willem turned seventeen with his defense of homosexuality. Willem had grown enough to face the asphyxiating confinement of his existence at home and stand up to the continual browbeating. The time had come to shed all intimidation. Not only did he dare to connect with new friends, other homosexuals but he refused to tiptoe around from mentioning it to his father. To Hendrik's great consternation, Willem's continued defiance led to daily escalating arguments. As his attention drifted off the commotion downstairs, images surfaced.

"There's nothing wrong with a man loving a man," said Willem, in response to one of Hendrik's irate tirades against degenerates, which as usual included Jews, homosexuals, and people with certain bodily deformities and characteristics different than what Hendrik felt was socially acceptable.

At first, Hendrik responded in a toned-down manner. "Stop

talking nonsense," he insisted.

"Nonsense?" A honeyed-sarcasm oozed from Willem. "What is nonsense about mutual attraction?" Willem looked at his father not expecting an answer. "Nothing nonsense about it at all. There is no logical basis in your rallying against men with men."

Willem's logical retorts reduced his father to prejudicial blathering. "Lowlifes. Inferior rats. They…" Hendrik had clumped Jews with homosexuals. "You defend those substandard animals!"

Willem knew who the "they" were that his father had referred to. "My Jewish friend Birgit is one of the kindest persons I've ever met. And my new acquaintances happen to agree with me that there's nothing wrong with men being interested in men. I've met a lot of fine friends, doing art, that share my opinion."

"Art! That's what got you into that mindset. If you'd have gone out and chopped wood—"

Hendrik's superior intoning, lip-smacking, and hand waving was a stick in Willem's craw to which he asserted, "I am who I am!" With that Willem would usually leave his father to hit the liquor cabinet or go out to a bar to drown his nasty, narrow-mindedness.

For a while, the tug-of-war between father and son was kept in check, with equal restraint and exertion. Hendrik expeditiously learned that a hand raised to his son brought an opposite and correspondent display of bodily force. Willem's unwillingness to continue to cower brought a defensive fist to his father's cheek and abdomen on more than one occasion. One black-eye to a man who cared about the impression he publicly made was all it took for him to back off, albeit it with grumbling and complaining. Once Hendrik succumbed to a calmer manner of display, Willem acted in like kind. It took Willem no time at all to see that when the fulcrum of aggression and passivity were in balance, the need for harmful actions halted. The ceasefire had benefitted Willem while Hendrik's insides were a wildly bubbling volcano.

The physical abuse had ended but the verbal abuse continued, with Willem finding ways to avoid encounters with his father, especially at night when Hendrik came home with the familiar smell of gin on his breath. To avert incidents with his father, Willem took to spending more time at Birgit's and Daan's. And with other new friends.

The racket on the first floor had eased into what sounded like Catharina leaving with the girls while Hendrik continued his enraged rumblings about something that had recently happened for which he blamed Willem. The loudness returned as Hendrik belted up the stairs and stormed to the hall outside Willem's room. "He will not bring shame to this house!" Hendrik slammed into Willem's room, the beginning of daylight appearing through a split in the curtain, casting illumination on his eyes; they were devoid of any softness, stones to be thrown, a vision of vile hatred. Out it came, "changing the consent age, those stupid Christian-based politicos," referring to the change that had occurred surrounding homosexual liberties. Hendrik had been in a tizzy about it for a week since he'd heard about Christian-based parties raising the age of consent for homosexuality from sixteen to twenty-one. "Those morons need to make it illegal! It is a sin! Allowing it?" His foot banged the floor, rattling the lamp on Willem's nightstand. "Throw the lot in jail!"

An electric anxiety ran through Willem's nervous system.

"They are worse than Jews!"

There it was, Hendrik's two persecutory topics, center stage, for the hundredth time in the last week. Hendrik had been up in arms for months over humanitarian efforts underway to protect homosexual men. Not to supersede his anti-Semitism, when one topic came up, the other invariably followed. Like two fingers in a glove. To add insult to injury, he blamed the Jews for their infiltrating, tainted culture allowing homosexual bars to be established. And a homosexual magazine! Worse, his stupid son protected the topic. There's nothing wrong with it, Willem's words rebounded in Hendrik's addled brain, building pressure, ready to explode.

Willem was out of bed, his back up against the window, the moist cool air saturating his pajama top. His father neared, his stale breath fogging the window. Brilliantly antisocial, he cornered his son with his two hands against the wall, enclosing Willem. Willem pushed him off.

"Sodomy!" Hendrik grabbed hold of Willem's arm, gripping it white, "that's what you defend!"

"Let go of me." Willem struggled to loosen the tight hold

his father had on him.

"You listen to me and you listen good." Hendrik's spit landed on Willem's neck. "No more favorable talk of homosexuality in this house. No more defending Jews. Why that cheapskate Levin refuses to assist me. Degraded, good-for-nothing, every one of them."

Hendrik's dialogue had reverted back to them and they, after Ernst Levin stopped loaning him money. Pronouns were all he could swallow when talking about a Jew or a homosexual. Red-faced, puffed-out cheeks, ranting at his son, he looked ready to burst. On and on he went, stopping only to throw a fist into the wall.

Willem shook himself free from his father. Casting-off his pajamas, he quickly dressed. One look at the deformed set of knuckles on his father's left hand and he knew it was broken. "Calm down," he pleaded, for both their sakes.

The hot pain seizing Hendrik's hand stopped him. A wide-nostril breath to sooth the pin-prick spasms moving to his elbow cooled some of the burn. "No more, Willem. You hear?"

Excitable angst moved through Willem, as he sotto-voce spoke. "I am sorry you hurt your hand." He stepped back from his approaching father. "I can't abide you, father. It is not right what you say about men loving men." Whether the timing was right or not, Willem refused to cater to his father's homosexual animus. He also felt that perhaps his father's painful vulnerability was the time to let it out, "they are not just someone out *there...*"

Hendrik, preoccupied with his hand, hadn't heard what his son had just uttered, that they lived in his home. And, he told his father, he had been seeing a man and it wasn't in the same way he socialized with Daan.

"Huh?" grunted Hendrik, not understanding. But he had heard him. Just like he had heard his friends snickering over their drinks about Hendrik's son, arm-in-arm with a man. "So, what! That's not from sex, you assholes," he'd taunted back to the drunkards.

Willem repeated, somewhat hesitantly and with concern over what the outcome would be, "I was seeing a man."

Once again, Hendrik heard the words but still not wanting to fully comprehend, he needed to be sure. Before he took action. "Seeing a man? What does that mean?"

"Like, how we've been talking over the last few weeks, months, what I've been defending…I can no longer avoid stepping around it, fearing your reactions. Today you could have seriously hurt me. I will not step down from your antagonism. Unfounded loathing. I will talk to you if you can be level-headed—"

"Oh, you will, will you." Uncharacteristically restrained, most likely from pain, Hendrik's pupils widened, his forehead furrowed, and his chin jutted out. Laconically, he said, "you are no longer my son. You will pack your things and leave my house immediately." With that he left the room, bumping the door on his way out. Blast the consequences!

Stunned, Willem stood there speechless, listening to the last time he'd hear his father's footsteps march from his room. A part of him felt relieved that a discordant hostile link in the chain of his existence had been broken, freeing him. He also felt sorrow. Sad at all the wasted opportunities with his family, never connecting with his distant mother or sisters, never knowing his brothers, and being at war with his father. The worst part was the battle Hendrik had waged against him to be someone he wasn't. Someone he wasn't born to be.

As Willem collected his things, he thought of his life spent in that room, his unprotected sanctuary in the house of abandonment. Gazing out the window he remembered the visions he had painted, the wisps of flowered limbs, a variety of birds lighting and leaving, the scattering of fluffy, cotton-like clusters of cumulus clouds and the condensation their vapors shed on his window. The nights when the moon was a sliver and his room was dark. The mornings when the sky was clear and the sun bright. Out there it was safe. Calm. Inviolable. Inside, it was perilous.

The contents of his drawers were emptied into piles. What to take and what to discard. He needed to reduce his belongings to what he could carry in a suitcase in one hand and a satchel in the other. His art supplies went on top of clothing and tied-together paintings went under his arms. His life had dwindled to what would shelter his body and what would earn him a meal. A heaviness of what could have been, the closeness he'd seen at Birgit's, at Daan's, and at the Rothsteins', in comparison to what he had lived, haunted his thoughts. He stood silently for an unknown amount of time, the sun rising and heating the room. In those last moments, he took cleansing breaths. He needed to release what had weighed him down for way too long. Release and let go, just like the leftover objects, things that wouldn't fit in his suitcase and satchel. He had to leave behind what would no longer serve him and that included letting go of grudges and painful thoughts.

Just before he walked out of his room, he turned for a last look. To the rumpled bedding. A pillow on the floor. Shirts and pants strewn about. Drawers opened. A vase. A lamp. The objects that meant nothing. The areas on the walls his paintings had hung now showed lighter rectangular areas devoid of dust and spiderwebs. He nodded a slow, pensive, final goodbye and made his way down the creaking stairs. How many times had that sound warned him trouble was marching up to his room? He would not miss those rampages. Eyes on the front door, he felt confident that what was on the other side would serve him well.

With each block he passed, his thoughts washed away, like words written in the sand as the tide came in.

# THE OLD GILT CLOCK

## CHAPTER TEN

Walking the streets of Naarden, Willem's attention drifted from the present moment to the dead past. Each step was a shovel of dirt on the grave he wanted to bury his pain in. A deep sense of aloneness. He was surrounded by people out and about, in twos, threes, more, a child being hand-held while his mother pushed a perambulator with squeaking wheels carrying a baby, sounds of laughter, sneezing, and a dog barking. Arriving at the park bench where earlier he had painted Adeline Rothstein, he sat. He needed to weigh his options but his mind wasn't ready to comply. Surrendering to images, he envisioned his father's eyes shooting daggers, his acid-burning words scorching Willem's insides. Pulled out of his reverie by another dog bark, he smiled. A bittersweet upturn of his lips as tears pooled in his eyes; he remembered the three-pawed dog, its matted, long hair with mangy, bald spots. The fingers on his left hand itched. That wide-eyed, black and silver mess of fur, alone and hungry, inhaled Willem's sandwich offering. Willem's hand patted his art portfolio, it contained the sketches of that dog, done several years ago, the same day he was hit and bullied in school. The same day

Daan and Birgit befriended him. Willem knew how alone, lonely, and detached that dog must have felt. Daan's and Birgit's faces came to him, his friends. Yes, he had friends, even made new ones through Peter, but something was missing. Always missing from his life was a sustaining intimate connection.

Another mother with two young children passed him, their closeness apparent, reminding him of the earlier day with Adeline and her two. Their bond, thick like plaster, glued like beautifully patterned wallpaper to a wall. They moved beyond him, not making eye contact. It made him feel isolated. The separation Willem experienced went deeper than the current sorrow washing over him. It was what he had always known. From the insecurity of not being held, as a baby. From hours of crying in his crib until soaked with urine. From solitary days in his room hearing the comings and goings of his mother and sisters, stomping from his father, the empty distance with two brothers he knew little about. Since arriving in this world, Willem had been on a raft floating adrift, seeking directions to a safe harbor, hoping for solid ground to land on.

Well-polished shoes passed before his downcast eyes, making barely a sound. The owner must have been content, thought Willem, to have such gentle, light bounce to his step. A gentle, light touch rang through his thoughts. Touch. Where was his? Where were the arms to hold him? The hands to give him a pat on his back to assure him there's more. Perhaps, with a little luck, he would encounter the affection he had hoped awaited. As long as I breathe there is hope. He chose to believe that. He had to believe that. He set his mind to accepting that what was behind would not repeat. He made himself envision that as sure as bright stars and planets are yet visible to the naked eye as a new soft-reddish dawn brought in daylight, a bright tomorrow awaited him.

A man donning a wide-brimmed hat with a woman wearing a small lacy cap walked by in silence. Willem's fixed gaze moved from their shoes – the man's, made of European leather and hers a beige, velvet-appearing, small-heeled pump with a meshed flower on top – to their intertwined fingers, loosely held. He took one taut inhalation after the next until the unyielding pressure eased from his chest and air facilely filled his lungs. Nature before him, a sea of tulips in shades of orange, violet, and pristine white danced around a small lake that was watched over by a majestic windmill. The gifts nature gave so freely were well received by Willem. Especially the wet bog area by the lake where water overflowed and marsh trefoil grew, a plant covered with pinkish-white blossoms. It was easy to commune with nature.

Willem was momentarily distracted by a drumming sound, a two-part hammering followed by a staccato roll, in between chirps. Next heard was a peculiar melody, cackles and other raucous calls, redirecting Willem's view to a red-headed woodpecker, its long black beak in motion on a nearby tree trunk. Willem's countenance softened into a half-smile.

Stiff from sitting, he rose from the bench, straightened a wrinkle on his pant leg, stretched his lower extremities, brought his shoulder blades together, and flexed his neck. Although he felt a little better, the sense of separateness was still present. However, it had mutated to a lighter sensation in his shoulders, to the realization that it was simply a fact of his reality. Reality, no different than the bits of wood falling from the woodpecker's work. Hungry and worn out, he shook his weary head. It was time for a decision.

Although Willem was equally close with Daan and Birgit, he felt more comfortable at the Levins' home. He'd had very little interaction with Daan's busy parents, their only real connection was meals involving light, superficial conversation. Feeling a warmth, he thought of Ernst and Gabriel Levin. When he went to visit Birgit, her parents engaged him, her brother taunted, per Birgit an indication he was well-liked by Ben. They had welcomed Willem into their home, telling him to stop by whenever he felt a need. Felt a need, struck him as an odd thing to say for an invite. What he did not know was all Birgit had shared with her parents about him. Further, he had no idea they sympathized with Willem's plight; it was not unlike the persecution cast against them. Although smart in business dealings and a close-knit family, they knew what it was to be rejected, obliquely and overtly. They had learned from their daughter that Hendrik was anti-Semitic and hostile toward homosexuals. Although Jewish, they did not strictly adhere to the Old Testament, especially aspects that shunned what they felt was a natural God-given phenomenon, like falling in love. "What man would choose to love another man in heart and flesh, only to be castigated," were words Ernst shared with his daughter; his way of letting her know that he harbored no ill-feelings on the subject. Quite the contrary for him, along with his wife, felt Willem deserved defending. "He's a fine young man, speaks up against prejudice," Gabriel espoused.

The Levins – intelligent, critical-thinking, compassionate people – refused to condone pejorative biases when some of their Jewish friends insensitively and pedantically espoused biblical quotes. When a distant friend paraphrased, 'it is written, a male shall not lie with a male as one lies with a female; it is an abomination,' Ernst ignored him. Trying to cite Leviticus 18:22 to Ernst was like squeezing an apple through a buttonhole. Willem had tasted a small segment of the sweetness that came from the Levins' tolerance. Soon, he would learn what it was to be accepted, unconditionally, wide-open.

One minute he had clarity, the next turbulence. Willem's head was a whirling vortex threatening to submerge him into the dark crevices of his past that he didn't want to think about. The centrifugal motion of conflicting emotions and ideas threw him off-center. The bright day ahead he had earlier envisioned, now cast shadows of disillusion. Desperately wanting to believe the positive things he'd talked himself into, he knew there were no guarantees. The sun was now high in the sky and sweat poured from his underarms, as one decision after another was disputed and discarded.

Never having been embraced by his parents, or

acknowledged for who he was, sorely lacking what it was to grow up being nurtured through developmental stages, the Levins' words of invitation rang hollow. He loved Birgit's family but, and much as he ached to connect, he had spent years building a protective concrete shield around his heart. To protect him from his mother's cold shoulder and his father's abuse. It would take time and kindness to pulverize the solidification keeping his shoulders tight and pushed back. Yes, it would certainly take time to relax years of knotted tension in his muscles. He knew it, he felt it with each abandoned solution until the sun began to drift to the earth and his stomach cried for attention. He hadn't eaten all day. He was hungry. For food. And help. Help? That was the door he needed to walk through, no matter how uncomfortable it felt, no matter his insecurity, he had to ask for help. Suddenly, the elastic band around his chest eased and breathing came without constraint. He knew what he needed to do. He knew where he would go.

*    *    *

The lights were on in the Levins' house, melodic laughter was heard inside and a slight breeze sent a cooling sigh to Willem's sweaty cheeks. The wooden door was smooth to his touch. Willem stalled, appreciating the workmanship gone into making it, letting the trembling calm in his legs. The agglomeration of emotions, reactions he was having, surprised him. He'd been here many times before but this was new. Everything was new. This was the first time he'd knock on that sleek door with no intention of returning home, of going anywhere. Feeling scared and lost, and also hopeful, his fist tapped the door. Once. Twice. On the third time, it opened.

"Willem!" Birgit looked at Willem's pale face, what he had in his hands. Without question or hesitation, "come in… father!" Opening the door wider to accommodate Willem, she stepped back.

"What is this?" Gabriel came to the door, a spatula in her left hand, dough dripping from it onto her right one. Wide-eyed surprise written on her face at the sight of Willem putting down a suitcase, satchel, and art, she motioned to her daughter, a head-nod and quick command. "Get your father." She placed the spatula down, atop a bowl, on a hallway table and wiped her hands on a handkerchief from a pocket. A few minutes of quietude to allow the white-winter-snow pallor of Willem's complexion to defrost, she let him compose himself. Nothing needed to be rushed. The boy needs some space. Let him speak when he's ready.

Willem breathed in the yeast aroma, contemplating what he wanted to say, anxious that too much might work against him. All he could think to speak was, "I'm so sorry to inconvenience you, Mrs. Levin. I didn't know where else to go." Wiping sweat from his face with the back of his hand, he began to tell her in a few brief sentences what had happened. By the time he mentioned, "a sensitive topic that my father and I disagreed on," Ernst was at his side, along with Birgit and Ben.

Furrowing his brow, "what's happening," Ben looked to Birgit like she must know.

"Shhh, Ben," came from Gabriel.

Seeing Willem's slack shoulders, bloodshot eyes, and trembling hands, Ernst took hold of Willem's elbow, averting his attention off his ghostly complexion. "Come, sit." Ernst led the way into their drawing-room, just off the entrance landing.

The large room was a welcome distraction from Willem's personal fiasco. Grateful for a brief reprieve from his story, he looked around the room. It was a contrast to the more ornate décor of the family home he'd left, with flashy, eye-catching, hand-painted porcelain vases, gold inlaid figurines and knick-knacks, top of the line wooden, hand-carved furniture, items for show, all lacking utility benefit. The Levins' home was in step with the changing times, catering to a simpler look; it was tastefully conservative. Less cluttered. Understated but elegant. The most striking features were on the walls. Adorned with brilliant art, a couple of paintings instantly caught Willem's eye. Could that be a Breitner, he wondered, referring to an exquisite painting of a woman in a long, black dress looking in a wall mirror. He was a relatively contemporary painter and photographer, a key Dutch figure in the new movement Willem had heard about from Peter. Impressionism. *In France, Renoir and Monet... and one of ours, Breitner.* Reminded of Peter's words, nostalgia moved through Willem's torso, as that small part of his past, tiny in time but big in impact, lingered like a played, piano note. His gaze yet on the artwork, his stomach growled. Self-consciously, he readjusted his position.

Gabriel looked at Willem as he was shifting about, his abdominal gurgles apparent.

Ernst, inattentive to his wife's slight hand wave trying to get his attention to curtail further discussion, started the conversation. "I will parrot my well-intended, nosy son," he smiled at Ben, "what is happening?"

Willem's stomach's noises became louder, he crossed his legs and shifted positions hoping to quieten them.

When Ernst did not take heed of Gabriel's repeated hand gestures, she said, "perhaps we can take this to the dinner table?" Without waiting for a response, she held out her hand to Willem. "Come, let me finish dinner and you can tell us while we eat. But first, Ben," looking at her son, "take Willem up to the spare room."

Surrounding the dinner table, set with a platter of gouda cheese, chopped liver, and a fresh loaf of bread, next to a bowl of carrots, green beans, and gherkins, the five sat. The warm sweet bouquet of freshly baked bread had Willem swallowing back the saliva pooling in his mouth.

The meal progressed with questions asked and Willem's answers. Coaxed by Birgit to feel free to be completely open with her family; "they know", was implicit in the expression on her deeply concerned face, the intentness of her glossy eyes – the unexpressed need not be stated. He had seen it in her countenance many times before when he shared secrets with her. About his father's anti-Semitism. Hatred of homosexuals. About the verbal and physical abuse. From Birgit's familiar expression, Willem knew the Levins also knew.

Willem was at the juncture of the bridge he needed to cross, to unburden a weight from his chest. Not buttressed, it would have been a long fall down to the solid surface of earth. Now supported, he knew there was no turning back. No hiding. He was ready to take the next step. To present himself. Unadorned. And so, he talked. He repeated things, as the Levins sat at the edge of their seats listening, nodding encouragement. When all was finished, exhaustion hit Willem, down to muscles, tendons, to the very cellular construct of his human makeup. Cleaned out to the core, raw and open, he took in the smiles and hugs. And a few tears from Birgit and her mother.

Later that night, when all was said and done, in his new room, surrounded by light colors and fabric, with a minimum of decorum, healthy and clean appearing, Willem felt safe. Warm and cozy, under a fluffy-airy, down comforter, reclined on a firm mattress, he had a deep, uninterrupted, restorative sleep.

## CHAPTER ELEVEN

Although Willem had a good night's sleep, the exhaustive emotional impact from the day before lingered and he awoke the next morning feeling disoriented. The first day in his new living place didn't feel right. It felt foreign and uncomfortable. Although grateful the Levins had taken him in and done all they could to make him feel welcome, he was unable to shake the sense of isolation heavy in his bones. He couldn't just snap a finger and suddenly feel like he belonged. The heavy suitcase of rejection into which he'd packed so many painful emotions was too tightly shut. It would take time for it to open, months before anything in the dark valise would meet sunshine and air-out. In the meantime, he did what he had always done, posture himself, with shoulders up, chest out, and did his best to walk tall into the next moment.

Barely audible voices and the aroma of what smelled like kroketten floated upstairs to the bedroom where Willem had slept. A quick look at the clock on the nightstand revealed it was nearing nine. Willem shot upright and out of bed. Nine! Never having slept in that late, he was mad at himself that he wasn't downstairs with the rest of them as he didn't want to inconvenience anyone by detaining their breakfast or any other of their daily routines. Making haste, he poured water from the vase on the washstand into a bowl next to it. After a quick scrub with a washcloth, he dressed and descended the stairs where he was met with laughter and a new voice coming out of an unknown woman standing next to the table where Birgit and her parents sat.

"Willem," Birgit stood from the dining room table and pulled out a chair, "come, sit." Motioning to the set table where her parents were being served by the new woman, "I hope you're hungry," she smiled at the five-foot-eight, stocky woman, with short brown hair, parted on the side like a male haircut, who held a tray of kroketten surrounded by mashed potatoes smothered in butter.

Ernst reiterated, "please, sit."

To which Gabriel nodded, adding, "yes, Willem, please make yourself comfortable."

Willem took his place at the table and not sure what to do next, remained quiet.

The pleasantly smiling, large woman was dressed in a drab, gray wool-dress covering her busty body from neck to ankle. Over it, she wore a white pinafore that had seen its fair share of use, with frayed edges and a few stains from meals prepared. Taking an unexpected liberty, she said, "you must be Willem. My little Birgit," she returned a warm, soft smile to Birgit, "tells me you're here to stay for a while."

*For a while. My little Birgit.* Willem had visited the Levins' house before but didn't recall seeing this woman who had served everyone and put the tray down on a side table. He startled when she placed a hand on his back.

"Glad to meet you. I'm Johanna." She caught Ernst nodding approval for her to continue. "I've been with these fine people for longer than I care to remember."

Gabriel stifled a giggle.

Ernst stood and to Willem's expanding surprise held out a chair for Johanna. Noting the head-tilted, furrowed-brow confusion written on Willem's face, he said, "Johanna was nanny to Birgit when I brought her home from the hospital. Gabriel was too ill to tend to her and so we hired our friend here," he said with a hand on Johanna's shoulder. "She's like family."

"Food's getting cold," piped in Johanna, her grin widening.

"Yes, she is family," added Birgit, "and bossy."

Laughter erupted, easing Willem's confusion.

"I hope you like kroketten," said Gabriel, eying Willem's untouched plate of food, "if not, we can—"

"No… no, I love it, especially with mashed potatoes. This looks delicious," he responded and cut into the breadcrumb crust. A mouthful of the crumbed coating, melting down, to tasting the beef ragout, convinced Willem he was in for a real treat. "This is delicious. I'm doubtful, I've ever had better. Did you make—"

"No," butted in, Johanna, "she can't take credit for this one." Johanna playfully winked at Gabriel.

"You made dinner last night…" Willem shifted his eyes

from Gabriel to Johanna, "I just assumed…"

"I have the breakfast shift and let the lady of the house have her go at some of the other meals from time to time," dallied Johanna, in a bouncing response.

Seeing Willem pull back and force a smile, Ernst surmised that the lightheartedness might be making Willem feel uncomfortable. "Johanna, speaks her mind, Willem," he gave Johanna a look that rang serious and not to be interrupted, enough with the levity. Ernst and Gabriel had spoken with Birgit and Johanna before Willem came down, as Ben was on his way out the door for school and suggested things be kept pleasant and by that they meant light-hearted. "We allow it…" Ernst hesitated.

Willem was sure he saw Ernst's eyes water.

"Were it not for this woman here," motioning to Johanna, Ernst pointed his emptied fork in his hand, "we would have lost Birgit." Wiping a quick finger across his eyes, "we've all had our share of hard times." His attention shifted to Gabriel. "It's always been my best guess my beloved wife would never have survived the loss of a child." He then went on to tell the story of how when Birgit was a few days old, just after a breast-fed meal from Gabriel, Johanna brought the baby back to her crib. She placed Birgit on her back supported by pillows but just as Johanna was at the door, she heard a commotion. Birgit had rolled onto her stomach with one of the pillows blocking her airway. Fast action, a slap on the back and the baby screamed bloody murder, much to the relief of the nanny. The Levins felt they owed their first-born's life to Johanna. When Gabriel healed from the birth and had her energy back, she could have easily tended to her baby, rather she decided to keep Johanna on. When Ben was born, Johanna took care of both children. As they grew and no longer needed a nanny, Gabriel asked her to stay on as their housekeeper and cook. They could have afforded more help but with Gabriel liking to busy herself in the kitchen it worked out well to let Johanna share some of the meal preparation. Johanna, being a strong, independent woman, never lived with the Levins although she would have been welcomed there, just like Willem. Johanna enjoyed her privacy and lived in a single flat within walking distance.

Willem listened and as the words washed over him, he felt a deep sense of connectedness with the strange, masculine-appearing, nanny-turned-cook-turned-family member. What he felt around her was visceral, and inexplicable. Not unlike how he felt with Daan and Birgit when he first met them. The meals continued, with Johanna being present for most breakfasts and an occasional dinner when she laughed about wanting to eat what they were serving that night. The days moved on and Willem looked forward to being around her; it was one of the few things that interested him.

A couple of weeks had passed. The Levins left Willem to do as he wanted, to allow him to decompress from all he had been through. Although they were affectionate in words, considerate in their manner, thoughtful how they presented themselves in leaned-back posture, and manifested delicate lit-up facial expressions,

Willem continued to struggle with a feeling of separateness. No matter how hard he tried or wanted to, he did not feel like he belonged. It didn't help Willem's feelings of aloneness that Daan had distanced himself. Birgit's making excuses for their friend, although well-intended, were unconvincing.

The hope Willem had built up, made of tissue-paper mental dreams began to pull apart, trapping him in a web of confusion that would not dissipate with encouraging words or promises from Birgit's parents that things would get better. They told him that he was a talented, gifted artist and his gift would serve him well. He didn't believe it and like a fly in a spider's web, Willem remained stuck. Without direction. Without purpose. In those few weeks, Willem was deeply distressed. Disillusioned. With no money, no job, no prospects, he sank into a deeper despair with each passing day.

Gabriel gave him odd jobs to do around the house, handyman work and assisting the gardener with the upkeep of the grounds, to keep his mind occupied. She knew, what Willem hadn't yet come to realize; all that he needed was time to decompress from the traumatic situation he'd recently been extricated from. The wounds needed delicate cleansing and balms to soothe them back to health, not bandages to cover them. He'd had enough of covering his distress, for way too long. Now, the raw part of his heart, his vulnerable core, needed fresh air, rest, nutrition, and people surrounding him with affection and appreciation. Then he would heal.

Change didn't come right away, in fact for weeks Willem wondered if his life was to be nothing more than aimlessly existing from one meaningless event to the next. Grateful for all he'd been given by Ernst, Gabriel, Birgit, and, yes, Ben who tried in his own young way to cheer up Willem, it didn't matter. Feeling like he was sinking in sand, he inertly went about his routine around the house.

Birgit was at Willem's side watching him dabbling in painting, sat next to him during meals, and joined him while they dug holes to plant new garden seedlings. She never complained about or objected to Willem's mood, the lingering shadow of gloom he tried to cover up with a camouflaged, smiling, stoic façade and mindless puttering. No, beside him she was a mirror of empathy, not in any way attempting to talk him into or out of anything, instead granting him the space he needed to evolve through the mist of thick, opaque fog that would disperse and become translucent on its own. Patience was one of Birgit's virtues, one which would eventually pay off.

At first, Willem's transition was hardly perceptible and if Birgit hadn't been with him to see his sunken eyes open wider and extrovert from a faraway look, it would have been missed. Little things like his noticing a prickly stem erupting from a neglected mound of dry weeds and decayed organic matter, then only days later, at that same spot, to run his fingers over a sprouting, dark-yellow rosebud and inhale the aroma spread over his index finger and thumb. To Birgit, Willem's nostrils flaring and chest expanding looked as if he had enjoyed a perfumed handkerchief. He never made comment about the fleeting experience. She never inquired. She didn't have to. It was answer enough to see his shaded-appearing skin, lighten.

That was how it was with them, experience, watch, observe, move on. Diminutive episodes continued. Another time, a small greenish-blue rock drew his attention until he picked it up and rubbed it between his hands, commenting on its surprisingly smooth pacifying texture. He put it in his pocket. The next day, wearing the same outfit as the last several days, Willem appeared agitated. Biting his lower lip, he took the rock out of the pocket and rolled it between his twittering hands until the spasms stopped.

Inconspicuous to anyone not observing, all the little things added up. Then, on a day he was in the backyard alone, raking fallen foliage, he happened upon what he thought was a clump of dead, dried White-Willow tree, leaves. On closer inspection, he saw it was an unconscious baby swift, its plainly-colored, charcoal feathers rapidly moving as it pumped air into its lungs. It must have fallen from a nest and banged its head, knocking it out. Tears pooled in Willem's eyes, as he kneeled beside it, wishing it to return to consciousness and find its mother. He knew not to touch it, for to put his scent on its body could cause the mother to reject it. A chirp from a limb above was his answer. The mother bird watching, Willem very slowly backed away. Wake up little fellow, he sent a thought to the small feathered creature. He sat there ten minutes and seeing the tiny bird's chest continue to rapidly move, he waited. Twenty minutes and the bird opened its eyes and wiggled its wings. Attempting to stand on its dainty legs, its tiny talons wobbled and it fell down. Willem's heart pumped simultaneously with the bird's breaths, fast and erratic. More minutes passed with Willem's attention frozen on the little creature struggling for life. Finally, it rose, flapped its miniscule wings and flew up to its mother.

With his eyes heavenward, large and wet, he let loose the tears he'd been holding back. Sorrow that had been building for years. Out came the floodwaters, triggered by the tender pain of seeing the mother with her hatchling, the bond so clear and visible, like the mom pushing her baby in a perambulator in the park the day of his expulsion from his home. Home. That was a foreign word. Where he had lived, it was a building, not a social unit formed by a family living together. No, that wasn't home, it was a boarding house.

The day of the fallen swift was the day Willem connected with a force greater than his own wishes and desires, it was a watershed moment for him. "Feeling outside of my own little self," he liked to call it, he connected with a new purpose in life. To care for and serve others while finding passion and joy in the moments of life. But how to meld this with his affinity to do art? Be kind in all you do. Be true to thyself. Forward the greater good. Do what you love. Not clear, on what this barrage of new thinking was all about, rising from submersion, his passion for art had been invigorated. There would be many days Willem would look back on that pivotal experience and ponder what it all meant, only to fall back on what he felt was the ultimate epiphany. Life will reveal things in its own way.

Whether it was because of that little bird, fallen from a nest, unconditional support from the Levins, the despair of hitting rock-bottom when he was kicked out of his house with nowhere to go but up, or a myriad of other possibilities, all he knew was that the rumbling thunder and torrential storming inside of his head had calmed. Just like a day after a cleansing rain brings dewdrops cascading off leaves and fresh air, Willem felt revived.

## CHAPTER TWELVE

Days came into being, as the sun pierced the darkness, casting off the ash of night and bringing in the intense scarlet dawn. Not all mornings were glorious, some were darker when the clouds obscured the sun, but all were different and ever-changing, like Willem's existence. With each new dawn came something new and unexpected. During overcast hours, when a dark canopy of grey shielded cauliflower puffs in the sky, Willem tried to conquer the diabolical forces of oppressive loneliness that had shrouded him. Although the sounds of his father's tormenting voice and the images of his mother's outstretched-palm-of-dismissal had become weaker in his memory, the impact was still present, creating a lingering insecurity. Despite Gabriel's urgings that he spend his time on his art, to be able to make a living for himself, he feared he was overstaying his welcome by spending time in his room or outdoors involved in painting or sketching, with less and less time delegated to chores around the property. Willem was plagued with worry wondering when the day would come that he would be told to pack his things and fend for himself. With Daan becoming even more distant, Willem had nowhere else to go.

Despite his anguish that he was overstaying his welcome, the kindness Birgit's parents extended to Willem knew no limit. Not only did they give him the space to work on his art but they allowed him the time to produce several paintings. They also lined up a few of their friends that they thought would be interested in purchasing them. Among those were the Rothsteins, whom Willem had seen little of since the breakup with Peter. Although they agreed to be amicable with each other, Willem felt uncomfortable continuing to cultivate a relationship with Peter's relatives. Willem had especially missed seeing Adeline and the children. Now invited there as a result of Ernst's promoting, Willem accepted the invitation.

With art in hand and the use of the Levins' car, Willem set out for the Rothsteins' house. On the way, his stomach felt like a hundred moths were eating through its mucosa; he lacked confidence that his work would be purchased other than as charity. He desperately wanted to become an accomplished artist but he needed more than charitable friends to buy his work. To him, it seemed impossible that such a leap could be made. It was situations like this when uncertainty reigned. Left to his own devices, once again he had to trust his insides. Glancing out the side of the car, he passed people walking and children at play. By chance, he saw a rodent scurrying underground and was reminded of something a teacher had taught while he was still in school. It was a lesson about trusting in the nature of things because nature knows how to trust in itself. Creatures know how to take care of themselves. When bees build a beehive, they don't consult an architect. Why? Because they already know what to do. Intuition resonated with Willem. It was then that he knew he would be okay, whether or not a painting sold as a gesture of charity or of its own merit.

In the time since Willem had been kicked out of his house, he had developed an embryo of faith. It wasn't a construct of a God on an altar or written about in the Bible. It wasn't something that came to him through proselytizing. On the contrary, it had arrived through an accumulation of what made sense to him. From many places and differing experiences. From the fabric of life, like seeing the rodent and remembering a lesson. Through his own observations, feelings in his body, Willem was guided. Little did he know that on this visit to the Rothsteins, he would put to use a tenet that would become his North Star, the heart of his inner constellation – the truth will set you free.

Parked before the grandiose home of the Rothsteins, Willem no longer felt small. Entering their large but warm home, Oscar met him at the door.

"Come on in, my boy." Oscar took hold of the painting in Willem's hands and guided him to the den, lined with filled bookcases, where he placed the art on a display easel. Motioning to an overstuffed, comfy-looking, velvet-covered chair he directed Willem to "have a seat."

Willem's hand moved over the silk twill, noticing the various shades of lavender and muted purple. The circular pattern, pleasing to him, matched other objects in the room, lacking showiness, mostly in good taste with the exception of a gaudy, gold clock sitting on Oscar's desk. Its mausoleum façade with pointed turrets looked more like a Victorian prison than a chronometer. It was clearly out of place.

Oscar met Willem's eyes squinting at the dull-gilt timepiece clicking minutes as if he wondered why it was tarnished when everything else in the room was in pristine condition, clean fabrics, polished wood, and neatly displayed vases and knick-knacks. Why amid all the understated good-taste was that piece of junk in the room?

"That," exhaled a breathy-sounding Oscar, rubbing a hand through his hair, "is a story… poor man," he reflectively said, as if Willem would have known who he was referring to. "He was in a bad way… I offered to help him but being too proud…" Oscar stopped himself, shook his head and sniffed in a runny nose. "Oh, you don't need to be bothered with my affairs. Let's see what you've brought." Oscar moved to the edge of his chair to get up.

Seeing distress written all over Oscar's expression, the repetitive movement of his fingers through strands of hair, Willem leaned back, indicating getting up to see the painting could wait. "I'd like to hear," he empathetically blurted out. Feeling somewhat self-conscious with his overly assertive tone, he lowered his voice. "If you don't mind telling me."

It turned out to be a risk well worth taking. Willem listened intently to Oscar when he spoke about a man who he'd been friends with, another Jewish man, who had migrated to the Netherlands from Russia. "Timing is everything, Willem. One week you wake up, go to work, come home, have a meal with your family and the next… things change. Sadly, they change." He took a handkerchief from his suit pocket, wiped his eyes, blew his nose and went on to deliver a heart-wrenching description of events that happened at the turn of the century in Russia in Kishinev. "My friend was away from his home… it was Russian Easter Sunday 1903. Anti-Semitic violence erupted." Pausing to catch his breath, Oscar looked past Willem, as if seeing an image before him of a time long gone. "Willem," he continued, lost in his thoughts, "rioting took the lives of forty-nine Jews," a long silence was followed by, "women were raped." He wiped tears trickling down his cheeks. "Buildings were destroyed, 700 homes… 600 stores."

Willem was motionless. Holding his breath. Listening.

"As I mentioned, my friend was not there. When he returned home, he learned of all the destruction. That was the heinous day he found out that his family, his wife and two small children, a girl three and a boy two, had been murdered." Oscar lowered his head and mumbled in a barely audible voice, "he was told he was one of the lucky ones, that he'd made it through alive."

Lucky? Trying to remove the stricture in his throat, Willem swallowed hard.

"Devastated, he buried his family the next day…" Oscar's eyes introverted, once again, appearing as if looking at some distant image. "I remember the day he told me what had happened." Pensively rubbing his upper lip, Oscar went on. "After he had been helped to emigrate, we met. Over and over, he moaned, 'why?' Not that he expected an answer. Innocents – young children, who can know why?" Shaking his head, Oscar picked up the clock and rubbed it like it were a valued pet. "Idiots told him that there was a reason, God's design, that all would be revealed in time." With a disgusted puckered sneer, Oscar redirected his attention back to Willem, "the world is full of stupid people. No, I tell you, Willem, from my perspective there is no seeing any big picture, nothing can explain pure unadulterated evil."

Willem's gaze followed Oscar's hand hugging the clock.

"This here," Oscar motioned his chin downward, to the object, "is one of the only things the man was able to find that hadn't been destroyed or stolen." Oscar finished up by telling Willem that when the man was destitute and in need of a loan, he refused to take money without offering collateral. The timepiece, at one time of great value in gold alone, was all he had to offer. Oscar lent him ten times what it was worth. Sadly, a week after securing the loan the man died of a heart attack. "It was as if letting go of his last possession, the last connection to his family and home, he gave up. That's what I believe." He sat back in his chair.

What transpired between Oscar and Willem that day was more than conversation, more than sharing the story of a horrific situation, it was something deeply intimate and personal. Willem felt saddened. Humbled. Honored, in a solemn way, that a man of great status, prestige, and wealth took his time to share. Took his time to include a teenage boy. Perhaps Oscar, in his infinite wisdom, knew that Willem desperately needed to be invited in, not just with words but into a place of deep trust. That incipient moment was when Willem began learning what it was to belong.

*   *   *

That same day, after tea and cake, when emotions had cooled, while the painting was being viewed, Willem wondered where Adeline and the children were. His curiosity was answered when a rather attractive, blond-haired, green-eyed girl barged into the den. "Uncle Oscar," she looked at Willem and stepped back. "Oh, I'm sorry, I didn't know—"

"Come in, my dear," Oscar waved a hand for her to have a look at the painting. "This is the artist I was telling you about."

"Oh," she glanced at the landscape, "that's really good."

"Yes, Willem here, is rather talented," he smiled.

Seemingly distracted, the girl's attention went to the door. "Where is Aunt Adeline? The children?"

Oscar, to Willem's disappointment, explained that they were out and wouldn't return for a couple of hours.

"Mamma dropped me off and will be back by dinner." She smiled at Willem, a warm wide grin, her eyes twinkling that she was not that upset to miss her aunt and cousins. "Femke," she held out a hand.

"Willem," he returned the introduction, feeling the firm, warm touch of her hand holding his a little longer than was comfortable.

Oscar, taking heed of the interest his niece seemed to express for Willem, said, "so then, we have a deal?" referring to the agreed-upon price for Willem's painting that he genuinely wanted to purchase. "And, we will discuss the others another time?"

They had talked about other people, friends who were art aficionados, that Oscar suggested he could show some paintings to. Now that Willem had a small collection, Oscar would arrange a get-together to display his work. Luck and good fortune shined on Willem that afternoon. With their business completed, Femke, who had been impatiently tapping a foot, grabbed hold of Willem's shirt sleeve and whisked him off with, "let's have a stroll around their garden, shall we?"

Without any time to reply, he was out the door, Femke's arm intertwining his, to a luscious garden filled with bulbs in bloom in every assorted color of red, pink, and mauve. Atop vibrant, verdant lawns were several bubbling displays of water, cascading down beautifully landscaped terraces. "My favorite part of uncle's home," she said.

"Yes," he looked around at the abundance of overflowing coloration, soothing to take in. Feeling her hand rubbing his arm, a flustered prickly sensation rose up his back. Hoping this wouldn't turn awkward, his mind returned to an earlier realization, the truth will set you free. By fluke, it was originally quoted to him from a religious friend of Peter's, an artist. An odd combination, he thought, art and religion. Why not, he smiled.

Mistaking his amusement, Femke asked, "would you like to meet sometime?"

Her alluring soft intonation and downcast eyelids made it difficult for him to unabashedly say, "although I find you a rather nice person—"

Quickly cooling, she removed her hand from his arm and stepped back. "Well!"

Sensitively responding, he reached back to her hand. "It's not what you think."

Her hand tensed in his.

The truth will set you free, and so he spoke his. "I like boys."

Letting out a relieved sigh, "oh…" she giggled, "like… Peter?"

Stepping into a new daylight, no further words were needed from him, a nod of yes sufficed.

"Well then," she tightened her grip in his hand, "we can be friends."

Willem had repeated visits with Oscar and Adeline but he never saw Femke again. Although he had met her but once, she was indeed his friend when compassionately revealing to the Rothsteins that Willem was homosexual. Like their beloved Peter.

A many stepping-stone journey to unwrap the cloak of shame Hendrik had dressed Willem in, had begun.

# CHAPTER THIRTEEN

Although the number of people espousing anti-Semitism was yet to grow into massive numbers and the Jews had prospered in the Netherlands throughout the 19th century, the blurring of boundaries between Gentiles and Jews had caused small pockets of resentment. A toxic segment of intolerant bigots was upset about Gentile-Jewish marriages, residential intermixing, and the increase in joint civic and political involvement. Due to the coalescing, fanatics feared Jews would form pillars (the politico-denominational segregation of a society into religious and associated political beliefs). Not dissuaded by the fact that Dutch Jews were a small part of the population and demonstrated a strong inclination toward peaceful integration into Dutch society and never having coalesced into a pillar, the anti-Semites still believed the opposite. To them, reality was the propaganda, merely lies allegedly spread by Jews and worse, despicable Jew-lovers. From their narrow-minded world view, they believed Jewish pillarization was already covertly occurring and surely would overwhelm the decent citizens, the true Dutch.

Garnering consensual validation was their aim, as their

whispers rang through dark alleys, where two or more shared a drink, in the privacy of homes, and behind closed doors, all the places it was safe to enlist agreement – where racism spread without dissent.

"They will band together and wipe us out."

"They are gaining momentum, why, one married our neighbor's daughter. Heaven forbid!"

"They'll overthrow the banks."

"They'll destroy our culture. The theater will not be worth attending."

"Their forbidden foods will ruin our restaurants."

As their voices grew louder, the words also took on darker tones.

"Filth."

"Pigs."

"They don't deserve to live in the Netherlands."

"They don't deserve to live."

"Something needs to be done about them."

Blinded by biased animosity, the insanity of the accusations, bearing no foundation, in fact, would never be seen for what they were, a hornet's nest of lies. Vigilante groups formed and made plans. A smattering of anti-Semitic events took place; a robbery here, a defacement of property there, a false claim of food poisoning from a store or restaurant, etc. Joining the mindset, in agreement with the covert hostilities ignored by police, was Hendrik. With his drinking buddies, he fumed and planned how to get even for his failing business. He'd get the Jew who stopped financing him.

First came the rumors of crooked financial loans. The gossip expanded into false claims that the government was wise to the criminal activities of the money-lenders.

"They can't be trusted."

"Steer clear of them."

"I know what I'm talking about," lied Hendrik.

Ears perked up.

Covert speech took place in important hallways.

Other institutions took note.

Other institutions stole business.

Ernst Levin's bank was a prime target. "Come-uppance for that bastard Jew," bemoaned Hendrik, who in his warped, twisted, alcoholic brain blamed Ernst not just for loss-of-business but also his son's perversion.

Willem would be spared from ever finding out about his father's involvement in the cascade of unfortunate events to follow.

\*　　\*　　\*

Well into 1913 and swimmingly content with Willem's progress, his children doing well in their ventures, and Gabriel's involvement with multiple charities keeping her busy, Ernst felt grateful to be living in a country not officially hostile to Jewish people. But with his business and social connections, he was aware of the rising anti-Semitic talk and actions against Jews. He also knew that he was not immune. With hostilities rising in Europe and wars breaking out, he was relieved that he lived in a place where peace was valued. Having just read a newspaper article about the opening of Vredespaleis in the Hague, he was impressed that Queen Wilhelmina had opened the Peace Palace, the Permanent Court of Arbitration. A drawing of the Neo-Renaissance building, with its massive bell tower, on the front page, had caught his attention. It reminded him of other articles he'd read, about the tensions between Italy and Turkey that resulted in the Italo-Turkish War several months back. And an anarchy bug breaking out, spreading its infection to the Balkan League and giving rise to the alliance between Bulgaria, Greece, Serbia, and Montenegro, which had declared war on the Ottoman Empire. Remembering those articles, he thought, they were not aligned with peace, like the Vredespaleis.

His thoughts shifted from the newspaper to his daughter's recent venture in helping friends in their Jewish bakery. Ernst sipped from the cup of tea he'd been drinking, proud of her. Smiling, he was glad that she'd taken on a part-time job to earn her own pocket change and to get out of the house to socialize. Despite his wealth, he had taught his children the value of money and the importance of being productive constituents in society. Ben, once finished with his schooling, would follow suit, earning his own way. As for himself, Ernst had plans. Expansive plans. He wanted to help more Jewish families succeed. To do that his bank needed to bring in new money. He foresaw doing that by partnering with the wealthy tycoon, Andrew Carnegie, who financed the Peace Palace – to the sum of $1.5 million U.S. dollars. The man has crazy ideas about religion but he's very successful, thought Ernst who didn't care that Carnegie had ideas about something called evolution. No, Ernst didn't mind doing business with someone who rejected Christianity. Unfortunately, he did not know the extent that his dealing with Carnegie pitted him against Christians. One falsely pious, non-church-attending, drunk Christian, in particular, whose son was living in Ernst's home.

"Disgusting! Christ haters!"

"I told you, they want to confiscate all our money," buzzed Hendrik, to listening ears.

Jealously permeated.

Hostilities rose.

Scorned institutions and businesses, left out of the Peace Palace transactions, paid attention.

Payback couldn't touch Carnegie, but it sure as hell could ruin Ernst Levin who foolishly attempted to partner with the enemy of Christianity. Carnegie was barraged by naysayers. The hassle factor turned Carnegie away from working with Levin.

Without ever fully understanding why, Levin lost the opportunity to do business with the rich American. Businesses pulled funds from his bank. He lost his health.

All this occurred as Willem smoothly strolled through 1913

selling art. While Willem's confidence improved and he navigated his days, satisfied, Ernst had grown despondent. While Willem was expanding and thinking of renting a simple flat and branching out on his own, Ernst had contracted into a shell of his prior self. Hiding his feelings under a mask of fake smiles and pleasantries, he fooled all around him who were too busy with their own lives. Too preoccupied, until tragedy struck.

*   *   *

Well away from the house, out at the far end of the garden, the day started uneventfully. In natural light, Willem captured the appearance of the outdoors. Wisps of wind moved through tree limbs, flushing birds from their perches. Filled branches shaded areas below, until the sun disappeared, changing vibrant daylight to gray. It was time to wrap up his outdoor work and head inside. Nearing dinnertime, his stomach complained that he had skipped lunch. Lost in the ardor of his work, he'd done that often, become so involved that meals were missed. Tonight, he felt a great sense of satisfaction with the accomplishments of the day and he looked forward to having a meal with the Levins and Johanna, who he knew was in the kitchen preparing dinner, as Adeline had a meeting that afternoon.

Entering the backdoor, the kitchen was quiet. The absence of an aroma was puzzling. Willem wondered what was going on. Squeaking floorboards upstairs, frantic tromping in and out of what must have been Ernst and Gabriel's bedroom, gave him a bad feeling. He listened to the hoarse, nasal tones that sounded like someone was crying. Willem was half-way up the stairs when the front door banged opened and in rushed Johanna followed by the family doctor, Jerome Koningberg. The overweight and bald man blurred past Willem.

Willem, crushed against the balustrade, smelled the medicinal ammonia odor coming out of the black bag in the doctor's hand. Smelling salts, he thought, remembering when he'd smelled them an earlier time during a doctor's visit. Fear coursed through his irregularly pulsing arteries, his fingers tightening on the handrail felt numb. Cautiously, he followed the doctor and Johanna.

"No!" a piercing scream came from Gabriel.

Birgit and Ben wept moans of disbelief when they were informed, with a sorrowful headshake, it was too late.

Willem watched the scene in slow motion, the loving wife crumbling to the floor, Birgit vomiting into her skirt, and Ben repeating, "no, it's a mistake," over and over.

Johanna, wiping sweat from her wrinkled brow and wetness dripping from her chin, caught sight of Willem at the door. She motioned him to her and in a slow funeral march, with sunken chest, he went to his friend. They had grown very fond of each other over the last couple of years, sharing meals together, becoming close. His heart felt like it would explode when she whispered in his ear, "it was a heart attack."

Willem sank into Johanna, her arms holding him up.

"Too much worry," she sobbed. "Too much pressure," she wept. "Persecution, it got to him."

Willem remained in Johanna's embrace, breathing onto her neck, crying onto her dress.

"Persecution for being Jewish!" Her words were overshadowed by the wailing in the room.

Persecution? What a thing to say at the deathbed of the man who had been like a father to him, the father he had never experienced with Hendrik. This can't be. Is it real? It made no sense, not here in Naarden. There were rumors persecution happened in other places in Europe. Not here. He couldn't believe that the things he had heard about since a young boy, gossip he and Daan spared Birgit from, had played a part in Ernst's death. Not Ernst!

There was no hastening the unbearable plodding the next hours brought. The body was taken to the doctor's office, which had a back room that functioned as a funeral parlor. A wooden casket was obtained, it was what Ernst wanted. In accordance with Jewish tradition, it was something that would decompose and he would join with the earth he so loved living on. The next day, standing around the simple coffin were the Levins, the Rothsteins, and a bevy of relatives and business associates. None, without wet, bloodshot sclera, sniveling noses, and wrinkled distress written on their faces for their beloved family member and friend. Birgit looked like she would fall over any minute from the weight of unbearable grief and Gabriel was frozen in disbelief. Neither one of them snapped out of it, not during the rest of Willem's days with them. Ben was stoic, strong for his family, as grief poured out of the surrounding black suits and dresses.

Grappling with the unreality of it all, Willem couldn't get air into his lungs, the heartache was too great. Over and over, his head told him it was a mistake, a bad dream, that they would all wake up and... whispering startled him.

"Damn anti-Semitism did this to him!"

"Shhh, not here."

"It needs to be spoken. The hatred has to stop."

"Shhh, not now."

"Not here... not here. Not now... not now."

"When!"

The last whimper drew attention and lip-smacking agreement, not here!

The funeral ended with silence.

Silence became a way of life in the house that had become a shell of loneliness without its soul. The walls were now a fortress that housed a family torn asunder, not just from the loss but the circumstances that caused it. They learned from Oscar Rothstein what happened; about the broken glass window at the bank that Ernst quietly replaced, never informing his wife, not wanting to disrupt the family's sense of tranquility. Oscar sat them down and told them all that he knew, about the clients who, under pressure and threat, left and worse, about the threats on Ernst and his family. Included were Ernst's plans for them to move to America. To get away from the hatred. To be rid of the underhanded, slowly spreading anti-Semitism. But the strain on Ernst's heart had been too great. Oscar would see his wishes to move his family to America were actualized.

Johanna was deeply involved in the move, the packing and shipping, the selling off items too bulky to transport, the unessential things that could easily be let go. She did what needed doing, suffering without complaint. She was there for them. She was there for Willem. Gabriel had asked her to go with them but she declined, saying she had a life here she didn't want to leave. What life was that? wondered Willem. Gabriel also told Willem that he was family. Family! Another time that would have brought him happiness. Now, there was only pain. He also told Birgit he wanted to stay when she said to him to, "come with us."

On the dock, the crying, shattered family choked out their goodbyes. Gabriel looked like she had aged twenty years and Birgit's eyes flooded pools of sorrow onto her dress. Ben, holding his mother's hand, sadly told Willem, "we'll stay in touch."

Willem wanted to help, to offer something that might lighten the gloom on their faces, the darkness clouding their vision but there were no cheerful words. How could he find the right thing to say when senseless prejudice had stolen so much? No, there was nothing uplifting to say, there never would be. Platitudes and euphemisms would never do. So, it was without a hope or prayer that they did what they had to, they said goodbye. And moved on.

\*    \*    \*

After the ship carrying the Levins departed, when the house was empty and all the belongings had been sold, Johanna told Willem about her life. It was then she opened up and spoke of what she hadn't earlier shared. It was what he had wondered about, the camaraderie between them, the familiar relationship from day one, they were from the same mold. The same tribe. It was this sameness that sealed their friendship for the rest of their lives. Sameness, Willem would look back on this time, this word, and remember she was the first lesbian he became close with.

Shortly after Gabriel, Birgit, and Ben moved to America, the Rothsteins packed up and also set off to meet Libertas, the Statue of Liberty. Once they landed, Adeline sent a letter to Willem telling him about the welcoming Roman liberty goddess, holding a torch above her head in her right hand and in her left a tabula-ansata. "A broken shackle and chain lie at her feet. It commemorates the abolition of slavery," she explained. "Freedom." The paper was smudged, the ink-stained by what looked like tear droplets. "That's what I wish for you, my dear friend. To be free." Also, in a postscript, she wrote, "Johanna has something for you. Oscar left it with her. He gifts it to you with love. And his hope that you live a good, long life."

Inhaling the scent of Adeline's perfume, Willem's fingers

moved over the silky paper. A good, long life. Relieved they were safe, a heaviness yet pressed onto his chest. It had been the only mail he'd received from any of them. He wondered how the rest were weathering. They were never far from his thoughts.

There was a knock on the door of the room above a bakery where he now lived. Helped by a bequest received from Ernst's estate, he had rented it when the Levins' house was sold. The knock grew louder. He knew it was Johanna, on time for their tea date and to deliver the mysterious thing mentioned in Adeline's letter.

## CHAPTER FOURTEEN

One look at what was in Johanna's arms and Willem was in tears. There was no holding back the emotions and loss that had been plaguing him since Ernst's death, the feelings he attempted to hide. The agony he shoved down, deep inside, as he tried to paint, to socialize and struggle to get back to living. All he'd held back, came pouring out. Tearful nostalgia sailed between them. Johanna held the object out and he ran his hand over the cool, dull surface. It looked exactly as he had remembered, how he envisioned it many times since that day in Oscar's den.

Johanna, stilled by his tears, remained unmoving, Willem's open front door dividing them, he couldn't take his eyes off of it. He had so many holes in his memory, like swiss cheese, things he wanted to forget, things he naturally forgot, but this, this he would never forget.

A couple more intense moments, taking hold of it, he moved aside for Johanna to enter his tiny one-room apartment. She looked around the familiar room, to the small kitchenette, the bed against a far wall at a ninety-degree angle to an adjacent window. Her eyes roamed to a two-seat table with a scattering of plates, saucers, cups, and utensils on it, next to his art supplies. The only empty space was atop an old, worn, wooden chest of drawers. She nodded at the dresser. "Are you going to put it there?"

He didn't answer. Instead, he simply hugged it. "How did this happen? How did this come to me?"

Warm from climbing the stairs to his stifling, closed-in room, she wiped perspiration from her forehead. "Can we sit," she simpered, pulling out a chair.

"Yes, yes. Forgive my manners. Please—"

"I understand."

At the table, she took a small note from her handbag and handed it to Willem. "This came with it."

The words on the paper went from his eyes to his heart. Right to the place beyond defensive barriers from hostile denigrating sounds, to the soft fertile ground where love grows. Unaware he had been whispering the message, "remember us," over and over, Johanna tapped a finger on the table drawing his attention.

"You asked how it happened? How this came to you?"

"Yes."

"When the Rothsteins were packing," she told him that Adeline had contacted her to say goodbye and give her a personal memento. It was during that visit that Oscar took her into his den, to his desk, to see the singular object left on it. "Oscar told me that it was for you and he repeated the story he told you about the Russian Jew." What Oscar told Johanna, that he hadn't mentioned to Willem, was that when the man gave the clock to Oscar, as collateral, he responded to Oscar's protests about not wanting to take it from him. "What the Russian said was, 'you hold it for me until I pay you back.' The man, having no wherewithal and knowing he would never be able to honor the loan, told Oscar, 'if something should happen to me before… well, then, I want you to have it. It needs to be where it will be appreciated. Where it will do some good.' So, Willem," she put her hand upon his and gave it a pat. "I guess it's to you now. To do some good."

Willem breathed in, do some good. Much had been unspoken between Oscar and Willem on that tender day when the Russian's story was revealed. The importance of the relic had been echoed through Oscar's words, Remember us. Over and over it rang in Willem's head, a melody that would linger and become a guiding force for him.

Johanna was the perfect person to share the day with. From when first they met and sat at the Levins' dinner table, to all the events after; watching him paint, partaking in a midday meal, taking breaks together, and exchanging stories, they had developed an enduring friendship. The adhesive that held them together was trust. For them, it came easy. When she first asked him if he wanted to have a cup of tea on a Sunday afternoon, on her day off, he responded favorably. Johanna's touch didn't create the same reaction that Femke's had. There was nothing sensual about it. No palpable ulterior motive. His gut told him she was safe.

Thinking back to times with her, he recalled a day sitting at a sidewalk café table when she told him she knew places he might enjoy visiting.

"What kind of places?"

Giving him a knowing look, "where people like us gather," as her face lit up.

Thinking he understood what she had alluded to but not being certain, he sat there waiting for clarification.

"You like men?" She knew. Willem had been open about it in their conversations. She appreciated he had nothing to hide. She respected it but it wasn't quite to her way of being. She was more circumspect.

"Yes."

"I like women," she confessed.

There it was, the first time she revealed to him that she was a lesbian. She also told him she felt comfortable talking about it with him. She wanted to share things with him. Especially about her excitement and subsequent disappointment concerning a friend, a woman, who had been thinking of opening a bar where homosexuals would be welcome. Where everyone would be welcome. The friend's name was Bet van Beeren. "It was exciting while she dreamed but then Bet had to shelve her plans."

"Why?" asked Willem.

"Money. Protests that too many homosexual bars were opening at the same time."

"That's too bad," Willem responded, not knowing then that years later Bet would open her bar and become an instrumental person in his life.

Sitting across from Johanna, at his little kitchen table, still holding the clock, he was reminded of his father's protests about homosexual bars. Irrational hatred of those who loved the same sex was at the root of so much affliction. A shiver ran down his neck as he rubbed the clock that had witnessed way too much torture.

"Willem? Where are you?" she murmured.

"Oh... just thinking..."

"That's dangerous," she quipped.

Yes, she was the exact right person to sit across from him as they spent time together and shared intimate conversations. Some light banter ensued before he made them tea and brought out a small cake he'd bought from downstairs.

"I admire your openness," came out of nowhere from Johanna.

"Huh?" he curiously squinted his brow.

"Take that," she tilted her chin to the clock, now next to him on the table. "I take it there was a very open communion between you and Oscar. Doubtful he would have told you about it if you were not open... and it goes both ways." She took a sip of the cooling tea.

"It's interesting how we know things." Placing the palm of his left hand over his abdomen, he said, "I feel it here. So, yes, in some sense we know... who to trust. And the converse as well, who we wouldn't bode well with."

"Right," she acknowledged. "I'm overly cautious... about

what I let out. In a lot of circles, it's very unsafe, who we are."

"Yes, that's very true." Noticing the muting of her tone, her sped up breathing, he asked, "did you think of something?"

Missing the only other person she had opened up to, about sensitive matters, Johanna puckered a pensive hesitation. She wanted to open up. She needed to. Today it felt right. "A few years ago…" Her eyes dulled and her pupils became wide. "I was in the kitchen making breakfast. Ernst came in to let me know he wouldn't be home for dinner and asked if I wanted to stay and keep Gabriel company. He was like that."

A solemn, "yes," replied Willem.

"Ernst was talking to me while I'm preparing the meal. When the sleeve on my dress rose up, he noticed a bruise encircling my wrist. I caught him looking and pulled my sleeve down. That would not deter the man. 'Stop for a minute,' he said. He made me show him my other hand. Sure enough, he must have sensed something, for when he saw the same bruise on both wrists, he had me sit down with him. He wouldn't leave until I told him what had happened. Not wanting him to be late for work, I told him." Johanna put down the cup she'd been holding and moved an index finger along the ridge. Streams ran down the sides. Thoughtfully, she continued, "a couple of days before, I'd been seen in public briefly holding hands with another woman. That's all it took. We were both dragged into an alley and held down by our wrists. I don't know what was viler, what they did or what they said."

"I'm so sorry," whispered Willem.

"I'm a private person, Willem. I never felt a need to tell the Levins I was a… you know. I mean who you're attracted to, or not, is not light chit-chat. Talking has consequences. It just was nothing I wanted to mention to them. Not until then but Ernst said he already knew and begged me to feel safe with him. To trust him. I always liked him but trusting someone, that is not easy for me."

"Understandable."

"That's the day I took a leap. Turns out that all my worry about what they would think of me was wasting daylight. Before long, Gabriel came to me with a twinkle in her eye and in a warm hug said, 'he told me,' but she went one better," laughed Johanna.

The changed lightness in her made Willem smile. "How so?"

"Next thing she said was, 'I love you, Johanna.' Can you imagine that? It was perfect."

The visit continued with topics shifting. When Johanna asked Willem about his friend, Daan, Willem revealed that Daan had a new girlfriend and he thought they were getting serious. "He spends a lot of time with her, when not helping his father with his carpentry business."

"Intimate relationships do change friendships," said Johanna.

"In this case, there's a wrinkle in her dress. She's Catholic." A sad-longing pain from the distance in their friendship, that had started with the confrontations Daan witnessed between

Willem and Hendrik, sat heavy on Willem's heart.

Johanna, ignoring the melancholic withdrawal painted on Willem's face, said, "oh, I see… and, it's interfering?"

"Yes, although Daan doesn't mention it, he looks stiff when he talks about what they do on Sundays."

"Church day."

"Right. I can smell the rejection of sin, including homosexual behavior, perfume all over her. I don't mind someone having an opinion, not favoring my behavior but why so much animosity? Why let her judgments create the distance between us?"

"Hmmm."

"No, you don't need to answer," he scratched the tip of his nose. "That was rhetorical. I've long given up on trying to understand aversion to differences."

"Touché." Johanna looked down at the clock, which was not ticking and shifting her view out the window, said, "where's the day gone?" Daytime's yellow-white sunlight was heading toward the horizon. Soon it would be dusk. Johanna took her leave.

\*   \*   \*

Tea dates continued. Painting, without sales, continued. Money spent on rent, food, and necessities continued putting a dent in the bequest Willem had received. At the rate he was spending, without earning, he figured he had only six months left to cover expenses.

He knew things would slow down when the Levins and Rothsteins moved to America, as they were his main promoters but he hadn't envisioned that sales would come to a complete standstill. Now, out on his own for the first time, having no one to rely on, he needed to plan for a future that wouldn't put him out on the streets. Johanna, like him, lived in a one-room apartment and had no extra space for him. Daan was never really an option, especially now that Daan's family, gravitating to their soon-to-be daughter-in-law and her religious family, no longer invited Willem to their house. Without any contingency plans, Willem became discouraged. He needed to get a job.

Luckily, he found part-time employment designing posters and tapestries for a local company. Once he began to earn enough to cover his basic expenses, he pursued his own art again, branching out to the nearby villages Laren and Blaricum. That paid off and, once again, he sold a painting here and there. He also took on jobs when they became available, such as working as an illustrator for the poetry of J.H. Leopold and Pieter Cornelis Boutens. Through these experiences, he made new friends. Some introductions came from Johanna, others were encountered through his art. One of his new friends, an artist named Guus, took a serious liking to Willem. A gypsy, Guus floated, as the breeze moved him, from place to place wherever work was available. Offered a job in Rotterdam, he convinced Willem to join him, even suggesting Willem could widen his circle of prospects by attending painting classes there.

"Influential people live in Rotterdam," said Guus, stroking Willem's chest after they had been intimate.

"Just pick up and leave?"

"Yes," smiled, Guus, "why not? What's keeping you here?"

Feeling Guus' hands moving over his chest, Willem reignited. With Guus, Willem's arousal went beyond sex, for he was a partner that was exciting, talented, and free in ways that attracted Willem like a moth to a flame. A magnetism existed with Guus, a contentment to spend time with him without a need for idle chatter. Quiet time, watching squirrels find acorns or ripples in rivers cascading over eroded soil, those incidents of doing nothing were sensually fulfilling. With Guus, sharing, appreciating together, Willem felt comfortable. Secure. Not unlike how he felt in his friendship with Johanna. But it didn't last. However, when Willem's relationship with Guus ran its natural course, they remained friends.

Like Ernst and Oscar had been successful bridges for Willem, so had Guus been. New men, new patrons, new locations, all came into being. All resulting in a steady income Willem could happily subsist on. Willem's life, now on track, allowed him to gain a comfortable sense of belonging. Relaxing among the homosexual community, Willem found kinship. Amity.

The same could not be said for tensions arising externally between European countries.

CHAPTER FIFTEEN

The disease of prejudicial toxicity, slowly eating its way through Europe, that Hendrik and his clan of haters tried to promulgate never really caught fire in the Netherlands. As rabid were the rumors of anti-Semitism, their bite fizzled in the shadow of the Peace Palace. Although, when the Great War broke out and some of the German Imperial Army marched through a small part of its territory during the invasion of Belgium, the Netherlands retained its history as a neutral country. Despite not entering the war, the Netherlands suffered hardships due to its geography, being surrounded by warring states. The North Sea was unsafe for commerce, decreasing food supplies, creating a need for the Dutch to ration. It had, however, remained a fairly protected place for Jews. Plus, with its tolerance towards homosexuals, homosexual magazines being published and homosexual bars opening, it was equally a safe haven for Willem.

Having ended his intimate ties but still remaining in touch with Guus, Willem returned to Naarden, back to Johanna and their mutual friends. He found another room to rent above a shoemaker's store. Upstairs in his room, the earthy smell of freshly tanned leather spread like overly saturated wetlands. He felt comfortable renting from the white-haired man with an aged, wrinkled face; it had a leathery appearing skin like the material he used in his craft. A pleasant, quiet man, he prided himself in making shoes from scratch. Scrapes and puncture wounds showed on his hands when he gave Willem the key. They were hands that worked long, hard hours to make quality shoes worn by customers with snobbish airs, who called his landlord, "a cordwainer." Who cares about highfalutin labels? scoffed Willem. He kept to himself and left the shoemaker and his haughty customers to their business.

Willem's hand moved rhythmically over the scenes he'd started to paint; first, the vast large lines to cover the canvas, with details saved for last. Clouds moved over the sun, changing the intensity of light and dulling the choice of color he was using. Pausing to see what the weather was doing he noticed a front forming. It was extremely unusual for the time of year, late summer, for fog and low-level horizontal layering clouds. The haze gave an eerie appearance. It was 1914 and a lot of what was going on was unusual.

The dueling masses of air, foreboding a storm, mimicked European powers in a tenuous seesaw counterbalance. The teetering had maintained a horizontal symmetry through Britain's diplomatic practice of avoiding permanent alliances, splendid isolation; the decline of the Ottoman Empire and all that transpired as a result; the Russo-Turkish Wars with their influences in the Balkans; the Franco-Prussian War, to name a few. The delicate balance finally gave way, like an overstretched rubber band snapping into parts, when on June 28, the presumptive heir to the Austro-Hungarian Empire, Archduke Franz Ferdinand, and his wife, Sophie, were assassinated in Sarajevo. Violence broke out, with a month of ensuing diplomatic maneuvering. Demands made to resolve the conflict proved unacceptable. Confusion existed among Central Powers. Talks failed and aggressive mobilization began. The alliances formed consisted of the Allies: France, Russia, Great Britain, Japan, Italy, and later the United States against a group of European countries known as the Central Powers: Germany, Austria-Hungary, Turkey, and Bulgaria. On July 28, twenty-five days before Willem's twentieth birthday, the Great War began.

During the chaos, when so many countries were at war, Willem sat in his room in a neutral country, contentedly painting. His involvement in the war extended to nothing beyond following it in newspapers, magazines, and in gossip parlors where people went to socialize. Willem's non-involvement was in contrast to Hitler, who voluntarily enlisted while living in Munich. As an Austrian citizen, Hitler's enlistment was an administrative error. Instead of being returned to Austria, which is what should have happened, he served as an infantryman in France and Belgium. Wounded in action and recommended by his Jewish superior, he received the Iron Cross. For Hitler, it was a hard accolade to swallow, coming from a Jew. It became another straw of hostility in his silage of hatred, the airtight tower of his anti-Semitic personality. At that time, Willem did not know how the pernicious seeds implanted in Vienna, in that vile man, would one day directly impact his life. Eventually, he would learn more than he cared to find out about; horrible things about Jews being considered inferior to the Aryan race, they are not human. What Willem did not catch wind of at the time World War I broke out, that he surely would have discounted as being rubbish, was the conspiracy gossip-mongering spread by the Jew-hater, Hitler and his cohorts. Their belief was that the majority of banks and financial lending institutions were owned by Jews and that Jews wanted to control the world banks and stomp on Germany for their own gain. Behind closed doors, Hitler spoke words that gained in volume and force. Once those doors opened, the corrosive sounds whirled in imminent winds, stirring to weaken and destroy. The scapegoat had been labeled. Eventually, the weakened Weimar Republic and the downfall of Germany would be blamed on the Jews. Hitler's psyche, filled with lies and dreams of arrogant annihilation, was to become the thing of nightmares. A masterful liar, a mysterious enigma, he was ultimately referred to as the beast who created the Frankenstein's monster religion of eugenics pantheism.

\*   \*   \*

Although the Netherlands was factually neutral, individual citizens had their own preferences. Some ministers were in favor of France,

Prime Minister Cort van der Linden privately favored Germany, even Queen Wilhelmina had sympathy for France and Belgium, while her German husband, Duke Henry of Mecklenburg-Schwerin, was openly pro-German. Willem was of the mindset that hostile aggressors, no matter the country, needed to be stopped and overthrowing areas of geography for political expansion at the cost of lives was morally wrong. Less concerned with the reason for the war, what bothered him was the victimization of the innocent citizens. He avoided discussions and siding with those who self-righteously took sides, while the sides were taking lives. Although some Dutchmen volunteered to serve in the French, British, German, or Austro-Hungarian armies, Willem was more concerned with living his life than becoming an aggressor. However, Willem indirectly felt the impact of the war years which were fraught with devastation, broken bones, bleeding limbs, lost lives, devastated families, and starving refugees.

Birgit wrote to him at the end of 1914 apologizing for being so remiss. She had sunk into a dark, irretrievable depression for months on end and feared she had nothing of any value to share; her thoughts being as black as the news of "that horrific war." Reading her words and missing her terribly, Willem wished he was with her. "Seems that anger has pulled me out of my morass," she wrote. "If that isn't a statement about how pathetic my life is then what else can I say. Fear not, my dear friend for that was tongue-in-cheek. Enough whimsy, I meant it about anger snapping me out of my doldrums. What in the name of all that is good are they fighting about anyway? It's a mass of conflicting confusion, the stories I read in the paper. Very difficult to read between the lines and I don't have my dear papa here to explain things to me. Mother wants nothing to do with talk of war. She's having a very hard time but I feel that, soon enough, with the help of her new friends and the good charity work she's involved with, she will turn around."

Reading 'my dear papa', Willem's airway constricted. The move of his friends and the death of Ernst were never far from his thoughts. Feeling lightheaded he continued reading about the good charity Gabriel was involved in, having to do with some prominent attorney named Louis Brandeis. When Birgit wrote about what her mother had been helping with, about what this man had been doing, her descriptive words seemed to sing a happier tune.

"A remarkable man. A Jew, Willem! There's no threatening him for being that, here. Here in the place where freedom is not a dirty word, this man is lauded." She went on with her lengthy composition, like a scribe, venerating the man who represented people helping the poor, who attended public hearings to promote investigations into conditions of substandard housing, and who rallied for the unemployed experiencing miserable living conditions where they were thrown together with the mentally ill and criminals. "Listen to this," she wrote, "Brandeis said, and I paraphrase, so don't hold me to this quote. 'Men are not bad. Men are largely degraded by circumstances. It is the duty of every man to help them up and let them feel there is some hope for them in life.'"

Birgit's words came from a different girl than the person Willem knew growing up. Just like she wrote about how circumstances change people, he deeply understood she had forever been changed. So had he. Imagine that, a Jewish man, a hero in America. Birgit's words showed a depth of maturity. Tragedy does that, he knew personally. Willem loved reading about a man doing something about those, who most in society, want to sweep into a pile of dust and out the door. It reinforced, in Willem, his own purpose to want to help others.

The letters between the two friends continued, pages mostly filled with talk of the Great War with an update about how Birgit had been right about her mother coming around. "She's continuing to work with the great Brandeis, who is fighting against big corporations, fighting against corruption of wealthy people who engage in conspicuous consumption at the disadvantage of the destitute, or," in other words as Birgit put it, "who were ostentatious."

Willem smiled at the way Birgit went on, explaining herself as if a teacher in front of a classroom.

"Listen to this," she wrote, as if they were sitting on a park bench in Naarden involved in conversation, "he," referring to Brandeis, "owns a canoe. What's my point? All... His... Rich... Friends... Own... Yachts."

Separated by the Atlantic Ocean, the two shared laughter. Feeling warm satisfaction, he continued reading about how

Brandeis backed up talk with action. It really struck a chord with Willem's strong sense of morally responsible behavior to read about an influential man who operated on more than lip service.

More letters came, along with relief that things had gotten better for the Levins and, also as Birgit had informed Willem, the Rothsteins. Relishing each time an envelope arrived, he was grateful for their friendship. He was also thankful for his relationship with Johanna and the few new friends he'd met at a bar or restaurant.

Through the war years, get-togethers with Johanna continued with one new addition, she had a girlfriend named Frieda, a lesbian cellist. She was also a closeted Jew, feeling one strike against her was enough. Willem took to Frieda like iron to a magnet, and, like iron, over time their bond would prove to be strong and show great determination. The three met in quiet cafés, usually at night when their day's work was completed and they had time to relax. Johanna caught Willem up on her part-time job, cooking for another wealthy family, which kept her occupied while Frieda was involved with her music. They were a well-suited couple, thought Willem; Johanna stoic and reticent while Frieda exhibited an outward, lively personality.

By the end of the war, Willem had found a new interest, not displacing his art but rather equally important; he began serious writing, considering the possibility of someday publishing a novel. He attributed some of his newfound passion to his correspondence with Birgit who exercised new usages of words, metaphors, and anecdotes to make her point. The effects of the war also influenced his desire to write. The scarcity of food, witnessing the influx of starving broken refuges, and neutrality violators becoming spies for personal gain. What also profoundly touched him was what he'd learned about prisoners of war (POWs). Adhering to international law, soldiers of warring countries entering a neutral country were to be interred until the end of the war. Among the prisoners were pilots who had flown into Dutch airspace and crashed, soldiers who had entered the Netherlands, to escape war or accidentally wandered into Dutch territory, as well as deserters who were not considered foreign soldiers and surrendered to the proper authorities. All were admitted to POW camps. Regardless of the fact that they received food and shelter, they were still prisoners. Feeling weighed down by all the senseless violence, the wounded and dead numbering over thirty-five million, Willem wanted to rip his hair out from the frustration he felt that there was nothing he could do about any of it. For what? Is there any insanity greater than war? Willem had plenty to write about, knocking open the portal in which he expressed his voice.

The travesties of war did not end, when after four years, three months, and two weeks, at eleven in the morning on November 11, 1918, a ceasefire was declared. The eleventh hour of the eleventh day of the eleventh month, however, was not the formal end of the fighting. That occurred when the Treaty of Versailles was signed in June 1919. But not everyone's combat would cease with the end of the war. The misbegotten Austrian-citizen-turned-German soldier, Hitler, went on to fight his own internal battle. Just as Willem turned to writing, so did Hitler, a few years after the war ended, with his toxic, abhorrent words in Mein Kampf. Sentences composed of devastatingly corrupt nouns and verbs were constructs designed toward inconceivable malevolence. Additionally, Hitler would go on to use the Treaty of Versailles to turn the world upside down.

## CHAPTER SIXTEEN

Willem compared the changes in his life to the metamorphosis of a caterpillar becoming a butterfly. His early formative years were when he painfully hatched from his larva and separated from the derelict and corrupt caterpillars which would never become butterflies. The tween years from 1910 to 1920 were when he spun his silky, shiny chrysalis, growing family roots and finely tuning his artistic muscle. Just like the butterfly goes through a radical transformation in its cocoon, for Willem the twenties were a time of great change. It was a decade when heartache was experienced from the ravages of war, selfless dedication was expressed in helping others and it was the beginning of a solidarity of friends that would play a key role in the Nazi resistance movement.

Although the war had ended and fighting stopped, ill-will endured. Over 100,000 Belgium refugees had fled to the Netherlands, most unable to support themselves and were housed in camps sponsored by the government. The Dutch blamed the mass influx on Germany's invasion of Belgium. By July 1919 most of the refugees had returned to Belgium.

Despite the majority of Dutch citizens being law-abiding,

an occasional altercation had broken out, mostly involving a gang of men against a German expatriate, sometimes ending in gunfire.

Willem had been out with Johanna and Frieda. They had shared a meal and said their goodbyes when Willem, on his way home, turned a corner and saw a crumpled lump of what looked like a stack of throwaway clothes. His view obscured by clouds moving over a crescent moon, he thought he saw movement. Discounting it, he continued a few steps until he heard a moan. It was a sound he'd heard before, from starving wounded animals, when venturing on walks through the forest. Assuming it was probably a hungry dog, he went and felt for the edge of the material. The foul-smelling wool coat shredded when a man jumped up pointing a gun. Seeing the dim moonlight reflecting on the metal, Willem knew what it was and that he was in deep trouble. He reflexively held up his hands giving a peace signal. "Don't shoot," pleaded Willem. "I mean no harm."

The tone coming out of Willem's small, trembling voice must have calmed the man. "Ich bin Fritz, ein deutscher Soldat," he uttered, in a raspy murmur, lowering the gun.

Willem knew a few German words and understood that the man had been a German soldier, named Fritz. "Sie Niederländisch sprechen?" He asked if Fritz spoke Dutch. To Willem's great relief, he received an affirmative nod. The momentary comfort was short-lived when Fritz winced and grabbed his abdomen. Despite unclear visibility, Willem could tell he'd been wounded. Without hesitation, he took hold of the soldier's arm, explaining he would help him. They just needed to go a couple of blocks to his place.

In his apartment, Willem looked at the wound. "Oh no, that looks awful." Willem felt bad the minute the words came out of his mouth. But the old, festering wound did look awful and smelled even worse.

"Kept opening. Couldn't stop the infection," squirmed Fritz, clearly uncomfortable. "Nowhere to go—"

Willem turned his head to let out the breath he'd been holding. "Let me get something." He gagged on his way to the shelf to get a clean cloth.

"A bullet wound," Fritz yelped, as Willem tried to clean and bandage it. He explained he was a deserter from the German army. He had hidden in alleys trying to avoid becoming a POW during the war; he didn't believe what he'd been told about internment being safe. After the war, he was afraid to go to a government-sponsored camp. "This," he indicated his abdomen, "because I German. Not safe here." He explained as best he could that a group of three men came upon him sleeping on the side of a dark road. It was his bad luck that they had been out drinking and would pass him on their way home. "They kick me awake… next thing, they hear my German accent and I see a flash. They run. A sharp burning in my side…" he told Willem. He stopped the bleeding with his jacket and moved as far away from that area as he could, into a wooded, protected field, where he prayed that he'd be okay. It turned out to be a superficial wound that grazed his abdomen. Having nothing to clean it with, no ointments for treatment, within days he felt flushed with heat. He knew it had become infected. Thankfully, he found a stream to bathe in and wash it, to try to keep it from getting worse. He remained there until his fever subsided.

Exhausted and filthy, half-starving, he found scraps of food in garbage bins, vegetables from farmland, apples and cherries from trees, raw potatoes planted in the ground, and raw eggs from a chicken coop as he had made his way from the southern border. How he managed to arrive all the way north to where Willem found him, Willem was never able to clearly discern. Through bits and pieces of conversation he'd learned that Fritz was eighteen years old, a couple of years younger than he was. Willem wondered what he looked like, what was under that unkempt dirty face, matted brown hair, and sunken sky-blue eyes. Medium height, he was very thin with ribs protruding and a concave belly showing when Willem patched him up. Despite the late hour, the way he looked in his pathetic situation, Willem knew he had to help the man. The problem; his apartment was small with only one place to sleep.

Willem fetched the pail of water he used for cleaning and began to scrub some of the encrusted, caked mud off Fritz's face. Although lacking the fullness of texture that goes with being well-fed, it was a handsome, youthful face, with finely sculpted features. Vulnerable and inviting, it made Willem feel warm in the chilled room.

By the time Willem finished cleaning the last mud off of

Fritz's chin, the man was nodding off. Willem gently lifted the spent vagrant and placed him on his bed, removing his clothing, sliding him under the counterpane and he, himself, went to sleep on the floor. Willem insisted that the arrangement remain that way until the soldier was feeling better.

Within a week, the wound's purulent draining and surrounding redness had lessened. Night sweats that Willem thought was a sign of recurring fever, finally ceased. What little food Willem had, he shared with Fritz. By the end of the week, Fritz had relayed what his life was like before being "forced by family, my father, to join the army." The kid, like Willem, spent his time hating war, counting minutes, fearful and anxious. Shortly after joining, while in combat, he panicked and fled in the middle of the night.

Willem made do for the pair of them, with the little money he had saved and with the help of Johanna and Frieda he increased his food supply. As long as he paid his rent, on time, the shoemaker downstairs never bothered him. Once Willem felt Fritz was okay to be left alone for any length of time, he returned to work. Through Johanna, Willem met Sjoerd, a homosexual with important family connections, who had been helping refugees. When Willem approached Fritz to get his agreement to let Sjoerd help him, Fritz broke out in a shaking sweat. Willem's attempts to calm the traumatized soldier were to no avail. Fritz did not want to leave Willem.

"Please, I help you. I clean here," he motioned his hand to

the small room, "and, you sleep in the bed. You sore. I see you stretch from stiffness."

The supplicating way his eyes pleaded spoke to Willem. His heart skipping beats, he weakened. Trying to come up with a different plan, he was distracted when Fritz took hold of his hand and begged, "I please stay."

A sensual electricity moved through Willem's limbs, down his back, and heated his belly. Taking hold of Fritz's hand and caressing it softly, he said, "okay." He needed this companionship as much as Fritz did; the sense of belonging, being under the same roof with another human being, if only for a little while longer. He knew that Fritz remaining in his room could be a serious problem for both of them. But for now, "okay," he gently repeated, "but we need to work out a plan to help you. You can't keep staying here forever."

That night, Fritz refused to sleep in the bed. "I sleep there," he pointed to the floor.

Willem felt the stiffness in his back muscles from sleeping on the hard wood but he was concerned that if Fritz didn't continue to get a few more restful nights of sleep, he may relapse. "I'm okay," he lied. "You stay there."

Fritz scrunched a troubled brow, when he responded, "you stiff. I see way you get up and move. No good for you."

They went back and forth another time with Willem preoccupied, that in bed, next to Fritz, his body so close to him would do more to keep him up than the hard floor. But to break the deadlock, he finally yielded. For the next several nights, they slept together, although nothing happened between them sexually. Willem had become extremely attracted to Fritz and equally frustrated. It preoccupied his days, disrupting work. It was time to reopen the conversation about Fritz moving on. He enlisted Johanna and Sjoerd to help. They would both come to Willem's room to meet Fritz, to establish a rapport, with the hopes of gaining enough trust that Fritz would agree to relocate to a safe house. Sjoerd had been instrumental, along with a handful of others, working underground, to help a few lucky deserters that, like Fritz, refused to go to POW camps during the war or government-sponsored refugee camps after it was over.

Over tea, in the crowded room, Sjoerd and Johanna sat at the table with Willem and Fritz on the edge of the bed. Small talk preceded, "you were in the German army?" Johanna asked, to break the ice. When she saw Fritz's forehead bead into sweat and his torso tighten, she sensitively walked back from diving into the deep end. "I have friends like you," she smiled. "They didn't like war either."

Without verbally responding, Fritz's relaxing breath indicated his anxiety had eased.

Taking the cue from his bodily response, Johanna went on to say, "Willem and I have had many conversations about how awful war is. We... I," she spoke for herself, "would have left also, if forced to join." She gave Willem a look.

"This is correct. I think I can honestly speak for the three of us." Willem looked from Johanna to Sjoerd and back to Fritz, "we think you did the right thing."

When Fritz looked at Sjoerd who had said nothing since introductions, it was an opening to revisit the plan that Willem had brought up a week earlier. "I not only would have done what you did, but I help those who did," said Sjoerd.

Tilting his head, indicating he didn't understand. "Help?" asked Fritz for clarification.

"Yes," Sjoerd moved his chair nearer to Fritz, closing the distance.

Fritz attentively leaned in.

"Yes, Fritz," he explained, "I have many friends. People who want to help... to help others who can't find ways to help themselves. Like you."

Aware of his dilemma, being a military deserter in a foreign country and relying on the mercy of one man who had already been inconvenienced enough, Fritz slumped forward, breaking eye contact.

In response, Johanna, rejoined with, "you've done nothing wrong and we'd like to... with your approval... with your permission, we'd like to help you."

By the time Willem joined in on the soft-toned conversation his two friends were involved in with Fritz, he knew they had achieved what they set out to do. When he said, "I think this is the safest thing for you... we've been lucky so far. But how long can it last? I'm worried that—"

Fritz interrupted, "I do it." Directing his attention to Sjoerd, in a half-whisper, he said, "I no more want to inconvenience Willem. He a good man. Help enough. If he says you safe... then you safe."

The day that Fritz left, Willem felt the void. Alone in his bed that evening, his feelings were bittersweet, lonely yet satisfied. He was pleased that he had helped, it reminded him of the time, many years before, when he had helped the hungry dog in the schoolyard. Smiling, tears came to his eyes as he thought of the dog. I am destined to help the underdog – the victims of injustices and persecutions – of course, it would make sense why he'd thought of that earlier time. Helping the downtrodden was the calcium holding his bones together. The foundation of why he'd been put on this earth. That's what the 1920s had done for him, transformed him from the protective casing he'd been cocooned in, into the colorful butterfly he now was.

The twenties were good years for him, when his talent reached a new level of recognition and he was commissioned to paint a large mural in Rotterdam. He also traveled to other areas for work, always returning to Naarden, though. Those were also the times platonic relationships blossomed and he found his clan; a compilation of talented, eclectic, homosexual, and heterosexual, intellectuals he felt at home with. They shone a light that he would follow; to help the greater good.

Across the ocean in America, where Birgit now lived with her new husband and baby girl, the Roaring Twenties were reaching an end. It had been a time when blues and jazz bled into the culture, a time of rags-to-riches for black entertainers when the American prosperity was a way of life. But as the end of 1929 approached, it all came to a sudden end with the stock market crash. Not limited to North America, the Great Depression created a worldwide economic desperation that would last well into the 1930s, impacting the Netherlands. It led to political instability and riots. Hit hard was Germany. Already in political turmoil with the rise of brutality in the form of the Nazi and communist movements and the economic destruction levied on Germany by the Treaty of Versailles' imposition of reparations in the sum of 50 billion gold marks, opportunity was provided for the rise of Hitler.

The end of the roaring twenties took on a new roar. At first, it was a low rumble but by the end of the thirties heading into the forties, it was deafening. The earsplitting grandiose contra-life outcry included talks of plans to create murdering machines. Sane ears discounted the oppressive rumors as madness. Just the talk of idle idiots. Sadly, as ears became unwaxed and able to hear, it became clear they weren't just listening to rumors.

"There's no such thing as a gas to kill people."

"Oh, there isn't? What of the poisonous asphyxiant gas used in the United States to execute condemned prisoners?"

Soon it would not be a far stretch from the talk of one criminal being put to death to a vast number of undesirables. Undesirables! They are not human, according to the proponents, remembered Willem, as electric ripples moved up his spine.

Just as Willem had heard about the dark shadows cast over Jews at the beginning of the century, again he listened to the horrifying descriptions of plans to hurt Jews. It was a topic discussed at length in the parlors he frequented, one in particular opened by Johanna's friend Bet Van Beeren in Amsterdam.

# THE OLD GILT CLOCK

CHAPTER SEVENTEEN

Willem woke early, next to a warm body. He reached out a hand to touch him and then drew it back into a fist. The man's knees were bent up to his chest, his posture curled and comfortable, he was fast asleep. Willem was reluctant to rouse him, to satisfy the engorgement in his loins. Just a few weeks ago, he had been wildly attracted to the curly auburn-haired, green-eyed man with inviting puffy lips. In the beginning, he wanted him… again and again. But now, something held Willem back. Something was wrong. The emotional vulnerability he had felt with Peter and initially with Guus, he never experienced with Henry. He doubted he ever would. He didn't know why and that bothered him. Things had been okay, exciting but now, even Henry's light snoring made him wince. With them, when the sex was finished, they had very little to talk about. Willem expected more. It was an odd relationship he had with this man he had met at Bet's bar. A loner, Henry intoned, "let's enjoy it, while it's here," he echoed repeatedly, "I'm not a talker." Puzzled, it made Willem wonder, then, what are you? Not only was conversation scarce but Henry didn't want to set times to get together. "Live spontaneously," he advocated when they'd meet up at the bar. Even though he had made his position clear right from the start, Willem wanted more from the man who shunned obligations.

Willem's thoughts were interrupted by a wheezing snort, a cresting-wave-and crashing-onto-sand heavy breathing. He opened his fisted hand and scratched the tip of his nose. It itched when he stopped paying attention to the feeling in his gut, when he stopped listening to the voice of reason inside his head. In this case, logic dictated it wasn't time well spent, getting involved with Henry when it was doomed to go nowhere.

Carnal glue; drifting back, he remembered that's what Johanna called it when she laughed about Willem being injected by a false widow-spider's venom. She further commented, "I don't know… you, with that sticky, icky mess," referring to Willem being in bed with Henry. Although in jest, her out-of-character frivolous manner when she'd say things like, "that female spider will eat you alive, they do eat their mates, you know," troubled Willem.

Not only was Willem bothered by Johanna's reaction, but it also disturbed Frieda. While Johanna was on one of her unusual sarcastic diatribes, masked as humor, Frieda whispered to Willem, "something's stuck in her craw. Just ignore her words, it'll pass."

Frieda was right. A few looks from her and Willem, and Johanna toned it down, justifying her flip-flop. "I suppose, if he's a friend of Bet's, he's okay."

Willem, hearing the lackluster resonance in Johanna's

speech knew that Johanna's last remark was disingenuous. He wondered what was so off-putting about Henry. Not one to cast aspersions on someone's integrity without good reason, he asked, "what's going on? I know you... you smile and poke fun, and make excuses about it but... it's not like you."

The glimmer in her eyes dulled. "It's just a feeling." A shadow moved over her face. "I'm sorry, Willem. I should just keep my mouth closed."

Johanna's regretful countenance brought up an image of being in bed with Henry, sending a momentary surge of aversion through him. He let it slide. Before long, Willem found fault in Henry. Petty things gnawed on his nerves.

Another loud gurgle from the back of Henry's throat tensed the muscles along Willem's spine bringing him back to his room, his bed, the man beside him who he found troubling. But why? Listening to the rolling-shallow air squeezing into Henry's nasal passage, Willem thought of the night when he met Henry. It was at the Café 't Mandje, which had opened in 1927, eight years prior.

On that warm night in 1935, Willem had been out with Johanna, Frieda, and Sjoerd. To those who knew Bet, the owner, well, she was a foul-mouthed, uncompromising lesbian but to customers, she ran her place with a velvet glove, friendly and unassuming. Masterfully finessing those she opposed overtly, she covertly supported persecuted victims of bigotry. Although all were welcome into her establishment, including Germans, Bet was staunchly anti-German. Johanna had once told Willem, "If you're a friend of Bet's, you're okay in my book." Henry would prove to be an exception.

Henry was friends with Bet and frequented the Café 't Mandje on Zeedijk Street. His ostensibly soft-spoken manner and light touch fit in well with the homosexual culture. Bet liked the quiet solitary way he sat at a barstool, politely asking for a gin and in return thanking her with a generous tip. He had been a customer of Bet's for several months before Willem made his first appearance.

"We're going to that bar," referring to the one owned by Bet, who Johanna had been telling Willem about for years. "Come along. Sjoerd will drive." Cars made traveling the twelve miles from Naarden to Amsterdam, where the bar was located, easy. Of Willem's circle of friends, Sjoerd was the first to purchase an automobile, a Fiat. He was more than willing to transport his friends to nighttime activities.

Willem had taken a breather from painting to concentrate on writing. Cooped up all day in his room and feeling frustrated that the poems and stories he'd written in the 1920s and recent work, had gone unpublished, he wanted to get out. He needed to get his attention off his writing. On the ride to the café, Frieda told Willem a little about the place.

"I like it because it's not just for homosexuals," smiled Johanna. "Bet is very liberal and will let just about anyone in, providing they behave themselves?"

"Behave? Hmm," smirked Sjoerd.

"Oh, stop it," Johanna giggled.

"She'll allow just about anything," added Frieda, "except violence."

"That leaves a lot of riffraff, like us, to feel welcome," clowned Sjoerd.

Frieda shook her head and rolled her eyes. She and Johanna were used to Sjoerd's sense of humor that tended to cover-up delicate subjects. When there was no glint in his dark-brown eyes, the women weren't fooled. They read him accurately when he feigned a smile with the edges of his lips subtly twitching. They knew that the minute he started to twist the ring on his right index finger it was a sensitive issue that he'd usually make light of before switching topics. His laconic style was appreciated by friends, especially in lieu of having to endure diatribes spouting from boring, pedantic know-nothings.

In a more serious tone, Sjoerd added, "she is the queen of tolerance. Prostitutes, pimps, seamen, lesbians... all are welcome." Rubbing a sweaty hand over the steering wheel, he digressed, "warm night."

Johanna mentioned, because Bet ran a tight bar, "where brutality was not welcome, it bodes well for the prostitutes who do frequent her place with the men or women who run them."

Prostitution; Willem knew people needed to put food on their tables. From the scarcity of food during the war and now into the aftermath of the Great Depression, wherewithal for food and shelter was hard to get. Willem harbored the viewpoint that as long as someone isn't hurting another what they do isn't anyone else's business, nor would it bother him. Listening to what he'd been told, Willem was looking forward to experiencing the often-talked-about Café 't Mandje.

Henry arrived shortly after Willem. At his usual seat, alone at the end of the bar, he caught Willem's attention. Sjoerd eyed Willem staring at the handsome man's backside, his contour with well-defined muscles. Elbowing Willem, he whispered, "go and meet him."

With the exception of re-ordering, the man at the bar hadn't taken his attention off his drink. Moving his glass in a circle, he spilled liquid on the counter. Behind the bar, a gregarious Bet gave the man an askance, nose-crinkled look, before cleaning it. That, plus not seeing any inclination of an invitation, gave Willem pause. But oh, he was so attractive.

Sjoerd sipped his drink and not to be deterred, nudged Willem again. "Go on," he swallowed the burning alcohol. "The guy is always alone. You're alone—"

"So are you," retorted Willem.

"Not my kind, my dear," smiled Sjoerd. "I have my kitten at home," referring to the man he saw from time to time that he refused to talk about. Winking at Willem, "he's rather attractive though, I do have to say."

After pestering and relentless prodding from Sjoerd, despite his initial doubts, Willem went over to the bar. "Can I buy you a drink," he offered the solitary man.

That sparked the relationship. They shared a drink or two for several nights before Willem asked him to come back to his place. That intoxicating night, the sex was great. Addictive. The best he'd ever had. Despite satisfying orgasms, the in-between sex times became less and less satisfactory.

Again, Willem's reverie had been interrupted when Henry stirred awake, stretched, glanced at Willem, and asked, "what time is it?" Without waiting for an answer, he looked over Willem's shoulder to the nightstand clock and instantly sat up. "I have to go."

There was a time Willem would have asked him to stay – for a morning quickie. Now, he didn't care that Henry got dressed, said his goodbyes and left.

Whatever they had between them ended abruptly when an incident happened at Café 't Mandje. It was an evening when Willem had stayed home and he heard about what occurred from Johanna. It explained the tacit disturbance he had felt with Henry.

Johanna had been out with Frieda and they stopped by Bet's to join up with a few other friends. The lively Frieda had just performed Camille Saint-Saëns' The Swan to a standing ovation. It is not an incredibly technical piece but it has a magnificent cello repertoire and played by Frieda, it was touted as "the beautiful highlight of the night."

Johanna, proud of her lover, vibrantly beamed to the friends they'd met afterward at Bet's, "we were transported to a lake, envisioning the elegant swan... and, oh, the best part, my lovely here," she reached for Frieda's hand, "played the notes that seemed to soar off the cello strings like the bird had taken flight. Brilliant—"

Flushed, and embarrassed from the accolades, Frieda rose and took her leave to buy drinks for the table. There, at the end of the bar, as usual, sat Henry. Not alone, this time. Two men sitting next to him seemed to have caught his ear.

"A year, that moron has been leading. A year of torture for the poor German Jews," said a middle-aged heavyset man sitting one stool over from Henry.

The hackles on Frieda's neck raised.

"Just be grateful you live here," replied a white-haired man sitting next to Henry. "How he ever rose to power and became the law of the land is beyond—"

The heavyset man slammed a palm down on the counter, drawing Henry's attention. "He helped restore economic stability. Heavy military spending got people jobs. Deficit spending... they took over public works. It was all diabolically brilliant. Put food on someone's table when they're starving and you better believe they'll get followers. All the power, the popularity, went to no good. Anti-Semitism became their central theme, Hitler's, I should say, ideology. He's an evil man."

"Yeaaah," burped the white-haired man. "I like 'em Jews."

"Of course you do, idiot, I'm Jewish," he nudged the man next to him. "It's all horseshit. And now, the bastards are rounding up Jews and carting them off to camps."

"How'd you heaaaar that," spat white hair.

"I have my connections, family in Germany for one." Tubby man took a sip of his drink, glancing over his shoulder to Henry whose head had been tilted in their direction. "What's got your tongue, mister?"

Henry smacked his lips, turned his back to the man.

Frieda's joy seeped out of her limbs like drying skin after a bath. Making no effort to order the drinks, she continued to listen.

The tubby patron reached over and poked Henry on his shoulder. "Don't be rude mister. Smacking those big lips—"

Henry turned to face the man, daggers shooting from his eyes, piercing and dangerous. His usual easygoing manner dissolved into an iron mask of terror. "Perhaps, the reason Jews are disliked is because of behavior like yours. Do not put a hand on me again!"

"Or what!" challenged the overweight man.

"It won't be pretty, you obnoxious Jew!"

Frieda gasped.

Fat man stood and without restraint went for Henry's neck. "Why you Jew-hating pig!"

Henry flew off the stool, landing on his butt on the floor. Livid, red-faced, he pulled a knife from his pocket and opened it. A slash at the fat man's left leg and blood was squirting. "I hope you all bleed," was clearly showing Henry's anti-Semitic fangs.

The last straw for the white-haired man, he threw his liquor-filled glass down on top of Henry's head, dizzying him.

Pow... pow... came from the gun in Bet's hand. Two holes in the ceiling and the place went dead quiet. "Out! The three of you! And don't come back," she pointed the gun at Henry. "No violence here!"

Ignoring the shots and the commands from Bet, like a wild animal, Henry grabbed for white-hair's pant leg and pulled him to the ground, the knife falling out of his other hand flew a foot away.

A cacophony of pandemonium broke out with Johanna up on her feet screaming over the noise, "Frieda! Get down!"

Henry went for the knife.

Another gunshot rang out, shattering a ceiling light. Shards of glass flew, one piece catching Frieda in her left forearm. Another grazed a customer's cheek.

Customers ran for the door, the back exit, and to the far end corners.

Frieda left blood streaks on the wooden floor as she crawled from under a barstool to where Johanna stood shaking.

The gun in Bet's firm grip pointed at Henry. "Up!" The barrel went to the other two men involved in the altercation, "all of you," she blasted, as the gun shifted back and forth. "Out! And don't come back."

Silence was interrupted by three sets of footsteps leaving the bar, the gun directed at them.

Frieda, dripping with underarm sweat, let out her breath. Shock coursed through her limbs; her heart visibly pounded through her blouse.

One look at her pale face and dilated, panicked pupils, Johanna knew that for Freida it wasn't just about the disturbance, the gunshots, or shattered ceiling light raining down on her, no, to her it was more personal. She had lost family in Russia because they were Jewish. Only her close, near and dear, trusted friends knew she was Jewish and what it had cost her family. Her friends understood why she rarely talked about it. Yes, it was personal for Freida and that meant it was also personal for Johanna.

When Willem heard about it the next day from Johanna, it made him sick. "You'd think a homosexual would have a different attitude," she said. "All the prejudice against us. Unbelievable the lack of compassion."

Willem felt nauseated. The hatred Henry expressed was what he had sensed but couldn't put a finger on. That was the same hatred that caused Birgit and her family to flee the Netherlands. It drove the Rothsteins away. For Willem, it was also personal. It left a bad taste in his mouth.

The disgust Willem felt over Henry's anti-Semitism intensified as disturbing new rumors spread about the madman in Germany. His abhorrence didn't let up as 1935 moved well into 1936 and the Summer Olympics were held in Berlin.

"The German Olympic Committee essentially barred Jewish athletes from participating in the Games."

"Why would they do that?"

"Nazi directive."

"Hitler's grand plan to promote his government's ideals of

racial supremacy."

"Follow orders or be sent to Dachau."

"Dachau?"

"A guy named Heinrich Himmler, Reichsführer of the entire SS, his bright idea. Forced labor, that's what the story is but I heard that it's not just for political prisoners. It's for groups the Nazis deemed undesirable. Inferior."

Inferior. Racial supremacy. There it was, once again, the horror refrain, subhuman. The sourness in Willem's mouth intensified as whispering continued and expanded into talk about something called "The Nuremberg Laws."

## CHAPTER EIGHTEEN

Sitting at his writing desk, the old gilt clock next to Willem was a reminder of what was important. People. What mattered to him were the friends he'd made along the way. He looked out the window of the one-bedroom apartment he now lived in, disbelieving how many years had passed. This blink of life we're all given moves too fast. Henry was now a distant memory. Willem's hand moved to touch the rough, scratched, dull surface of the timepiece that stopped clicking over time long ago. Willem needn't have been in Russia, no, he didn't need to go anywhere to know the hatred that took the family of the man who gave the clock to Oscar Rothstein. Through the years, he had experienced more than he cared to remember about the ugly images housed in his memory drawers. If only he could keep them shut but too much devastation kept happening, the drawers were overflowing. Willem and his close circle of friends agreed that something needed to be done about it.

Distracted from writing the piece he'd been working on for Brandarisbrief, the underground periodical that he had recently started, he heard marching boots a floor below. The Nazis had been there two years. No one believed it would actually happen, not back in 1937 – the year after the Olympics had been held in Berlin – no, no one thought that the evil Nazis, who enforced the despicable Nuremberg Laws, would ever invade the Netherlands. Even in 1938 when the abomination of the pogrom Kristallnacht tortured and terrorized Jews throughout Nazi Germany, the Netherlands was safe. It didn't take long for the citizens of the Netherlands to realize that safety was just an illusion when on May 10, 1940, Hitler ordered an invasion.

Hearing what sounded like boot heels clicking together, in concert with "Heil Hitler" and a sharp metallic click that sounded like a gun hammer getting ready to fire, Willem's stomach churned. Edging from the desk to see what was happening below the window, he saw two uniformed Schultzstaffeln (SS), one pointing a gun at a filthy man on the street. Butted up to the bent man, the two in black uniforms wearing Allgemeine-SS officer caps stood like starched, stiff-shirts, rigidly tall, sneering down at the humbled man. The one pointing the gun kicked the man's chest, yelling, "dirty Jew!" while the other, tight-legged, to the side, laughed, "vermin."

Willem had learned some German words from Fritz, the German soldier he'd found wounded and had helped years earlier. So, he understood the gruff command from the rigid finger-pointing officer when he looked back over his shoulder, out of sight from Willem, to what must have been others with him and ordered, "take that pig away!"

Slithering down, away from the window, Willem swallowed hard. Taking in a deep, slow breath, he quietly sat back in his chair as the sweat-drenched man was carted away. It took him a while to get his attention off what he'd just witnessed.

A slight breeze picked up creating a waving motion on the blackout curtains pulled aside from the window. The sun was rising in the sky, it was yet hours before curfew. He hated looking at those dark, heavy drapes, another reminder of the enforcement imposed not just on Jews but all citizens. Curfews and blackouts had been imposed on all. But restrictions for Jews were more severe than for the general population. Confiscations of Jews' gems, jewelry, gold, art, radios, and guns, etc. sickened Willem because he knew that Jewish property helped finance the Nazis' war effort. Confiscating Jewish property did more than rob them of their expensive items, it also intentionally robbed Jews of their culture. The Nazis wanted to remove all traces of the influence of Judaism. Pathetic, thought Willem as he grabbed hold of the blackout material and twisted it into a knot. Mumbling to himself, damn curfew, his thoughts reflected the notification distributed that the populace was not allowed out after dark. It increased the risk on him and other resistance workers who operated at night when it was safer to move and hide Jews. He let go of the curtain, the constant reminder of oppression. Restrictions. Windows had to be covered. Doors kept closed. Matches and flashlights were not allowed outside. Enough! He'd had enough.

Lately, things had gotten worse. Initially, at the time of the invasion, he tolerated the occupation, back then it was a lighter touch as the economy was doing well. He was doing well with success affording him a move to a larger apartment. As the war intensified and Germany demanded higher contributions from occupied countries, living standards declined and Jews were targeted. Repression and deportations threatened the entire Jewish population of the Netherlands. No more! Lip-biting anger surfaced. Again, he grabbed for something. Willem's hand was tightly clutching the clock, his wrist throbbing a rapid beat, his knuckles pallid. *I'm not doing enough!*

Even though he was now a published author of novels, a well-known artist, and contributed to the resistance movement through the subversive periodical he had created, it didn't satisfy his need to want to do more to help. The gilt clock reminded him of Oscar's note; remember us, prompting a desire to be more involved in the Dutch resistance movement.

Shoving his writing material aside, he took his overcoat and left. It was early but he knew several others active in the underground cell he was involved in would be present where he was headed. Driving his six-year-old Citroën to Bet's place, he was able to relax. His second-hand car was purchased from Sjoerd's friend who left the country. Although unknown how resistance workers circumvented gasoline rationing, Willem was grateful to be the recipient of enough to get him to and from where he needed to be. He was glad to be out on the open road away from marching soldiers.

At Bet's, the downstairs bar area had a few early stragglers while upstairs was where the action was. "Go on up," she tilted her head to the door at the back of the room.

The smoke-filled room had several people in it; Willem knew everyone except one. Sjoerd, Frieda, and Gerrit van der Veen, the latter a man he'd met at Bet's a couple of years earlier, were there. Gerrit was a sculptor and a clever, committed resistance worker. Among them and unknown to Willem was a man named Jan. Of average height, the brown-haired, blue-eyed man had a cute curved nose that scrunched when he looked closely at something as if he needed glasses. Something about that look made Willem smile. Anxiety sitting in his tensed muscles, eased, when Jan's thin-smiling lips propelled a friendly outstretched hand greeting, "hello."

Jan's hand felt warm and soft. It took Willem a few minutes to unfix his attention from the heat that moved up his arm.

"Sit," Gerrit motioned to an empty chair, "be comfortable, Willem. We were just talking about a dilemma I'm faced with." He went on to explain that he was being harassed for refusing to sign the Arierverklaring, the Declaration of Aryan Ancestry. "Oh, they tout the benevolence and benefits of the anti-Jewish regulations as being rather harmless—"

Sjoerd slammed an open palm on the table before him. Jan jumped at the sudden motion.

Frieda's face flushed. An artery in her neck visibly sped up.

Willem's stomach tightened.

Sjoerd repeated the noisy bang.

Frieda spoke in a forceful undertone. "Keep the noise and your voices lowered. We never know who is entering downstairs."

"Yes," Willem joined in, "the uniforms are everywhere." He then turned to Gerrit and asked, "what do you plan to do?"

"Continue to refuse to sign!" adamantly, responded Gerrit. "A few others have also refused. It's not to highlight those who register but rather to catch Jews. Particularly Jewish civil servants. Filter them out and get rid of them."

"The Nuremberg Laws all over again," mentioned Frieda.

Sjoerd's lips twisted into a half-smile. "Laws for the protection of German blood. German honor." He cynically rolled his eyes. "What a bunch of crap. When did a human not become a human? Don't answer that," he smirked at Gerrit. "The drivel in those laws... you can't marry a Jew. You can't employ a Jew. You can't do this or you can't do that!" He outstretched his palm like he wanted to give the table another bashing.

"Don't," Frieda warned him, "we need to protect our efforts to help."

"True," added Willem. "So... we know what the Germans have done... are continuing to do. Before they round up and send every Jew to be killed in extermination camps, what more are we going to do? We're heading into 1943... the longer we do nothing significant, the more are killed."

The downstairs door opened. The upstairs room hushed. It wasn't unusual for a Nazi soldier to enter for a beer. Light footsteps moved up the stairway. Bet opened the door. "It's okay. No Germans here."

"Thanks, Bet," Willem breathed out. "Do you have time to join us? I have some ideas about what we can do to expand our resistance efforts."

"That's why you came today?" she asked.

"Yes. We... I... need to do more."

Another sound, the outside door opening and Bet rapidly excused herself.

Willem, waving smoke away from his face felt Jan's attention on him. He liked the way it felt. Making eye contact with Jan's blue eyes was when Willem noticed the permanent dimple on his chin and others on his cheeks that showed when he smiled. The little concave hollows on Jan's chin and cheeks were spaces that allowed for something else, something inviting. It felt comfortably inviting, to Willem.

Sjoerd, winking at Willem, asked, "what more do you have in mind, my dear?"

The downstairs outside door slammed open. What they feared had arrived.

Gerrit put a finger to his mouth.

Frieda's forehead bubbled perspiration, she fanned herself with a periodical left on the table before her. When the title caught her attention, her skin turned to gooseflesh, a hot itching, sandpaper feeling spread up her arms. She wished Johanna was with her and not at work. Bundling the print in one hand, she quickly grabbed some matches and made haste to the brick fireplace in the room.

All eyes were on her when she burned the paper.

Willem slumped back down in his chair; it was his periodical. Bet had been careless to leave it out in the open like that. The already smoke-filled room became unbearable as plumes from the fire spread through the room. Jan stepped lightly to open a small window. Cool fresh air flowed in as they waited, each lost in their own thoughts, for the Nazis below to leave. Willem hoped they would clear out in time for him to be on the road before curfew.

Getting restless, Sjoerd filled Willem's ears with whispered words. Around an hour before dusk and not having had a chance to discuss expanding their resistance activities, Willem was driving along the open roadway on his way home. He thought back to Sjoerd's whispering, which began with a sarcastic comment about being grateful the Nazis weren't as rabid toward homosexuals or they'd all be dead.

"It's no mystery to me why we're tolerated," Sjoerd pinched Willem's cheek, an affectionate gesture leaving a red mark.

"Are you planning on sharing this mysterious information?" Willem rubbed the sting left on his face.

"Ernst Röhm."

"Huh?" questioned Willem, not understanding.

"Doubtful Hitler was ever close with a Jew, Right?"

"I'd imagine so. But what does that have to do with Röhm?"

"He was homosexual."

"And?" prodded Willem.

"No one ever told you this story?" Seeing the furrowed-brows, blank expression on Willem's countenance, he continued, "I guess not. At the beginning of the thirties, when the lunatic assumed supreme command of the Sturmabteilung (SA), the Nazis' original paramilitary, he sent a personal request to Röhm to serve as the SA's Chief of Staff. Röhm brought in personal friends and changed the command channel from subordinate to Nazi Party leadership, to no party oversight. SA numbers grew to over a million members and their intimidation contributed to the rise of the Nazis and suppression of the right-wing. Eventually, their tactics of street violence, drinking, and open homosexuality became a hindrance."

Wide-eyed, mouth agape, Willem was astonished. "He was a homosexual... that high up?"

"Yes," Sjoerd, twisting the ring on his index finger, continued, mumbling in a hushed undertone, "Hitler was aware of it."

Willem sat there shaking his head. In utter disbelief, he replied, "but, I've heard that some homosexuals are being sent to camps and—"

"True but that's now. And certainly not in the same numbers as are Jews. Jews are the target. The main area of concentration. Plus look at how many homosexual men and women the Nazi boys are aware of at Bet's and yet nothing has happened with them."

"This is all news to me," Willem rubbed the back of his neck.

"You're young."

"Not that young."

"Well, Röhm's reign didn't last," Sjoerd finished off, telling Willem, as spittle landed on his cheek, that tensions grew between the army and the SA. The army officer corps viewed the SA as a bunch of unruly gangsters. The conflict between them resulted in the Röhm Purge. Hitler, at the urgings of Göring and Himmler, ordered Röhm to be locked up. While in prison, he was murdered.

A chill filled the car. Despite the less belligerent way the Nazis treated homosexuals, there was a need for precaution. Reminded of caution, he cringed when he remembered he left his writings blatantly out on the desk in his apartment. Should an unsavory intruder see and report him, it could mean similar treatment for him as the Jewish people he wanted to protect. Lax behavior would have to change. Clandestine activities needed tightening. This, he knew, had to happen before he ventured into what he had in mind about expanding his periodical's operation.

\* \* \*

While Willem and his friends in the resistance movement continued to meet and socialize at the Café 't Mandje, all traces of resistance material were kept well hidden. Once 1942 met 1943 and with no security breaches, Willem made his move. He merged his periodical the Brandarisbrief with another publication called De Vrije Kunstenaar, which was edited by Gerrit. After the amalgamation occurred, the two men spent a great deal of time together becoming close friends. For Gerrit, it was a trial. A baptism of trust. Gerrit had heard about Willem before meeting him the year before. Several of their mutual friends confided in Gerrit that Willem was dependable and his desire to help the Jewish people was in earnest. Weeks collaborating with Willem would let Gerrit know directly if he could confidently depend on him.

During the time Gerrit was establishing how far he would go with involving Willem in his secret activities, another relationship had been nurturing for Willem – with Jan. After several dates, getting to know each other, Willem took Jan to his bed. It was the first time Willem felt an enduring close emotional bond with a sexual partner. Before, with the others, affairs began intensely heated only to fizzle. With Jan, each new encounter intensified their intimate connection. Willem's emotional needs were being met. The fearful protective raincoat Willem wore to ward off abandonment and rejection, he hadn't needed with Jan. Jan listened, nurtured, and valued Willem not because of what was in it for him but out of love, a love that was reciprocated, in kind, by Willem. Night after night, Jan stayed over at Willem's to avoid being out after curfew. Two months after they met at Bet's café, Willem asked Jan to move in with him.

"So Gerrit wants to meet with you?" asked Jan, repeating what Willem had earlier mentioned. "Today?"

For Willem the timing was right. Being in a stable relationship with both partners, his lover and business associate, he sensed something big was about to happen. "Yes," Willem responded.

Jan knew Gerrit from before meeting Willem, from his work in the resistance movement. He had also worked closely with Gerrit. He had a good idea of what was about to take place but let it play out without butting in. "I'll see you later.... let's see," he thought of the handyman work he had scheduled for the day, "around supper time?"

"Depending on what happens with Gerrit, maybe we'll have something to celebrate?"

Heading out to Gerrit's studio, Willem was grateful to be a part of a large number of men and women who put their lives on the line to help Jews. Willem's bloc was interconnected with many larger groups; churches, independent collectives, and the Dutch Communist Party. They rallied together in houses, offices, and parishes to arrange the hiding of tens-of-thousands of Jewish people. A number of resistance groups specialized in hiding children. Yet, despite all their efforts, Jews continued to be rounded up in droves and transported to death camps. Willem knew the activities he'd been involved in, mainly disseminating information, wasn't enough. It plagued him that what he was doing wasn't enough.

# THE OLD GILT CLOCK

CHAPTER NINETEEN

The red-brick exterior of the building where Gerrit worked loomed large. Behind the extensive brickwork façade, through the wide halls, upstairs on the fourth floor was the studio where he created sculptures and planned resistance strategy, sometimes alone, sometimes involving another. His endeavors began back in 1941 when arbitrary hostilities had escalated, with Nazis deporting several hundred Jews. That stimulated not just Gerrit but the entire resistance movement. The people Gerrit and Willem associated with who frequented the second floor at Bet's café were but one of the many conglomerates of resistance cells. Motivated, Willem had been doing what he could, spending time helping to disseminate subversive material, to enlist resistance help. Now, with things getting worse and the evil corruption against Jews escalating, Willem wanted to do more.

Entering the building, he thought back to the 1941 February events two years before, stirring into action the multifaceted resistance groups. Among them, the Dutch communists immediately established a cell-complex, military-type groups formed, and collective lay groups joined together with the common purpose of helping Jews escape oppression and deportation. Many groups had trouble continuing to exist because of betrayals. Those that didn't fall to the wayside, grew into a vast counterintelligence, domestic sabotage, and subversive communications network. Willem's involvement, initially, concerned working under the umbrella of the communications network. Today, that would change. Feeling anxious and excited over what was about to happen, he approached the last door in the hallway and knocked.

The shuffling of feet and the unlocking of the door took a couple of minutes.

What's going on that it's taking so long? Willem looked around the empty, cold hallway, hoping he wouldn't be seen. Every extra pair of eyes on him or any other resistance worker was cause for concern. The SS had spies everywhere. Insurgents were hunted by plain-clothed Nazis. Civilians, for a loaf of bread, ratted out resistance workers resulting in imprisonment or deportation to Mauthausen, from where few rarely returned.

"The lock stuck." Gerrit waved Willem inside and quickly closed and relocked the door. The curious expression on Willem's face lent to the explanation, "if someone comes, I have locks because of my valuable sculptures," Gerrit loudly spoke as if for effect in case someone was in hearing distance of the door. That was the story he used to gain time to hide things and be ready.

Willem smiled at the cleverness of the tall, lanky man, before him, wearing a tight-fitting black-and-blue argyle sweater and beige pants. On his feet were brown leather sandals worn without socks. His straight, short, dirty-blond hair had bits of dried clay at the sides near his left ear, most likely from swiping a hand across the side of his face while working. Sure enough, when Willem glanced down at Gerrit's hands they had traces of clay on them. He had been working on a bust of a man, which sat atop a long, wood, work table.

"Is that what you've been working on today?" asked Willem, heading toward the interesting looking head with a small, bulbous nose and mildly pocked complexion. Willem held back a smile for the head looked like Gerrit, right down to the short, straight hair, parted-on-the-right and combed back off the forehead. The only missing feature was color, the dirty-blond hair and the amber eyes. Willem gave those vibrant amber eyes a look, deep into the passionate resistance worker's whom he had grown very fond of in the last several weeks since he had been working closely with him. Gerrit was a philanderer and bragged about the multiple women he had been involved with who he deemed lucky to have a part of him. That was the curious side of Gerrit, who was a vigilant and dedicated fighter for justice of the oppressed. We are all multifaceted. We all have our faults; Willem knew this about everyone he'd encountered. The cream rose to the top, none without impurities.

Gerrit's focus moved from Willem's studying the bust to his looking at Gerrit's facial features. Smiling, he responded, "yes, it is a self-portrait."

Willem had seen Gerrit's work before but from a distance.

Here, paying attention to the wrinkles, indentations, and infinite other geometrical curved lines was an exquisite likeness. "Your work is stunning." He wanted to reach out and feel the nearly completed work. He thought of one of his favorite pieces of sculpture, only having seen photos, David. That was marble using a different method than clay where one adds to the piece to form it. With the marble sculpture, Willem had read "take away what isn't David and what remains is the finished piece." The artist is like a river, his body is the bed where the natural stream of water flows leaving an impression through his hands making art, thought Willem appreciating the artistic work before him. The two sculptures used different methods, both to beautiful results. With art, differences were accepted. If only we could accept differences in each other.

A gentle pat on the back from Gerrit accompanied a quietly voiced, "thank you." With his hand still on Willem's shoulder blade, he walked him to the far corner of the room. It was the space in the room farthest from the door, the wall adjacent to an empty lot. This is where business was conducted. "There's nothing built there," Gerrit pointed to the wall next to him as he sat. "But we still need to keep our voices down."

Willem nodded he understood. Excitement swelled through him, his heart racing, he kept his ears close to the ground.

"I am not going to talk about trust. What will talking about it possibly achieve? Too many say, 'oh, you can trust me' and then you sadly learn that isn't the case. Truth is, I have to judge for myself. Based on actions. In that, time is involved and consistency."

Willem hadn't moved, intent on listening.

"That's why I wanted to work with you a few weeks before mentioning... asking you if you..." he hesitated.

Willem, on the edge of his seat, thought he felt a breeze at his feet, rising up his pants. Was it coming from the opening at the bottom of the door? From what? Could it have been made by movement outside?

Willem's quiet side-glance toward the door stopped Gerrit.

A few swishing sounds, a cough, and then silence outside the door. Gerrit held up his palm to stay put for a few more minutes. Convinced it was okay to continue, that trouble was not afoot and no one was spying, "let me make haste," smiling, he continued. "Being laconic isn't my strong suit." He then went on to explain that when the Nazis first occupied the Netherlands, Jews were excluded from public office and, "as you know, later from public places."

"Yes." Willem's eyelids drooped and a heaviness pressed in on his throat making it hard to talk. An image came to mind, a specific time he had been out with Johanna and Frieda having a coffee.

No sooner did a woman enter with her young daughter, maybe four-years-old, clutching to her hand, when a uniformed German entered behind her. His baton banged her shoulder. "Out!"

The little girl, hiding behind her mother, held onto her

mother's dress, as the woman pleaded. "Sir, I am only wanting a piece of cake for my daughter's birthday."

Curling his upper lip in disgust, he asserted, "she shouldn't have even been born!"

The little girl, now in tears, lost her bladder. Dripping down to the floor, pools of urine at her feet, she cried, "mamma, I want to go home."

When Willem spontaneously stood to protect them, Johanna grabbed hold of his jacket and whispered, "no. It won't help."

Frieda's neck flushed red, her pupils eclipsing all color from her eyes.

Willem sat down. All they could do was watch the rest of the monstrosity unfold.

When the woman turned to comfort her daughter, the soldier swung his wooden weapon across the back of her head with such force she fell to the floor. A pool of blood flowed from her ears as she took her last breath. The little girl fell on top of her mother. Screaming. Wailing. Until silence followed, from another blow by the officer's baton.

Willem's eyes were riveted on the Jewish star they wore – their death sentence. For what! He wanted to scream.

"You okay?"

Willem woke from the trance he'd drifted into.

"Where were you?"

He was in a bad, ugly place. Happening not just in the

Netherlands, as from what he'd heard, it was much worse in Germany. Over and over the stories repeated about what had been happening in Germany, Poland, Austria, and God knew what other territories Nazi troops occupied and plundered. Willem shook his head in an attempt to rid it of the lingering, haunting nightmare image of the little girl and woman. "My apologies. You must have hit a nerve. Please," he wiped the palms of his wet hands on his pants.

"Yes, yes, we all have raw nerves." Seeing the hue dim from Willem's face, Gerrit asked, "do you need a minute? A glass of water? Something stronger?"

Willem refocused his attention on Gerrit. "No, please, I'm okay."

"Where was I... hmm." Gerrit swiped back the hair from the side of his head. "Oh yes... the point I was getting to," as he lowered his voice.

Willem leaned in.

"The Germans ordered that damn compulsory census."

Willem understood he was referring to the registering of people having full or mostly Jewish blood. After the registration, agitators of the Dutch National Socialist movement attacked Jews in public places, especially in the Jewish quarter. When the brutality intensified and a Dutch Nazi was killed all hell broke loose for Jews. Over thirty Jews were deported to concentration camps. From this escalation came the intensification of searching any questionable citizens for identification. Questionable meant they looked like what anti-Semitic Nazis considered Jewish characteristics; red or brown curly hair texture, dark beady eyes, large hook-noses, and a swarthy complexion, an overly exaggerated stereotype used to taunt Jewry, in cartoon characterizations.

"The census is responsible for forwarding orders coming from Adolf Eichmann to deport 40,000 Jews!" Attempting to keep his tone lowered, spittle flew from Gerrit's slightly opened lips. "The murderers want this to be the year every Jew is deported."

"I heard about that from Karl," said Willem referring to the young doctor, Karl Gröger, who was a part of the resistance workers who frequented Bet's.

"Yes, a good man. Rational and thoughtful. Extremely loyal. He shares a secret in common with Frieda."

Without mentioning it, Willem knew what Gerrit had alluded to. Karl was part-Jewish, hiding it well.

"That brings us to what I wanted to talk to you about, more specifically, to elicit your help. Our newsletter, calling for resistance to the occupation, has recruited a lot of new people. Many will be taking up the torch with writing and circulating press. What's badly needed are forged documents, identification papers, passports, and to get them to Jews in hiding."

"You mean… identification papers that distinguish Jews from non-Jews?"

"Yes. We have a plan."

Without hearing the details of the plan, Willem eagerly

countered. "Count me in."

\*  \*  \*

That night, wrapped in Jan's embrace, Willem felt complete. Whatever that missing part was, that he had been sure for many years he'd recognize it when it came, had arrived. Guided to this moment, this place, to Jan, to Gerrit, to the resistance work, Willem had walked through a portal of involvement and responsibility and there was no turning back. He knew he was home.

Jan stroked Willem's face, the tenderness, a reflection of all that was good between them. Tolerance. Compassion. Integrity. Compatibility. Being there for one another without the need for words. Jan continued caressing Willem's cheeks until he fell asleep.

The next morning before Willem met with Gerrit, he said a hugging goodbye and for the first time told his partner, "I love you."

Jan stepped back, eyes bubbling with sparkling tears, gazing at Willem. He put a hand to his heart, letting the joy overflow down his smiling features. "In a world that creates Buchenwald, that kills thousands upon thousands of Jews, there is still love. There is still happiness to be had. We must never lose sight of that."

# THE OLD GILT CLOCK

## CHAPTER TWENTY

As Dutch resistance workers labored to sabotage the Nazis by cutting their phone lines, distributing anti-Nazi leaflets, tearing down Nazi posters, destroying swastika flags, hiding and sheltering Jews in attics, basements, rooms in houses with false walls, and anywhere a secure space could be found to hide the enemies of the Nazi regime, Willem was set to begin his work with Gerrit. Also involved would be another man, a printer named Frans Duwaer. In the intransigent fight to help Jews, local printers, with their printing presses, were invaluable commodities.

The notion for the meeting arose a few months earlier when Gerrit dropped material off to be printed by Frans and saw something on his press. In his studio waiting Willem to arrive, Gerrit mentally replayed that earlier event.

"Is it difficult to make those?" asked Gerrit, walking to the press and picking up the small maroon book. Running an index finger over the word on its cover, PASSPORT, "what I mean is, can you get a blank book and make a forged one?"

Frans wagged a finger at his friend. "What do you think

that is?" His focus shifted to the double-locked and bolted door. "You don't think all that hardware is to protect my printing press."

The smell of Frans' sweat, mixed with the inked-press chemical stench, was perfume to Gerrit's nostrils. "Really! How marvelous."

Frans nodded the satisfaction he did not speak.

Gerrit lit up like the celebrations on Koninginnedag. "Aha, this is most fortuitous. Of late, I've been pondering ways to expand my involvement. There are several groups already working on making false identification papers from stolen plates."

"Yes, I'm aware of their activities. The printers' team, we call ourselves—"

"We?" queried Gerrit.

"Why of course, I'm involved. That there," indicating the passport, "wasn't just a fluke favor to one person. I do more than make passports," he smiled. "I receive stolen papers from team members." Looking toward the door, he stopped a minute to listen and when he felt comfortable, continued, "a group of undercover men and women – our people – working close to occupying Germans, in one capacity or another, have stolen official paper to allow us to make documents necessary for Jews in hiding."

"Brilliant," smiled Gerrit, lost in thought.

Frans gave Gerrit a minute to come out of his faraway countenance before asking, "did you have something in mind?"

"Yes," he went on to explain that seedlings were planted in his mind when the Germans enforced Persoonsbewijzen. Today the germination of his thoughts bore fruit. "We'll join your efforts to help get identification papers to more people."

"We?" Frans gave Gerrit a puzzled head tilt.

"I've been working with another artist, Willem Arondéus, a reliable, trustworthy worker. And, friend, I might add. We can work with you to combine the effort and help more people."

"If you say he can be trusted—"

"He's a friend of Johanna and Frieda," Gerrit interrupted Frans. "A homosexual with steadfast sympathies toward Jewish people. He's got history there. Purpose. I've no doubt we three can get a lot done."

A knock at the door and Gerrit refocused his attention back to the room. Willem arrived first, shortly followed by Frans. The introductions were made and a strategy was worked out. Gerrit and Frans took turns discussing the best way to achieve the greatest result, with Willem listening and concurring. They would work out of Frans' shop, taking turns, around-the-clock, to make the documents. Frans would obtain the necessary material and orient them to his equipment. Further discussions resulted in uniform agreement on who would do what at what time, how they would travel, enter the building and how the one, on night-shift, would have to work under very dimmed conditions. The risk was greater at night but they all agreed it was worth taking, as Jews were being carted off and killed in droves.

Their work began with great vigor and vitality. Names were obtained from the go-betweens and documents were constructed.

Identification papers and passports were then forwarded to the next person in the link for delivery to the Jewish person or family in hiding. In their time working together, before trouble began, the three produced some tens-of-thousands of false identity papers.

Hypervigilant, Willem felt eyes upon him, ears listening, noses sniffing out information when he was out on the street, opening a door, or at Bet's bar. No time was without suspicion. Even in his apartment with Jan, he was acutely attentive. It made it hard for Willem to relax, to make love, to enjoy life. Despite the burden, the squeezing pressure on his chest at times making it hard to breathe, he never regretted his commitment. Doubt didn't enter into his decision. He was sustained in his actions, by the thoughts of saving as many Jewish people as he could. And Jan as well, for Jan understood that the winds could change and sweep down on homosexuals like they had in Germany. Either one of them could be next in line to be carted off. Between them, nothing was left unsaid, including the danger they were involved in.

"Helping someone else," espoused Willem, "is helping ourselves."

Jan understood what he meant. He would never forget what he heard from friends fleeing Germany, about the escalation of discrimination against homosexuals. "We are now in the same category as Jews in Germany, but thankfully our fate here has been slower to progress. I don't feel safe." A chill ran up his spine, into his heart, when he remembered what Frieda had told him about changes in Germany that had been validated by other friends who escaped. What was relayed to him concerned the German Criminal Code, Paragraph 175. Under Propaganda Minister Joseph Goebbels it was changed from punishable by prison sentence to: "We must exterminate these people root and branch; the homosexual must be eliminated." Jan remembered hearing how things had changed for the worse. The first couple of years into the Nazi rule in Germany the law was lenient, stating that specific evidence of a sex act being committed was necessary for a guilty verdict. Of course, difficult to pursue, many charged with the crime of homosexual behavior were exonerated and released. Now, although the law stated if found guilty per evidence, punishment was confinement in a penitentiary, in reality, per Goebbels' implementation, it meant proof be damned, kill them in the camps. Why!

"I don't feel safe," Jan spoke out loud echoing Frieda's words.

"You shouldn't feel safe. We are in the rule of madmen."

"Working very hard to restore some semblance of sanity," Jan looked through the descending darkness to the window, a sliver of moonlight came through the crack between the blackout curtains. "Look," he pointed to a shadow on the floor where leaves on a tree limb filtered the light. A breeze lent to a moving form that looked like little chicks scurrying about.

Willem the storyteller, turned the dancing shadow on the floor into a fable, a needed distraction. "Once there was a well-formed egg—"

"A chicken egg," chuckled Jan, playing along.

Just then a cloud moved over the moon and the room went black. The dancing-chick breeze now felt like a thick gray ominous fog. "Hmm," Willem whispered into Jan's ear. "Like all good stories, there's a villain. The protagonist needs to overcome the evil powers exerted against him. So… let's see. Hmm," he grabbed hold of Jan's hand. "Ah, okay, here is the twist. The well-formed egg has been fertilized with hatred. The little healthy chick was intentionally being poisoned with intolerance."

"Ooooh no," facetiously moaned Jan.

Unwittingly tightening his grip on Jan's hand, Willem, now carried away, kept at the story. "The little guy pecked at his shell, seeking fresh air. Desperately wanting to be freed from the toxic seepage percolating into his home."

Too reminiscent of things he'd heard about the camps, Jan loosened Willem's hand. The buoyancy was gone from his tone. "It's really getting to you." That was no silly, little nursery story, it was a metaphor for what had visited Willem in dreams, waking him in groaning night sweats. Perhaps the only way to release the tension was through story, nightmares, talking about the shocking hardships indirectly.

Perchance Willem had premonitions causing the bad dreams, that sick feeling in his gut, the fear at every corner that they'd be found out, for it was no surprise when he received an indirect message from Gerrit to see him immediately. At a lunch with Johanna, who had come from a meeting with Gerrit, she said, "not at the printing shop, at Gerrit's apartment." Fearing that Frans' place had been discovered, Willem quickly left. Turned out that the shop hadn't been compromised but Gerrit felt it best to limit the number there to one-at-a-time. That way if the place was found out, the other two would be safe and could relocate with another printer and continuing working.

"We have a problem," Gerrit stated, facing Willem, after latching his door. Heading to the back of the room, he murmured in an undertone in Willem's ear, "I feared this would happen. That damn registry has been a nemesis since day one. It seems… more like, it has occurred, that the Nazis are checking the registration lists against papers, for suspicious people and determining them to be fake."

"How did that happen?"

"From what I heard, it started out unintentionally in a coastal village. A boat carrying Jews was spotted. The identification papers were then in question. The guards reported the names of the suspicious people fleeing in the middle of the night. The names were compared with names at the registry and deemed to be false."

"How many have been detained?" asked Willem.

"At present, it's fewer than twenty but soon the numbers will increase. It is a horrible deterrent to our efforts."

"The Municipal Office for Population Registration is the place?" Willem nervously scratched the tip of his nose.

"Yes."

"We need to do something about this," replied Willem, bent at the waist, elbows resting on his thighs, looking up at Gerrit.

"Agreed."

Willem sat up. He fidgeted. They went back and forth. No ideas popped-up. Twenty minutes passed. Heat and frustration filled the space between them. As nothing arose, Willem suggested they sleep on it and touch base tomorrow. Gerrit had to relieve Frans at his printing shop soon anyway.

Back home with Jan, Willem paced. Had no appetite. Unable to think of anything helpful, thoughts banged around in his head giving him a bad headache.

"Sit for a minute," pleaded Jan.

"I have to think."

"Don't you feel you've done enough of that for one night?"

"Imagination helps me survive. I can't survive if I can't imagine."

Jan shook his head at his failure to get Willem to calm down. "Can't you be a little more patient with yourself?"

"No! I'm allergic to patience." Realizing how ridiculous that sounded, he smiled back at Jan. "Honey," said Willem, finally sitting down by Jan, "too many are dying. I can't forget it. For me to relax is like dancing on someone's grave."

"But you haven't hurt anyone. Why do you take it so personally? You're on a relentless mission that is threatening to destroy you. You need a breather from time to time. Some distance from all the—"

"Jan," Willem stopped him. Looking into Jan's deep-blue, worried eyes. "For me it is personal." Willem had never told Jan the full story of the Levins and Rothsteins. He lowered his head, put a hand to his throbbing forehead and said nothing further.

Worried and wanting to know what Willem was so reluctant to talk about, Jan said, "I'm here... talk to me."

Willem was hesitant. The topic of Birgit and the Levins' move, plus the Rothsteins, was painful for him; he missed them still, so many years later. That pain had been reinforced every time he saw a crime committed against a Jewish person; a hateful injustice levied on an innocent victim. Perhaps it was too close to home, being homosexual and the rejection cast upon him from his own family. He never wanted to spend the time self-introspecting to figure it out. Now, here with Jan, it felt raw in the safe confines of their intimate relationship.

Willem's lack of response, his quiet demeanor, prompted Jan to say, "I don't want to push you. I don't want you to ever feel obligated to explain anything to me. It's just that... it's so dangerous... and if something happens—"

"Jan," again Willem interrupted, "remember Birgit Levin... I told you about my friendship with her in school and how when I met her family, they were good to me?"

"Yes," replied Jan.

"There was another family I haven't mentioned, the Rothsteins." Willem wiped the wetness blurring his vision. "See that clock over there," he motioned to his desk.

"That old antique?" Jan gave Willem a tight-lipped smile. "The one you won't let me touch."

"Yes. It was a gift from Oscar Rothstein," explained Willem, continuing with the rest of the story through tears and sorrow. The very sorrow motivating him now. "It never leaves, that burning in my chest. It's a searing, dug deeply into my flesh, the bones that hold me up, engraved in my heart, resounding in my soul, all the unthinkable things that are being done. What is wrong with us?"

Jan knew the rhetorical question wasn't meant to be answered. Instead, he reached for Willem's hand. "I've read of the Russian pogroms. The repeating events being parroted by the Nazis. It's hard for any empathetic person to take." What words were there to speak? What sounds could possibly do any good? It wouldn't unpeel the relentless pain that continued to be stimulated with each new persecution, each indignity, each act of bigotry, each blow with a baton, each bullet shot through the flesh of innocence. He could think of nothing more and so for the next many minutes they sat still until Willem got up and went to his desk.

"Here," Willem smiled, with a face flushed with wetness, "you can hold it."

Jan delicately took hold of the gilded clock and hugged it close to his heart. Next to the deep love he felt for Willem.

Doing that – handing the clock over and seeing the expression on Jan's face, released something Willem had been holding onto. It made room for something new. It was then a bright idea hit him.

# THE OLD GILT CLOCK

## CHAPTER TWENTY-ONE

"You want to do what!" Gerrit was flabbergasted, his face bright red, his hair looked electrocuted. He wildly shook his head to clear it of distraction, confusing cobwebs. He couldn't believe what Willem had just said. "This is your plan?" Sucking in a mouthful of saliva that went down the wrong pipe, he broke out in a coughing fit.

Frans went into fits of laughter; he understood. "It's genius. Willem is on to something," he slapped a hand on Gerrit's back. "You okay," he asked, banging another blow to try to stop the whooping spasms.

"Breathe slowly," Willem piped in, concern growing that Gerrit might lose consciousness. "Breathe."

A gulping inhalation, interrupted by another outburst of hacking and finally, Gerrit swallowed calmly. Once quieted, his face still red, he looked at his partners with amazement written all over his face. "You're both crazy."

Willem and Frans looked at each other and broke out laughing. There was nothing funny about the situation, the pressure-cooker, built-up stress needed release.

Gerrit tried to quiet them down, reminding them that walls have ears.

Eating half his words, Frans waved a hand in the air for emphasis, "crazy genius, that's what he is. It'll work." With a stern narrow-eyed look directed at Gerrit, "anyway, you don't have a better plan," was said with another slap on his back, this time for emphasis.

Another slow breath through his nose, Gerrit hoarsely replied, "another suicide plan? No, I don't have one. But since you two find this to be so brilliant, let me hear all the details." He leaned back in his chair, awaiting a fantastic story, something he was sure would come from one of Willem's novels and not work in reality. One he was sure would be dismissed, once it arrived in the light of day, to be seen for what it was. Loony!

Out of habit, Willem looked at the door to be sure it was indeed locked. It had become an obsession since doing the forgeries, to check doors, double-check, triple-check. Not to mention the windows in his apartment, windows where he was working and windows he passed on the street where he could see reflections of anyone who might be following him. Overheard, whispered conversations felt personally directed at him. Overly friendly waiters and shopkeepers were suspect. No one but his close circle of friends was to be trusted. Words meant nothing, no verbalization or assurances would convince him of reliability. Nothing but time, a good long stretch of time and a steady relationship that sat right in his gut, that didn't make him feel queasy, guided him toward people to involve in his activities. New people had joined his group, the one that continued to meet at Bet's. It was convenient to continue to meet there, at a place where crowds gather and homosexuals were known to frequent, an establishment where they were left alone for the most part. Newcomers put him on edge.

"Okay, so here's the deal," he looked at Gerrit to be sure he wasn't going to lose it again. "MOP," said Willem, dropping his volume, referring to his acronym for the Municipal Office for Population Registration so they wouldn't have to continue mentioning its name and risk exposure, was easy enough to use and if needed they could switch to talking about mopping the floor. Silly as it sounded, it wasn't unusual. Nazi destruction needed cleaning up, brooms, mops, cleaning items were all being put to good use.

"Mopping?" Gerrit's dismissal, a tightening of his facial muscles forming into a grimace; he wasn't buying the plan. Willem was not going to convince him of it and he was ready to protest that they needed to drop it when Willem demanded Gerrit hear him out.

"MOP is the major handicap to the achievement of our goals. Since what we do," he lowered his volume even more, close to whispering, "can be checked against the registration lists revealing inconsistencies…" He picked up a pencil from the workbench and wrote out, "checking against the registry reveals forgeries," then erased it.

Frans nodded.

Gerrit's chin was tucked down. Looking up at Willem, he remained skeptical.

"So, here's what we do." Willem outlined the remainder of the plan on the piece of paper, ending with, "we bomb the building." Willem watched Gerrit shake his head. "Think of the lives. Theirs, not ours. Thousands!" he loudly whispered.

Gerrit stood up and rubbed a hand through his hair.

Again, Frans laughed as sweat poured from his pores. He pulled his shirt from his chest.

Willem felt the February cold on his feet. Putting his knees together to stay warm, he tapped a finger on what he'd just written. "It's the only way." He moved his finger over, "destroy the registry then the comparisons are gone," to reiterate his point.

Gerrit stopped resisting; that got his attention. "Hmm," he rubbed his chin as he added, to the two men, "that would work, but..." he scratched his neck, leaving red streaks. As soon as it had made sense, doubt surfaced. "No, it's too dangerous."

Finally, Frans added his comment. "Our activities have already subjected us to immediate arrest. This is no more dangerous than what we've been doing."

"I beg to differ," countered Gerrit.

"It's true, what he said," Willem added in. Looking at Gerrit then Frans, he said, "Gerrit's right. It is more dangerous. But it would..." he started to reach back to the paper to write then continued in a barely audible sound, "it would save lives.

Thousands of them." The utterance, instead of pencil and paper, was his way of saying I'm willing to risk it all. We need to move on this!

Frans puffed out his chest, raised his shoulders, and proudly whispered, "what would my life be worth if I continue to sit back and do nothing. To continue to work, as we have, doesn't guarantee safety. I don't want to just go through the motions, I want to…" fervent passion, caught in his belly, silenced him.

Gerrit empathetically felt what Frans wanted to say, what they were all feeling. "Yes, my friend, we all want to save lives." A long pensive silence. A look at Frans. The same look at Willem and then Gerrit's eyes lit up. "We do it!"

The change in the room, the glue of commitment, purpose, and selfless behavior bonding them together was palpable.

"Okay then," Frans held out his hand to Gerrit, "we shake on it."

Their agreement, sealed with a handshake, set Willem's plan in motion.

"We need to include others for this to work. I've thought through a way to implement it but it will require more than the three of us." Willem elaborated on the plan to bring in some of the others in their group, the Bet gang he called it, who were already risking arrest to help Jews. People who were trusted. Among them were, Johanna, Frieda, Sjoerd, and Karl Görger, who had risked his life as well as his profession and had proven to be invaluable with his help. There was no question in Willem's mind that Karl, a doctor in Amsterdam, who had joined the resistance movement under Gerrit, was credible.

"That makes sense, but," Frans interjected in a concerned tone, "the larger the group, the greater the risk."

"Correct," Willem responded. "That is why only our most reliable, trusted friends in the movement will be included. Not one iota of uncertainty must exist."

"What about Jan, Bet, and anyone else that might be needed?" asked Gerrit.

"Yes, of course, those two. I haven't told Jan yet but I'm sure Bet will be on board," said Willem. "And, as for others, we'll see what's needed and move accordingly. I agree with what Frans said, that we need to keep the numbers small. However, if we need someone to accomplish the goal then that person will be considered."

"Meeting at Bet's will work," said Gerrit, referring to an earlier mention that it was a centralized place where they were already congregating with the others.

"That's for sure," Frans' lips turned into an affectionate smug grin. "That is one good lesbian, helpful to a fault."

With limited words and a few more written, erased, and burned comments, they worked out a rough plan. The less to discuss at Bet's the better. They would need surveillance of the Population Registration Office for the layout of the building, the list of day staff and night guards, how many German soldiers patrolled the area, all the details to determine how to best implement the plan for success. But, before anything else, they needed to discern who was in. With the day moving on, it was time to break up the meeting.

Frans went back to work on documents.

Gerrit stayed put.

Willem went home.

Arriving at his place, Willem smiled, at the table set with a half loaf of bread, a section of rookworst, and dipping mustard, next to a single bottle of beer. Sitting for the luxurious meal, Willem never asked Jan how he acquired it with their ration cards. Willem felt the cold beer, a chilly reminder of his father's drinking. He never ventured further than a small glass of wine or cold beer. Tonight, though, he needed something to help him unwind, unknot the muscles in his neck and back.

Jan served himself, watched Willem put some on his plate, and held up the beer. "Here's to... well, you tell me," he smiled, took a swallow and passed the bottle to Willem.

Appreciative of Jan's effort in getting the food and obvious wide-eyed curiosity about how the meeting went and having not told Jan the details yet, Willem briefly mentioned, "the MOP plan," and told Jan that once they finished their meal, he'd fill him in.

"How am I supposed to wait?" he fondly nudged Willem's arm. "Willem, don't keep me waiting." A sheepish look and flushed neck from Willem and Jan knew it wasn't good what Willem had in mind, not good at all. He knew that anxious response in his partner, the one that had hidden stress written all over it. He put down the knife he was about to use to cut a slice of bread and wasted no time in demanding, with a sharp insistent edge, "you better tell me now, before I completely lose my appetite."

Willem looked like he had swallowed an orange, whole. His Adam's apple bobbed up and down. A sip of beer to wet his suddenly dry tongue was needed before he said, "can we just finish our meal? It's really not a topic to discuss while eating."

Jan grabbed hold of the edge of his plate, his knuckles going pale. "You're scaring me." He moved his hands off the plate and put both hands, palms down on the tabletop, waiting. Staring at Willem. "Now! Please!"

Willem took another sip, contemplating his reply. He knew Jan would react as Gerrit initially had. His plan most certainly crossed the line of cautious safety. They had a tacit agreement to keep safe and be smart with their resistance activities. What good would an arrested, imprisoned, or dead resistance worker be? They had talked about not signing up for something so dangerous it would risk too much. Now, stepping into too much, Willem wondered what was too much? Prior, it was merely a rhetorical question. No longer, supposition, he knew the answer. He also knew Jan wouldn't like it. Willem would risk everything, including his relationship with Jan. On that day, he was guided by a higher purpose, to act for the greater good. At risk of his life, imprisonment, so be it, whatever may come. He hated to jeopardize his close and loving relationship with Jan but knew he couldn't live with himself if he didn't give it his all. "Jan…"

"Go on," responded Jan, solemnly, tight-lipped, grabbing his thighs.

Willem pushed his plate away, wiped his mouth with a napkin, folded it and put it on the table, leaned toward Jan across from him and softly breathed the plan as close to Jan's ear as he could reach.

Jan reflexively stood, pushing the table back, rattling plates and tossing the beer to the floor, spilling the remainder. "What!" He walked in circles. "I can't believe you're going to—"

"Shhh, please," Willem went to him. Grabbed him in his arms and continued to gently explain his rationale. In a low, soft voice, he said, "I know how you feel. And… I'm sorry." He knew he'd be sorrier if he didn't go through with it. Then what would that do to them? To their relationship? They thrived on integrity. On helping others. They knew the dangers involved in what they had been doing. They had talked about the impact of being caught. Being interrogated. Being sent away. Being killed. They knew the risks. They knew before entering into the relationship what was at stake. For each of them. Now, here it was, in their faces. They were both scared. But for Willem, the fear pumped him up. For Jan, it was deflating.

Jan knew there was nothing to say. Nothing to do. Fate had grabbed them and, as Jan's father had said so many times in the past when destiny catches up, it's in God's hands. Feeling depressed like the concave dimple on his chin, a sinking feeling pressed in on his shoulders. He remained in the tender embrace of Willem, who tried to comfort his crying spell. A few minutes, not even sure how much time passed, when the heaves of painful tears stopped, there was a quietness. Like what is left from a passing storm. This one had been weathered. Who knew about the next one?

# CHAPTER TWENTY-TWO

The next morning, when Jan had calmed down a bit, Willem asked him if he wanted to be involved in the plan. Not sure who else would agree, they needed all the help they could get to pull it off. Yet subdued and muddled, he told Willem he needed to think about it, to be sure he would be doing it out of his own determination and not just to be at Willem's side. After Willem left, the confused, sticky fibers in Jan's head had dissolved enough for him to think more clearly. It didn't take him long to realize he had no choice. He too was intently and irrevocably invested in saving lives.

\*     \*     \*

Rushing off to the first group meeting, arranged orally through messages passed along person-to-person, Willem was stopped by a commotion blocking the road ahead. He pulled over, parked and hid in a small storefront alcove. Close enough to afford a view of what was occurring and within earshot, he waited. A malnourished man and woman, ostensibly married, for she was wearing a wedding band, stood in an apparent state of panic before a towering SS officer. Lording over them in a somber, authoritative, dark-gray uniform, tailored to project domination and promote fear, his movements were stiff, loveless, and perfunctory. He coldly stood there with outstretched palm as if waiting for something to be placed in it. By the sound of the increasing stomping from his left boot on the road, the rigidity increasing in his shoulders, it was clear his patience was running thin.

Slumped down, the woman postured her hands in a meek, folded position resting against her sunken chest while the man dug through his coat pockets looking for something. The first, a left front pocket, drew nothing. Before the trembling man reached for the right one, the towering Nazi unfastened the snap on his gun's holster. While he tauntingly rubbed a finger on the gun, the man took a minute to wipe sweat from his face with the back of his sleeve.

In a helter-skelter rapid motion, what looked like a Walther P38 was pointed at the man's right temple. The stiff SS man nodded to the whimpering woman, "you! Get the papers!"

*Papers*, thought Willem. Taking it all in, he felt like he was going to vomit. Trapped in the small recess, he continued to watch, hoping the couple would be safe but fearing the worst. Willem's eyes widened when the woman reached for her husband's shoulder; she tried to steady his shaking body while her other hand dug into his right front pocket. Out came the passports and folded identification papers. The Nazi forcibly grabbed them from the woman and upon opening them looked back and forth to the faces of the two. "Liars! Filthy scum." He shot the man.

The woman fell to the ground beside her husband, wailing, "why? Oh my God, why?"

She never took her eyes off her dead husband. Not while the contemptuous Nazi pointed the gun at her back, nor when he said, "why? Your frizzy brown hair. No Dutch Jew is named Kuiken! Goodbye pig." A bullet sank into her back, splattering blood.

Nooo! The inside of Willem's head screamed, over and over, no. Feeing like it was going to explode, he waited while the vile SS officer walked off with their papers and left the couple in the street for others to clean up. That damn bastard didn't even take them away for a crosscheck of the documents. Feeling sick to his stomach, Willem had just witnessed the harsh punishment against Jews with suspected falsified papers. How many more had been shot on the streets without checking? How many murdered or sent to concentration camps once their papers had been crosschecked? Willem hated imagining the number of times this scene was replicating throughout the Netherlands. Throughout occupied territories. In Germany.

By the time Willem arrived at Bet's, everyone was there.

Frans, looking at his wristwatch, cast an annoyed expression at Willem for being late. "We've been here—"

Johanna grabbed hold of Frans' shoulder to hush him. One look at the drawn expression on Willem's face, his bloodshot sclerae, and she knew something terrible had happened. "What?"

Willem struggled to get air into his lungs, through the constricted band compressing his chest. In clipped sentences, he gave them brief snapshots of what he'd just witnessed. "They didn't even cart them off? Didn't even check—"

"The brutality," interrupted Frans, "has increased since the boat filled with Jews was discovered off the coastal town."

"But he didn't even crosscheck their IDs," mourned Willem. "Executed them. Left them for the vultures... What of their families?" His hands grasped hold of his lowered forehead.

"They don't care. Why waste time interrogating. Why be fair when you can just kill a Jew outright and be done with it," Sjoerd, filled with rancor, dug his nails into the palms of his hands.

"The hostility is self-righteousness at its worst. The very essence of hatred. Weak, cowardly, ineffectual men need to hate so they can make themselves superior. They hold no power other than brutal, bullying force. They have sunk into immoral quicksand, never to see the light of day," said Gerrit, feeling the need to say something, wanting to break the tension in the room and move things along. Now more than ever, they had no time to waste.

A few more attempts at a breath and Willem sat up, wiped his eyes, and sensing the urgency in the room, said, "we need to act and act fast." Willem bit down on his lower lip to calm his rising volume and to slow down. Sucking in a slight amount of blood from the inside of his lip, he deliberately added, "fast but smart."

"Absolutely," added Gerrit. "Haste without prudent

planning will lead to errors."

Speaking of prudent planning, none of them knew that while they were meeting, downstairs an overly curious patron and friend of Bet's, Ans van Dijk, had entered the café and wondered where Bet was. Taking a liberty, she tiptoed up the stairs. Without a knock, she twisted the door handle overhearing something about wise planning.

Ans, a lesbian Jewess, was a former hat shop proprietor. She was also a black marketeer with an ardent sense of self-preservation, known to be cruel and devious to her own kind. Wearing a chip on her shoulder, she had a reputation for being off-putting. Ans and Bet had an intimate history and everyone knew that Bet did not readily throw people away. Especially an ex. Especially someone Bet suspected of spying. Keep them close, acting ignorant of their devious ways was found to be more prudent than shunning them, which only increased their curiosity. Just stay guarded!

Johanna, facing the door, was the first to see her. Instead of greeting her and switching them all off of what looked suspicious, she smartly said, "yes, you don't want Jan to find out." Eyes facing Johanna scrunched in confusion until she said, "oh, hi, Ans. Now that you're here you're going to have to be sworn to secrecy. We're planning a surprise party for Jan's birthday."

Ans looked around at the familiar group, nodding hello.

Bet stood, went to Ans and taking hold of her arm, said, "I knew I shouldn't have left the place alone this long. Is there any of the liquor left? Have I been robbed blind?" she joked to Ans. "Come on with me and we'll catch up." Turning to the room, before exiting, with her back to Ans, Bet winked at the others. "Feel free to plan what you want for Jan, just let me know when, and if anything special is needed." She escorted Ans out.

When the door was closed and footsteps gone from the stairway, they all let out a collective sigh. Sjoerd in his usual sarcastic levity said, "that Bet... she could talk her way out of a robbery."

A finger to his mouth, indicating quiet, Willem reached for pencil and paper. "Next time we meet, Bet needs to stay downstairs and guard the door."

Frieda, her attention yet on the door, had concern written on her scowling countenance.

With alertness and sensitivity to every new and unfamiliar sound made, pencil and paper were used to outline plans and jobs. Arrangements were made for messages to be passed word-of-mouth. Nothing in writing. Nothing incriminating. A note written by Gerrit said, "we're lucky it was only Ans. Next time could be a German soldier." It wasn't unusual for them to frequent Bet's. It also wasn't unusual for them to see Bet's friends congregating upstairs for social privacy. As long as they kept low-key and didn't arouse suspicion, the Germans left them alone.

Just as they began to elaborate a bit more, Jan entered. Willem, glad to see Jan, had his curiosity piqued when he saw the look on Jan's twisted face. Once the door was closed, "Ans van

Dijk is downstairs. Did you know?" asked Jan, looking to Willem and the others. Bet was downstairs schmoozing with her right now, keeping her preoccupied. Jan ran into them when he arrived. It left him with a sour taste in his mouth.

"Yes," answered Sjoerd.

"I'll fill you in later," said Willem.

Jan nodded.

The meeting ramped up, as Sjoerd, with infinite connections and wherewithal, wrote about a friend, a writer Johan Brouwer, who could indirectly help. A longtime acquaintance of Sjoerd's, they all knew of him, of his impeccable reputation with the resistance movement. "He can't come to meetings," he mumbled. "Too busy and involved in other activities." Starting to write something else, the pencil lead snapped off. Frieda handed Sjoerd a pen to continue to write that Johan would provide a detailed layout of the building to be kept in a secret safe. That was the only thing to be allowed in writing. Once subjected to memory, it would be destroyed.

"Excellent," said Frans.

Frieda, scribbled, "What else will be needed?"

"Disguises, my dear," noted Sjoerd. "I can make the uniforms."

Frieda added, "I'll help with that."

Noticing the hat on Jan's head, Sjoerd took the liberty of whispering, "only thing I can't make is hats."

In an environment that was never without peril, where

walls don't protect conversations and no one is safe, "Shhh," came from a hypersensitive Frieda. "Use the pen!"

Further notations jotted down included Frans and Willem continuing to make documents. Willem also added, "I am sure I can find someone to make hats."

When they got as far as they could for the day, before breaking up, Gerrit whispered, "no discussions. No sharing with friends, trusted or not. We must keep this on the hush-hush." Although it didn't need to be said, Gerrit needed to speak it. "It's not just our lives at stake here."

"Not a word," agreed Willem.

All concurred.

Frieda burned the notes.

"You'll explain to Jan that his absence from future meetings will be needed," smiled Johanna, referring to the story told to Ans. If they were to pretend to throw a party for Jan as their excuse to meet, he couldn't be present.

Leaving Bet's Jan caught site of Ans watching him with one squinty eye as she conversed with another woman at the bar. Quickly, he broke visual contact but not before a deep cutting sensation struck his belly.

"Who dropped you off?" asked Willem, needing a distraction from the lingering sick feeling in his gut from the bloodshed earlier in the day. What he had mentioned to the others before Jan arrived, did not need to be repeated to Jan. Willem did not want to resurrect a replay of the night before. The less said of the horrors they saw, the better for both of them.

"Coors," Jan replied, indicating a resistance worker he knew. "He had to come out this way."

"Karl's friend? The medical student?"

"Yes."

"That was nice of him. I'm so glad you came," he gently squeezed hold of Jan's hand.

"You said you'd fill me in regarding Ans?" Jan reminded Willem.

Willem relayed what had happened earlier, including the surprise birthday party ploy.

"I got a bad feeling from her. I know she's Jewish. And I know that her millinery shop—"

"Maison Evany in Amsterdam?" asked Willem.

"Yes, that was hers. As I was saying, her shop was closed in '41."

"Right, when the Nazis seized Jewish property," continued Willem, "she had it bad. Also lost her partner, Miep Stodel."

"Yeah, Stodel fled to Switzerland. I wondered why Ans didn't go with her." Jan looked at the car window fogged from the heat of his exhalations. Distracted, puzzling over why that woman bothered him so much, he rubbed a finger across the glass. Crying streams of water ran down the cold surface, pooling at the ledge. A pat to his face, the coolness felt refreshing. Near the horizon, dark clouds were moving in. A distant flash of lightning and a muted blast of thunder and he knew they were heading into rain. A few gray cauliflower clouds parted just as Jan was looking in their direction. "Oh, how beautiful. Do you see it?"

"Yes," Willem smiled at the orange, blue, and violet rainbow that had formed between the splitting fog at the murky distance. "The first beautiful thing I've seen today, beside you."

That night they made love. Desperate and passionate. Exhausted afterward, they fell asleep intertwined, awaking early the next morning ready for work.

## CHAPTER TWENTY-THREE

February drifted into March and plans were well underway. The layout of the building was mapped out. Uniforms were being made. Someone had been contacted to make hats and a progress report indicated they would be done in time. Guns had been obtained. Thankfully, Karl assumed responsibility for arranging chemicals for drugging the guards and the most effective explosive for the best result.

"Be careful," ended conversations.

With a tiny glimmer of light from the moon, Willem sat at his desk rethinking the events of the last several days, when his attention shifted to the old gilt clock. He had conversations in his head with the remnant object, a survivor that remained after the disintegration of so much. The last trace of a tragic past. It made him feel better to personify it. Into the mysterious unknown, Willem asked; "how many have perished since you stopped ticking?" He wondered what the clock would say if it could speak. If it could tell the stories of lives uprooted and destroyed; would it scream from rooftops to stop the madness? Would it whisper to the dead there was hope, that some good is being done? Or would it weep from the rusted turrets on its mausoleum façade that it came from a place that once had mobs led by priests who stormed in yelling, "kill the Jews!?" Would its mechanical insides bleed for the citizens who were unaware of the approaching tsunami that swept through the town, slaughtering them like pigs? Would the clock dare to tick again if it knew babies were torn from their horrified mothers crying for mercy? No, the clock would never speak. Now its motion had stopped, never to tick again and Willem knew it would never be able to tell the last cold, brutal details about Kishinev. About how, at dusk, the streets were piled with corpses and injured. About how the police made no attempt to rectify the criminal brutality and about how those who could escape, left in shock, away from the town rid of Jews. Like its owner who fled, the clock's heart stopped ticking, for they could no longer bear to live in a world where the unthinkable continued.

Doing some good, inspired Willem and kept him from sinking into an irretrievable morass of melancholy. Although being actively involved, planning the MOP mission had invigorated his purpose; the past month and beginning of this had been bad for the victims of war. He thought back to last month, the middle of February, back to a speech delivered at the Berlin Sportpalast by the vilest of men, Hitler's mouthpiece and spreader of vicious lies, Goebbels, calling for a total war. The headlines covering the speech read, "TOTALER KRIEG – KÜRZESTER KRIEG" ("total war – shortest war"). Envisioning the Nazi banners and waving swastikas, sent a cold chill up Willem's legs. A total war meant warfare that included all civilization-associated resources and infrastructures. Shortest war meant an escalation of lives lost. More murders. Once again Willem's focus returned to the clock. How many had already perished in the Warsaw ghetto? From the Bialystok ghetto? Salonika? Other places? How many were gassed and burned in Auschwitz-Birkenau? In other extermination camps? Too many! Too many! He wanted to break things and howl like a foghorn. "Stop! Stop! Stop!" His hands clenched into fists, his nails digging into his palms drew blood and he knew there was nothing to say to anyone. Not with shouting. Nor pleading. Words were of no use. Do some good. He replayed the MOP plans in his head.

Willem continued to make mental notes of the tragedies, offloading his mental anguish to the clock when it was too painful to share with Jan. It was in the silent, unspoken moments he swore with his life he would never stop resisting, even onto his death. Willem knew that up against Hitler's army, what he was planning, the bombing of the registry building and destruction of incriminating lists, was merely a spit in the sea. But, if through the saliva of one mouth, one human being, was saved then Willem had done right by the memories the clock had generated. Very soon, the day would arrive when the plan would be implemented to do away with the lists the Nazis used to check for fake IDs for Dutch Jews and others on the SS watch lists.

The smell of smoke from a neighbor's chimney seeped through a crack on the windowsill. Sneaking a peek through the side of his blackout window, Willem wondered who had lit a fire in their fireplace, an illegal act during the blackout. Was it a mother helping an ill child stay warm? What would cause such a risk?

Suddenly distracted by Jan, waking from a deep sleep, Willem heard, "you still awake? Come to bed?"

"A minute... maybe two." One thought leads to another. The thoughts, a million-man firing squad, wouldn't let him rest. In a perpetual state of exhaustion from lack of sleep, the thinking wouldn't stop. How do you sleep when so many are dying? He felt for the clock. How can those foul, foul animals sleep at night? Hitler, you brutal tyrant, why have you no mercy? No decency? What kind of psychotic madman does what you're doing? There is nothing but hatred residing in your cells!

"Willem, it's been way more than a couple of minutes. Come to bed," entreated Jan, patting the pillow on Willem's side of the bed.

Willem, ignoring the plea, stared into dark space, images rolling through his head like a horror movie.

Jan, not to be deterred, stretched, got up, and went to Willem. Putting his hands on Willem's back, he kneaded the tight muscles. "Come on, I'll give you a nice massage." A few more firm strokes and Jan slid a hand down Willem's arm to grab hold of his hand. Leaning over, he kissed Willem's cheek. "Come, lie down." Gently coaxing Willem to their bed, he had him position himself facedown. Straddling his hips, he gave Willem a massage until his breathing slowed and his body twitched in what Jan feared were nightmares that threatened to wake him.

The evenings continued like that while the days were occupied with finishing up the plans. It was March 20th, a week from the day to stand up and be counted. The finalization of every aspect occurred at Bet's on Tuesday, March 23, 1943. Later that same day, a fabricated surprise birthday party was held for Jan in the Café 't Mandje. Present was the MOP resistance group, also present Ans van Dijk. Jan kept a distance from her.

Sjoerd, pretending to have had one too many, cozied up to Ans who was at a table with another woman. "So, I see the great millinery proprietor is gracing our party with her presence," he slurred. Wiping the sides of his mouth, he wobbled and sat. "A bit too much… you know." He tipped his hand like taking a sip from a drink. "Mind if I sit?"

Ans gave a lopsided counterfeit smile to Sjoerd. "It appears that question is perfunctory. You seem to have already taken a seat."

"Kaatje," the woman with her, held out a hand of introduction.

Sjoerd, in good theatrical form, took her hand to his slobbering lips and planted a wet kiss on the back of her hand. "And, I am Sjoerd, my dear. Lovely to meet…," he sagged to the side, then jerked as if to catch his balance.

Kaatje wiped the drool from her hand.

Ans cynically rolled her eyes, sliding her chair to create

some distance from Sjoerd.

Might as well put it on thick. Distraction is the best form of relief. A quick side-glance over to where Willem, Jan, Frieda, and Johanna sat, Sjoerd was sure he could see Willem biting a lip to prevent himself from laughing. Sjoerd knew there was nothing funny about buddying up to Ans. Nothing amusing about anything he and the MOP gang were involved in. Not understanding why Ans would show for Jan's pretend party was a curiosity. If nothing else he wanted to occupy her ears, to keep them diverted and emptied of any slipups.

"A new friend?" Sjoerd looked from Kaatje to Ans.

"Hardly," derided Ans, "a fond customer. From, well… never mind."

"I frequented her lovely shop. This," Kaatje pointed to the brown felt cloche on her head, "is one of hers."

"A rather nice flower design," Sjoerd reached a hand to Kaatje's hat, tilting it sideways on her head. "Oh, my clumsy hand. My apologies."

"You are a bumbling idiot." Ans reached for the hat to correct the mishap, her eyes shooting needles at Sjoerd. "Let me fix that," she directed her comment to Kaatje.

"I sincerely," spittle flew out the sides of Sjoerd's mouth before he completed the sentence, "do apologize." He wiped his wet face with the back of his sleeve. "Perhaps, I've overstayed my welcome."

"I certainly agree with you on that point," caustically

burned from Ans.

Kaatje looked on, an embarrassed glow covering her cheeks.

Attempting to rise, he awkwardly stood, shaking the table as the women grabbed their drinks. He bid them adieu and wobbled off to Willem's table.

"Have another," said Willem, as he passed a glass of water to Sjoerd. "The best hard stuff," he said in a loud enough voice, going along with the pretense. The levity was a relief. Good old Sjoerd to turn this into obtuse entertainment.

Sjoerd winked before quietly saying, "I don't think the birthday boy will be bothered. They're not about to slide their way over here any time soon." For good measure he floundered in his chair, looking like he was about to fall over.

"Yes," laughed Jan, softly responding, "that was a perfect gift."

"Speaking of gifts," Willem's tone turned serious and in a lowered voice, he muttered, "if anything should happen to me—"

"Nothing's going to happen," interrupted Jan, now dampened like Willem.

"Hear me out. As all here are my witnesses, it's important."

Willem's directed attention at Jan made Jan's stomach irritably bubble. Waiting a minute, he calmed when he heard the tenderness in Willem's voice.

"The clock is my gift to you."

Sjoerd and the women understood. Johanna knew the story.

She had relayed it to Frieda as well as Sjoerd. All were tearing up.

Johanna broke in, questioning, "why bring that up now?"

"Seemed to follow appropriately, as a gift," smiled Willem. "But seriously, it's been on my mind. And... well, you never know. What we see every day. The violence. The people who randomly disappear. The insecurity we live with, especially as homosexuals."

"Point well taken," abruptly came from Frieda, wanting to truncate the conversation from turning maudlin. No one wanted to speak the unspoken about the risks. Or allude to them. Tonight, was a night to forget, or at least try. A movement across the floor caught her attention. Ans and Kaatje were leaving.

Taking the cue from Frieda's stiffened posture, "okay, darling, say your speech to lover boy and let's get it over with," piped in Sjoerd.

Willem also got the hint. "Jan understands why. That is one object that needs no words."

"I beg to differ," Jan said, reaching for Willem's cheek. Caressing it, he softly said, "what did that Russian say?"

Frieda's attention still preoccupied watching Ans head out, caught only the last two words Jan said. Her palms grew clammy. "Russian?"

"From long ago... you know, what I told you about the clock." Johanna offered a word of comfort, "it's a loving gesture what Willem is doing. Poignant, to say the least." Reminded of the bittersweet gift Willem received from Oscar, her sight became blurry.

"Oh, we're still talking about the clock." Frieda's breathing eased.

Willem looked to Jan. Then Johanna. Seeing the liquid pooling in Johanna's eyes, he said, "Johanna why don't you say it. You remember what you told me." He knew neither of them would ever forget.

Johanna sniffed in the tender moment. She sat still. Head held up as if looking beyond the second floor where the meetings took place. Way up to an invisible God in the skies. To the heavens above where prayers are heard. "Do some good."

Knowing what the next week would bring, they all breathed in, do some good.

*　　*　　*

Stress and tiredness had proportionately increased the growing dark circles under Willem's eyes, as March 27th approached. Willem's loss of several pounds since the beginning of the month concerned Jan. Jan was worried that Willem would be tired and distracted tomorrow; it was the day the MOP plan was being implemented. Despite worries, they both knew there was no turning back. The plans had been gone over. And over. They were ready.

"Come, let's have a drink." Jan motioned Willem to come sit down at their table. "Calm the nerves. A shot of relaxation to help you sleep." Without receiving an indication from Willem, Jan poured a hefty glass of gin and handed the gift from Frans, to Willem.

Willem looked at the clear liquid swishing in his glass, a never-ending reminder of his father. It had been a long time since he'd dwelled on his painful past. As soon as images of his drunken father entered his consciousness, he let them go. Think of something else. Do something else. He knew that booze could act as a reminder or a distractor.

Jan poured himself an equal amount to what he'd given Willem. "That should do us nicely."

Rubbing a finger over the room temperature bottle of Hollandse Graanjenever, Willem thought of Frans mentioning that it was for a medicinal purpose to help bring a good night's sleep. "Frans gave a bottle to everyone on the team. Said it was distilled by producing malt wine and then something about, what was he saying, about herbs being added?" smiled Willem, the image of Hendrik was now restored back in his memory banks, to a locked vault labeled, images to forget.

"I think he said it was to hide the flavor. The old pedantic showoff," Jan affectionately jested to make light the heaviness they both felt. "Juniper berries are used, so he says... So what!"

"I know. That whole long spiel about some false tradition... something to do with a Dutch alchemist claiming he invented... what a bunch of nonsense," yawned Willem.

The yawn was infectious. Jan's mouth opened wide and

took in a long breath that ended with what sounded like a kitten wanting food.

"Repeating Frans' tirade about the benefits of gin is what will put us to sleep faster than the drink," grinned Willem. "And what the hell did he say about... oh never mind. I had no idea what the hell he was talking about."

"Me neither." Jan took a sip.

Willem raised his glass, "Wait a minute. A toast."

"Yes," Jan licked his lips.

"To success," said Willem, his glass ringing against Jan's.

"To success... and all that it means." Jan tasted the smooth, subtle juniper flavor, glad that it didn't burn like other hard liquor he'd occasionally imbibe. Neither one of them were regular drinkers. Willem rarely venturing beyond a little wine or beer, hard liquor was for special occasions. Tonight, certainly warranted it.

"And to our professorial printer, Frans, a hearty thank-you."

"That's probably why he was so loquacious," laughed Jan.

"Why is that?"

"He's a printer. All that intake. Something has to come out."

"He's a good man, that Frans," said Willem, finishing his drink, before another yawn.

The liquor did the trick. Loosened up and tired, they went to bed. Middle of the night Willem woke and went to his desk. "Bring me luck, old guy," he murmured softly, as he rubbed the clock like it was possessed with a magic genie.

## CHAPTER TWENTY-FOUR

No longer painting. Nor writing. Not involved in sitting down with friends over a cup of tea, nor a meal, Willem's life had been reduced to a concentrated well-thought out plan. Interest in the things that used to capture his attention, like walks in nature, smelling its perfume, feeling its textures, communing with others hiking along paths, had been substituted with attention to watching people. Before, it was something he used to love to do. Walking outside in the fresh air, sitting on a park bench, or involved in outdoor painting, he had enjoyed noticing demeanors, the language the body expresses that speaks clearly about relationships. Soft voice tones, handholding, skipping, distances between couples, closeness of a parent and child, clinging, and all the patterns and forms of clothing that they wore told him so much about how people interacted, what they liked and didn't care for. He had reached acclaimed success as a painter and writer by paying attention. To people out among the living, the artistic design in the skirts, women wore, the curvature of scarves around necks, the flow of material, the buttoning of a tight-fitting sweater, the nuisances and vagaries that come unexpectedly with the tide of life, rising and falling, ever-changing. Yes, once his life held an array of colors, sleepy and crescendo symphonies, the aroma of freshly baked bread with melted butter, the feel of soft soil beneath his bare feet, all within differing viewpoints of metamorphosis. That was then. Now his focus was tunneled, through the thoughts in his head and people-watching had turned into paying attention for spies, snoops, undercover Nazi agents, and, sadly, Jews turning against their own. What used to be a pleasurable leisure activity had become a watchful-and-prompt-to-meet-danger necessity for survival; it was no longer relaxing recreation.

Willem had been at war for as far back as he could remember. With his family. With bullies. With anti-Semites. With prejudice and bigotry. His strategy to level the playing field manifested before him, starting with the uniform hanging next to him. Tonight, he would dress as a police officer and march his team into the Municipal Office for Population Registration. He felt paradoxically settled with the anxiety in his gut, if you can't get rid of it, might as well make friends with it, he convinced himself. He'd learn to live with the paradoxes, the differing sides to his emotions that counterbalanced him. He'd long given up seeking upside emotions like excitement, happiness, and joy; he knew all too well disappointment was never far behind. Hope is a double-edged sword. He knew there were no guarantees.

The uniform represented the fifteen men and women who would partake in the do-or-die activity. Not all would be directly involved in the bombing, some helped with behind the scene jobs, setting up hiding places, assisting with uniforms, supplying Karl with the chemicals he needed. Each person involved was a known and committed resistance movement loyalist.

After today, Willem's life would not be the same. As long as the Nazis reigned, he'd be looking over his stiff, knotted shoulder. Never trusting anyone but a handful of longtime friends, the ones who he knew would rather sacrifice their lives than betray a friend, the very idea to them was unconscionable.

He reached for the uniform, feeling its thick texture, the firm, double-layer, charcoal shoulder boards and slid his hand over the braided pattern. His eyes roamed from the jacket to the pants, down to the polished boots on the floor. The hat and a gun, the last parts of his disguise sat on his desk, next to the old gilt clock. The proximity of the objects, so close together, sent a prickly sensation to his skin. His eyes moved from the face of the old stilled clock to his wristwatch. A warm flush moved through his chest. His heart sped up. It was time to go. But first, he had something to check, something vital.

He slid his bed over several inches, bent down, and gently tapped a tightly-fit floorboard that only at close view showed the slight fingernail abrasions at the side. He elevated the board just enough for him to slide his hand in. He felt for it. What he wanted to keep, not just for future writing were he to live, but as a testament to those who perished. Remember us, that's what he titled his notebook. Remember us. That's what was written on the note from Oscar. The note that came with the clock. Willem had no guarantee he would live through the night and were he to die, this was his legacy. The only thing of worth he felt he had to offer a future generation, the value of remembering the lives that were unjustly truncated. The millions upon millions of lives.

Discerning that his journal was safe, he returned the floorboard to its place, put the bed back and went through his mental list of things to do, one last time. The room looked normal. A large sack with the neatly folded uniform and accouterments had been packed and stood ready by the door. All else was in order, as he ran his hands over the old gilt clock before heading to the rendezvous destination. Jan, who was assigned to help Karl, would meet him there.

*　*　*

It was a cold, clear night with the sky filled with a million twinkling eyes shining down on a small army of brave members of the Dutch resistance as they broke into the Artis zoo; it was just outside the civil registry office at Plantage Kerklaan 36. Of the three entrance gates to the zoo, the one farthest from the main roadway was the penetration point; it was a distance from the busy thoroughfare where a Nazi night patrol passed. Willem put a finger over his mouth and outstretched his palm, indicating to keep quiet and wait. Wait to be sure there was no one inside the zoo, guarding it or tending to any of the animals.

Huddled together, the temperature of their jittery overheated bodies rose, a discomfort to be ignored as sweat dripped and evaporated in the night air. A low grumbling, what sounded like a lion stirring, generated lip-biting, breath-held anxiety. A swishing sound and the rustle of branches, perhaps an orangutan descending from a perch to settle into its bed, was heard fairly close to where they had settled in a heavily landscaped area, behind tall bushes. Waiting to be sure no footsteps followed the noise where silence infiltrated the space. An unearthly quiet to experience in a zoo. A very long couple of minutes passed when a grunting noise broke the stillness. It sounded like a hungry pig but Willem knew it could also be a vulture that makes that kind of sound, sounding similar to a pig or a barking dog. When the deep-short sound changed to a raspy drawn-out hissing, Willem knew it was a vulture who must be fighting for its meal. Some unfortunate critter must have landed in its cage. Images of vultures circling above carrion left a pungent taste in Willem's mouth, as the squawking silenced and the zoo once again stilled.

Willem smiled when he saw the half-moon reflecting in Sjoerd's eyes, his face holding a beseeching countenance as if in prayer. Willem wanted to ask him if he was praying but instead, he held firm to the order he'd given everyone during preparations the day before. Bent on preventing Nazis from identifying Jews marked for persecution, arrest, forced labor, and death, wanting desperately to accomplish their mission, Willem told them to; "remain frozen until you get your cue."

The first cue came when all activities had long ceased at the registry building. They had arrived at the zoo well after dark, long after the Municipal Office for Population Registration was closed. They waited to be sure there were no after-hour stragglers returning to work. No one needing to enter the building for a record. It was well into the hours when the city calmed into curfew, an unlikely time for there to be interruptions.

While the others stayed back, Willem, Gerrit, Frans, and Karl slithered in close formation to the building's main door. Willem, in a perfectly-duplicated, starched, police officer's uniform, knocked. A guard immediately at the door was met with heels clanking, raised arm, and a very convincing, "Heil Hitler!"

"Heil Hitler," returned the guard, stepping aside to allow the foursome in uniforms to enter. Obsequiously at attention, his hands shook.

"We need to inspect – there is no time to waste. We have received a threat there are explosives in the building. Where are the other guards?"

"This way, Sir," the guard's brittle voice cracked. Half-running, he brought Willem, Gerrit, and Frans into a back office where two other guards sat, involved in what looked like a break, with food and drink before them. Karl stayed just outside the door, readying for what he needed to do next.

Willem gave the salute. The guards instantly stood, saluted, and looked at the first guard with accommodating quickened-breath anticipation. As Willem, in an authoritarian, condescending tone explained their purpose for being there, he could feel his heart racing. A head nod from Willem and they drew their guns. With barrels pointed at the guards' heads, Karl entered.

"Not a sound out of any of you," commanded Willem.

Karl heavily sedated the guards with phenobarbital. They waited the twenty-minutes for the drug to take effect. "They'll be unconscious for hours," said Karl, looking at the slumped bodies of the three guards. "They'll be okay."

"Good. No casualties," Gerrit nodded approval. The group had been adamant that they wanted the destruction confined to the records. Letting out a breath, Gerrit hand-waved, "Quick, to the zoo. Tell the others all clear."

In accordance with the plan and no time to waste, the guards were dragged to the hiding place at the zoo, an area of thick foliage, back behind a row of wide tree trunks, far enough from the animals to not disturb them. Leaving them covered with leaves and broken twigs, Frans gave the others the go-ahead. The entire group rushed back to the registry building.

There was no time to think. No time to do anything but be present in the heart-throbbing, adrenaline-filled moments that demanded absolute attention. They went to work.

Filing cabinets were tipped over and drawers emptied.

Records were scattered across the floor.

Methodically, the files were heavily doused in benzene.

With clockwork precision, Karl and Sjoerd arranged the series of timed explosives throughout the building. Sjoerd, with the help of other resistance workers, had obtained the explosives from a munitions store at Naarden.

The timed explosives ticked down as the men continued to spread the flammable liquid.

When the last can of benzene had been spilled, they set the files on fire. There were two minutes left to clear the building. With a quick sweep of his right hand, Willem gave the sign to get out. Fast!

With barely a second to catch their breaths, they got out of the building and fled to their prearranged hiding places, all but Willem and Karl. They had one last thing to do.

Spasms moved through Karl's legs and a cramped right calf muscle held him back for a few seconds, a stretch of time that made him feel faint. He banged his leg down to relieve the cramp and hobbled to catch up with Willem, who was back far enough to ensure their safety. When the first explosive went off, Willem grabbed hold of Karl's arm. Waiting to be sure the rest ignited, he squeezed so hard on Karl's limb it went numb. With the accuracy of a well-designed train crossing, the rest of the bombs exploded right on schedule.

Not staying long enough to discern the damage, Willem and Karl ran. Behind them, concrete, bricks, and wooden structures hailed down on soaring flames.

On the night of the attack, no one was caught. No one was injured.

*   *   *

Fumes billowed through the air, inflamed files flew, papers rained down on Amsterdam and people in nearby homes, hearing the blast, peered out through blackout curtains. Some scared that a bomb had been dropped on the city, feared they were under attack and ran to backyard bomb bunkers.

In the haste of the moment attempts to start the firetrucks caused flooded engines that refused to start. Those actions gained the fire time to do greater damage. Once the firetrucks did arrive, the firemen accidentally used too much water, way over what was needed to put out the fire, excessively long beyond what was necessary to extinguish lingering embers.

When the SS arrived to check the exact damage and what documents were salvageable, one high-ranking officer was particularly aggravated when he saw that a good amount of what had been spared by the fire had been irretrievably ruined with water damage. "The water has made these documents illegible," he stomped, kicking wet ash onto his polished boot.

A fireman on the scene bit his lip to prevent himself from laughing.

Known to have sympathies with the resistance, a few of the firemen had been alerted beforehand. They played a vital part that night.

# THE OLD GILT CLOCK

## CHAPTER TWENTY-FIVE

The brave assault on the Municipal Office for Population Registration, the MOP mission, had a significant emotional impact on the residents of Amsterdam and nearby areas. In the privacy of their homes, citizens cheered the attack. Standing up to the hostile, destructive Nazis was an encouraging balm. Many felt proud that the bullying giant had been knocked down a notch. Considered by the vast majority as an act of defiance to protect Jews against unfair treatment, for many, it went deeper than that; it meant standing up to aggression against the Netherlands. It stood as a symbol of hope at home and for other countries oppressed and ravaged by war at the dictate of Hitler.

Instantly offering a large reward, 10,000 guilders, to find the perpetrators, the daring attack also had a significant impact on the Nazi occupiers.

Interrogations intensified, driving fear into the hearts of residents.

Examples had to be made. "You! You there," pointed a German soldier's finger. "Your papers!" echoed in alleyways, on streets, in stores and restaurants. The stench of harassment crept through every crack, into every crevice.

People stayed home.

Doors were banged on so fiercely that several came off their hinges.

The angered Nazis needed targets. Statistics. Reports were demanded from higher-up's in Berlin.

Cruelty escalated. Batons splintered on body parts.

"They will be shot," spread through the streets.

"Many will suffer until we find the Jew lovers," seethed from the vile mouths of humiliated Nazis.

They didn't care how, they simply wanted word to get around that the cruelty would continue until the perpetrators were found. Bodies were left in pools of blood, children were torn from their parents' arms, couples were ripped apart, men carted off, women raped.

Orders to the staff at the registry office demanded they work round-the-clock. "Clean the mess. Restore it to order." So more Jews could be identified and carted off to the killing machines, the workers were threatened, "hurry up or you'll be sent with the Jews."

Terror rained down on Amsterdam.

Hitler was watching. Anton Mussert, who Hitler had declared to be the Führer of the Dutch people, was ordered back to Germany, for what he was told would be, "your last meeting with Hitler."

Goebbels got word from Heinrich Himmler, after a meeting with Hitler. "He wants you to spin the propaganda in our favor. Underplay the destruction. We need heads... numbers..." Dead Jews was what he really meant. "Hitler is not happy."

Resistance workers hiding Jews took extra precautions. Prying eyes were everywhere. Deceiving ears listened; their mouths professing loyalty, up until the threat of punishment. Interrogations were ruthless, a quick death was not an easy out. First torture, prolonged and ruthless, then execution.

\*     \*     \*

Rumors seeped, like water through a sieve, arriving to the hiding places the next day. Willem, Jan, Gerrit, and Karl were in the attic of Cornelis de Vries' farm. He was a resistance worker, a good man who Frans had helped with documents. His wife and her parents were Jewish, which meant his three boys were also considered tainted. He was indebted to Frans that his wife and sons were now safely residing in America. He had stayed behind to tend to his elderly mother, Beatrix, who lived with him. His small farm had a barn with an older milking cow, that the German's didn't want and a garden, growing potatoes, other root vegetables, and fruit. Additionally, with the three chickens he'd hidden from the Germans, a good amount of food in his larder and enough water in his well, they could all make do for a while.

The Nazi-controlled newspapers played down the story but

that didn't stop information from spreading. The morning after the MOP mission, the four hiding in Cornelis' attic were exhausted. None had gotten any sleep from replaying the events and wondering if everyone made it to their hiding places safely. Each person or group knew only where they were to go. The least amount shared the less chance of revealing anything if anyone was taken into custody. None were deluded about the Nazis' interrogation methods – torture chambers they were called. The best of men broke.

Not having had a good night's sleep in weeks, Willem's sallow complexion held deepening, dark circles under his eyes. As neuron-sparked energy pulsed through him, he tapped his foot and rubbed the tip of his nose raw. He knew the Nazis would be out in full force looking for him and the others. The strange place brought new, unfamiliar sounds, there was no way for him to relax or try to get some sleep. Jan was just the opposite and had trouble keeping his eyes open as they talked and rehashed the events well into the night and early morning when Cornelis came up with news.

Arriving holding a tray with food and drink, "mother fixed you boys up a little snack. Scraped together some ingredients she had and made a loaf of fresh bread. And that there," he motioned with his forehead to the small bowl of yellowish-orange jam, "is pear." A proud smile lit up his leathery-wrinkled, prune-like face. "Had a crop of big juicy ones. We hid some… you know, to keep for ourselves and friends, like you good people."

"You're a lifesaver, Cornelis," said Jan, reaching for the

container of milk. "Fresh milk and all this." Jan put the milk down and relieved him of the tray.

Gerrit, more concerned with news than food, asked, "have you heard anything yet?"

All eyes were upon him, Jan the only one spreading jam on a piece of bread while the others waited to hear what Cornelis would say.

"Oh, there's a lot of talk alright." He explained that he ventured out to bring some milk to a neighbor who would know. "The Nazis are livid. Dragging people in for questioning."

Karl sniffed in and with a hard swallow asked him, "any idea who?"

"No specific names were mentioned. Sounds like they're just lashing out all over the place. All because they hate the Jews." Cornelis' shoulders slumped, as his attention shifted inward. "Hate to think of what they'd have done were my wife and kids—"

"They're safe?" asked Willem, not knowing they were in America.

Seeing sadness cloud Cornelis' features, Gerrit answered, "Frans helped them. They're in America where—"

"I'm glad they got out and I'm hoping that our actions last night will help more," interrupted Willem, breaking off the segue. He was anxious to get back on the topic. Wanting to know what the fallout was from the bombing, he asked, "you mentioned the Nazis questioning… I was wondering if you heard anything else? Anything about the registry building?"

THE OLD GILT CLOCK

Cornelis leaned forward. "I got an absolute earful. My neighbor has relatives who work somewhere near the registry building. Couldn't get to work so they went to my neighbor's place for an early breakfast."

"Why," asked Jan, finishing the last bite of his bread. He took a swallow of milk to wash it down then added, "why couldn't they go to work?" He cut pieces of bread, spread jam on them and handed them to the others while they waited to hear what Cornelis found out.

"It's a mess down there. The SS don't want anyone tampering with any possible evidence till they can clear it out. They are up in arms. Using all their manpower to find those responsible. People are sneaking around putting up notes, written on them, 'we are fighting back.' Oh, that's got to be churning them up good."

"I'm sure you're right," said Gerrit. "Any information on the amount of damage?"

"Not yet but I'm going to head out soon, to get me some supplies for my broken plow," he pulled a face indicating he wasn't serious. "Funny how it breaks down every time I need an excuse to go to town. If I don't till the soil, those Nazi boys lose some of their food supply. They won't argue with my need to fix equipment to help them." Under his breath, as if not used to speaking the words out loud, he protested, "I hate giving them food when so many of ours aren't getting enough."

"We sure understand that, Cornelis," said Karl.

"Well... okay then, I'll be back and tell you what I find out."

Willem took hold of Cornelis' upper arm and gave it a pat. Gratitude clearly written all over his drawn, weary face, he said, "thank you for all you're doing. For this," he moved a hand to indicate the food, matting to sleep on, and blankets and pillows that must have been arranged beforehand in concert with the resistance workers. "Your help is deeply appreciated."

Cornelis thought he saw tears pooling in Willem's eyes. The clouding in his burning cataracts caused him some doubt. Nonetheless, he said, "you owe me no thanks. I owe you. This is just payment for all you have done to help me." He took a handkerchief from a back pocket in his pants to wipe his eyes and blow his nose. "You sit tight here," he gave them each a warm half-smile, "and I'll be back soon enough."

*     *     *

Six Nazis stormed into the Café 't Mandie, guns drawn, attitudes as stiff as their starched shirts and as harsh as their loud lumbering gaits. An especially boisterous, "Heil Hitler," arm salute, heels snapping together, came from a rotund short, must have been five-foot-three-inch German officer, whose voice was as big as his belly. It spoke a very frightening message to Bet, made worse by the fact Ans was at the bar.

Ans had arrived around forty minutes earlier. Nonstop

chattering about the bombing with questions to Bet about what she'd heard, what she knew, gave Bet a queasy feeling. Ans was blatantly forthcoming when she commented, "plenty of people out asking questions." She pulled back her shoulders, stuck out her breasts, in a self-righteous pose. "With that sizable reward on offer, why not?"

Bet knew Ans was in need of wherewithal. She'd been low on funds since her shop was closed by the Nazis. At least that's what Ans preached. But what if she had been fictitiously poor-mouthing. If so, then where was her money coming from, enough to get by on? Also, it was odd that she was Jewish and yet had managed to avoid excessive Nazi scrutiny and abuse. Not openly spoken in Bet's circles, it lent to suspicion about Ans' loyalties.

The way the fat Nazi officer looked at Ans, gave Bet a chest pain. The prickling feeling around her heart squeezed tighter when the group of six storm-troopers wreaked havoc.

Batons banged stools, chairs, and tables, turning them into splinters.

The mirror behind the bar was smashed.

Liquor bottles were thrown to the floor.

The money drawer was robbed and left empty.

A customer, not answering the question, "what do you know?" fast enough, was beaten. His left hand was smashed, clearly broken by the sound of bones crunching.

A cowering, perspiring fifty-something Dutch patron was at a table alone, nursing a drink, when the obese, frustrated Nazi saw him. Seeing an oblivious smile, like he was either intoxicated or stricken with dementia, he screamed, "you think this is funny, old man?" The Nazi kicked the table, overturning the drink and pinning the man to the floor.

The scared, gray-haired, balding man looked up; a protective hand raised above his face. He didn't have the time to respond when the fat Nazi lost all patience and shot him in the left leg.

"Is it funny now?" He smacked his lips, "you Jew lover. We know who frequents this bar. Homos and Jews!"

A searing pain cut through the man's leg as Bet motionlessly watched.

Patrons slid out the door as the other Nazi SS men searched the kitchen and upstairs areas.

"Please," the old man with the leg wound pleaded," tears streaming down his face, dripping off his chin. "I just come here to drink," his words slurred together. "I don't like Jews or homosexuals—"

"Liar," the officer exploded, gun still drawn he pulled the trigger and this time aimed for death, right through the heart.

Bet jerked back.

Ans didn't take her eyes off Bet before she got up and left.

The murdering Nazi took a cigarette from his breast pocket and as if to no one said, "I'm going outside to have a smoke." Threateningly approaching Bet, he added forcefully, "tell them," motioning to the stairs, "where I went."

Bet felt chilled, the blood running through her veins no longer warmed her. A washrag clenched in her fist, squeezing it with all her might, she wanted to scream. She wanted to pull the gun out from under the bar counter and do some damage. But she knew that any activity on her part, other than staying put and keeping quiet, would be the last action she ever took.

Once the soldiers left, she closed the bar and went to get help from the neighboring shopkeeper. On her way there, she saw Ans across the street talking to the rotund officer. Bile rose in her throat.

At her neighbor's she asked, "can you help?" She explained what had happened. She needed to remove the corpse. Thank God for help that is still left. Later, as she cleaned the bloodstains from the floor and tabletops, she swore she would fix the place up. Everyone welcome. Unless violent. She hoped that day would come again.

\*     \*     \*

Cornelis returned with a pot of soup and hunk of cheese, telling them he'd heard an earful. "The bombs destroyed less than a quarter of the registry office. The estimated damage was to several hundred thousand identity cards. None of the perpetrators have been caught but the Nazis are livid, rounding up Jews and anyone suspect and sending them to concentration camps. Violence has broken out in the streets with innocent citizens, out minding their own business, being shot."

"Revenge." Gerrit rubbed the nape of his neck. No amount of rubbing would work out the tension he felt over all the guiltless being targeted. The only benediction was the vast number that would be helped due to the bombing.

"Any word on the guards?"

"They were found wobbling out of the zoo." Cornelis puckered his lips and pathetically shook his head. "They were accused of being drunk and not protecting the building. They got off easy and were only fired." He yawned and stretched. "I'm tired. Been a long day," he turned to leave then looked back. "Hope you get some rest. I'll see about getting you some clean clothes. Get you out of those uniforms."

"Cornelis," Willem reached for him. "I know you're tired. We all are. Anything else you caught wind of?" He was anxious to know more about any news of damage to the files.

"Hmm," he replayed his day and rubbed his eyes. "Oh yes," he remembered, "someone mentioned that because of the tight stacking of the identity cards, a lot of information had been preserved. There was an enormous mess... hmm," he scratched the back of his head. "Wait a minute, yes, something was said about the estimate of the damage. Figured it amounted to around fifteen percent that was completely destroyed. That's about all I remember," he said, before leaving.

"That's all," Jan sunk back. Feeling defeated his torso slumped. "All this and... how many are left? How many Jews will still be unprotected?" He put his head down in his hands.

Willem put a hand to Jan's back. To help him feel better and give it perspective. "Don't you remember what Cornelis said about what that fifteen percent represents, that's several hundred thousand. That's a lot of lives."

Jan looked up. It did help to get the context.

"And how many were illegible due to water damage?" asked Karl, before including, "we didn't do too badly."

"Agreed," added Gerrit.

## CHAPTER TWENTY-SIX

The attic was windowless, dark, and musty. Safety being the only necessity, the foursome would make do with all of the inconveniences. At least they were able to view the outside through a few cracks in the wooden walls, which also allowed a small amount of light to seep in and brighten the space. The view through the tiny openings was to the front of the house. Cornelis had assured them that no one was expected and the noise from anyone entering the long drive should alert them to keep quiet, to not move. Any noise or movement would immediately draw attention to the attic, which had no soundproofing. Taking turns watching through the small holes helped ease some of the claustrophobic feelings they all felt in the dark, crowded space.

It was their second day in hiding, the 29th of March, at what Willem assumed was a little before daybreak. The lack of any news of the others who had been involved in planning and carrying out the bombing was a mixed blessing. Not learning of any bad outcomes allowed the foursome time to unwind and breathe, to even catch some sleep but the vacuum created from the lack of information made them nervous. They talked and repeated back what Cornelis had shared. The Nazis' repulsive bragging had spread like ignited dried compost. There were no surprises in what the foursome heard the Nazis were doing on the streets and in interrogation rooms.

"That's enough of that," said Jan, wanting to steer clear from the discussions of broken bones and blood. "We're here. Nothing we can do about it until we get word and figure out what our next step is. I don't want to keep regurgitating all the—"

"I need to vent," interrupted Willem, elaborating on what Cornelis told them about people being dragged off the street, innocent citizens who had nothing to do with the resistance movement but just happened to be in the wrong place at the wrong time. Some were taken into the SS headquarters, never to be seen again. Some were shoved in the backs of trucks headed for trains and there was no mystery as to where the trains went. The death trains, for if someone made it through the airless, packed spaces after days of no food, or water, they were marched into showers. Gassed. Burned. Willem needed to talk about the women who were raped and murdered in front of their children. Of the babies ripped from the breasts of feeding mothers. The violence was near impossible to entertain. Yes, he needed to say things, like, "how could a human being do that to another—"

"Stop!" Jan had heard enough. "That's enough!"

"It's not enough," resounded Willem. "It's never enough."

"The talk isn't helping. What good is it doing? It's just upsetting me more," Jan's words came fast and furiously, escalating.

"Me, me, me," Willem lost control. "That's all you're thinking of now… there are others here who are also upset and need to—"

"Okay, now," came from Karl's soothing, calm voice. He was the level-headed one. "Let me have a say here for a minute…" He paused, to de-escalate the conflict, to cool the other two off. When neither Jan or Willem lashed out at him, he continued. "We're all under pressure." Karl's soft, hazel-eyes lowered as if looking away was less directive, less intimidating, like a dog's averted eyes when displaying submissiveness. His words were silky when he said, "we need to do our best to find a happy medium. For all our sakes."

The sound of breathing and wood squeaking from shuffling positions occupied a long silence before Willem responded, "you're right, of course." He reached for Jan's arm. "I'm sorry," was followed by another lengthy pause. "But…" Willem's attention went to their apartment, to his notebook under the floor, his way of venting built-up emotional pressure. He didn't have that luxury with him and so it came out orally, in ways that, in the past, he'd tried to spare Jan from. Feeling Jan's presence so close to him, hearing his breathing slow, he decided that he would let go of the but, which was an excuse for the ranting he was about to subject the rest of them to. Instead, he added, "I understand," to Karl, before affectionately giving a squeeze to Jan's bicep.

Gerrit, the quietest of the group, opened up. "I don't know

why we like to dwell on all the awful things that are happening, forgetting about how much good is being done. The mind is an oddity I will never understand."

"True," added Karl. "Perhaps the brain's function is to remind us of threatening things… to protect ourselves. But then, it's so misplaced when a repetitive thought process doesn't let go when there's no danger."

"But there is danger," Willem piped up, "right here, right now, in this space."

Karl tried to explain. He added that in situations where there are no imminent perils, thoughts create worries about what might happen. "Worrying about something that isn't present just burns daylight. Why get all worked up over—"

"Karl," Willem broke in, trying to contain the reignited anger he felt. He paced his speech so as to not let his reaction creep into his tone. "I disagree. It doesn't have to be in my face, in this attic, for me to know what's going on." A flood of mental pictures sprang forth. "As far back as I can remember, I could never see a time without danger. In school, the whispers about anti-Semitism spreading throughout Europe. Then my friends leaving," his voice cracked. A familiar lump in his throat pressed in on his airway. A sign he was heading into a conversation he knew would upset Jan and so he muted it. He let thoughts of the Levins and Rothsteins float to the ether. "But," his attention shifted to Gerrit, "you're right. About how much good is being done."

A few minutes passed when suddenly Jan perked up and as

if reminded of something pleasurable, laughed.

"What," poked Willem, "are you laughing at."

"Oh, this is funny," his laughter increased, saliva went down the wrong pipe and he coughed. When the coughing didn't clear the spasms, he started to choke. He waved a hand indicating he was okay. It was hard to understand him through hacking laughter when he mentioned something about, "cutting the phone lines to a Nazi detention center."

Karl gave Jan a hearty slap on the back.

It was déjà vu for Willem, remembering when he told Gerrit his plans and Gerrit went into a coughing fit similar to Jan's. But then it wasn't over something funny, no, then it wasn't entertaining at all.

"I'm okay," snorted Jan. "I just thought of... oh, I needed a laugh. Do you remember when some of the resistance workers cut the phone lines," he interrupted himself, unable to contain fits of giggling, making it impossible to get another word out.

The laughter, like a yawn, was infectious, spreading to Willem, who started to chuckle and then Karl. When the three looked at Gerrit sitting there shaking his head, their laughter grew more hilarious. Smiling, Gerrit commented, "it feels so good to hear you all laugh. It was funny," referring to the incident when the Nazi phone lines were cut and one of them was so angry, he'd run out of the building to find the offenders. "The idiot pulled his phone out of the wall and had it in his hand, while stomping around in his big black boots, like a child having a tantrum."

"You saw it," smiled Willem. Not having been directly involved in that event, he curiously asked Gerrit, "you were there? You were involved in that one?"

"I was. Night before. Heard about the reaction the next day. One of the big, important Nazi officers went to use his phone and, well, you heard the rest."

"Big tough Nazi," inhaled Jan, sniffing in and swallowing before he could continue. "The rest of Amsterdam got a good laugh out of that one. Big tough man, screaming and pounding a foot, flailing his arms, like a three-year-old having a conniption fit."

The cheerful moment didn't last.

The hatch to the attic creaked open, letting in light. Cornelis entered, panting like he'd been running. He wiped dewdrops from his jacket. It was unusual for him to come up so early, on the edge of daylight and wearing a jacket. His distressed demeanor was evident by the cursing under his breath and the hurried way he shuffled in. "It's not good, what's happening and," his shoe caught on the edge of one of the sleeping mats and he lost his footing, tumbling on top of Gerrit. Squashed in the already tight area, it took a couple of minutes for Cornelis to right himself and remove his jacket from the stifling heat building inside him. Hot from fear and anger combined, he had just been to the neighbor's house with the morning milk, risking curfew, to get an update before the neighbor went to work.

Gerrit stretched his legs while Cornelis adjusted himself.

"You okay," he asked.

"Yeah, yeah…," Cornelis responded, then shifted his position, his knees bent under his body resting on his calves but he couldn't get comfortable. Physically and emotionally, he was too unsettled. "No," again he paused, fidgeted and twisted his mouth into a crinkled-nose disbelief, the look that didn't need words. His expression clearly saying he wasn't okay, that it's madness what's happening. Senseless. From the dark place where hope never germinates and fear grows, he spoke. "Heard a lot of bad things."

"Go on," anxiously prodded Willem.

"Hate to bring terrible news. Hate to."

"We understand but we need to hear everything. Hold nothing back. It will determine where we go from here," Karl smoothly responded.

"That's right, Cornelis." Willem had an uneasy feeling in his gut. Pieces of an unformed puzzle were coming together, painting a picture he really didn't want to see, a future that he couldn't exist in. "We knew what we were getting into. We certainly know who the enemy is. They have the empathy of a dead snail. No compassion. Those who benefit from deluded self-important peddling of hatred only bring harm to others… oh hell, what is this babbling nonsense coming out of my mouth." Willem stopped beating around the bush and spat out, "they are killing machines! Bent on catastrophic revenge! Deaths of unthinkable magnitudes! And they call Jews pigs!"

They listened to Willem's tirade, what he'd earlier held

back. There it was and what his lips sounded, made it easy for Cornelis to continue. "There was a death at Bet's"

"Bet!" Gerrit sat up straight. His eyes widely dilated, he feared that it had been a close friend. "Who?"

"A patron," Cornelis relayed what he'd heard, all that had happened.

Jan bowed his head.

Karl remained silent, while Willem asked, "is Bet okay?"

"As far as I know, she's okay. They tore up her place pretty bad but she's got a crew in there cleaning it up. Hard to knock her down."

"True," Willem nodded.

"That's not all," Cornelis swept a few strands of hair off his perspiring forehead. "Hitler's enraged. He wants heads to roll and...," he stopped himself. The air was thick and it was hard to breathe. Trying to make room for oxygen to get into his lungs, Cornelis pulled his collar away from his neck.

"We expected that," said Gerrit, filling the vacuity that was devoid of everything but a deep, throat moan from Jan. "You know we expected that but you're having so much difficulty relaying what you heard, I'm concerned you're leaving something out." Without quibbling, Gerrit asked, "are you?"

Cornelis nodded yes.

Feeling lightheaded, "what is it?" questioned Willem, shaking his head to clear the haze.

"Hitler has ordered resistance workers to be shot on sight."

"But they don't know who's with us," said Karl.

"Exactly," murmured Cornelis. He took a handkerchief from a pocket in his pants, wiped his face, and continued. "To them, everyone is guilty. The streets are flowing with blood. Anyone suspected of helping is dead. Or soon to be. Trains are packed with Jews – thousands are being carted off to camps. The numbers are staggering. And Mussert was ordered to Berlin."

"Head on a platter," said Willem. "No doubt Hitler's making an example of Mussert to scare the hell into his team of ruffians... as if they aren't evil enough."

"He's out for blood. Lots of it. The crackdown at Bet's was the tip of the iceberg. Anyone suspected to be a resistance worker is doomed, one way or another," he repeated, his voice growing gravelly.

"What do you mean by that?" asked Karl.

"If they're not shot, they're put in detention cells and interrogated within an inch of their lives. As I said, they want numbers. They're using extreme duress to get names. Addresses." Cornelis, hearing footsteps below, stopped talking. A minute passed. Two. The tension in the room became tangible. Another minute passed and when no boisterous Nazi invading sounds rang out, Cornelis said, "it must be mother shuffling about." If she was up, he needed to get back downstairs, to not offset his routine with her. She was elderly, frail. An hour or two in the kitchen and after that she needed to rest. Lately, she'd been having dizzy spells. Cornelis found her on the floor when returning from town last week. After that, he hated leaving her alone. Especially now when it was too dangerous to seek a doctor's help. "I need to go. I'll be back in a little bit with breakfast and to empty your waste pots. I also have a few more sweaters and items of clothing to bring up."

"Cornelis," Willem blinked away a mote of dust that got in his eye. "I don't want us to jeopardize your mother's—"

"Gotta do what you gotta do. She knows it. We'd both hate it more if I didn't help. She'll just have to try to stay put till I return from being away. I'll just have to work faster," he smiled.

A pat on Cornelis' arm, Willem returned the smile with, "thank you for coming right up here to let us know—"

"Thought you'd want the news more than food," he feigned a brief smile, let himself out, and closed the hatch.

Jan belched regurgitation.

Karl, seeing Jan's haunted look, knew there were no encouraging words to lift the mood. Anything that came out of his mouth was sure to be devoid of his usual lilting confidence.

Even Willem didn't have the heart to unleash his feelings. Deep down, he knew they were in trouble. What good would vapid words do? In that isolated farm, up in the shadowy attic, there was no doubt that they were in serious trouble.

*　*　*

The next forty-eight hours passed exceedingly slowly. It was March 31st and the bad news kept getting worse. Any talk of feeling they'd escape had dimmed. Cornelis had told them about several of their team, not directly involved in the bombing who had been hauled in. Fearful they would talk, the four men in the attic waited in pools of perspiration and wrinkled smelly clothing. Their hideout felt like dugout protection during battle and the enemy was closing in.

Jan hadn't yet entirely given up hope. "I don't believe our friends will rat on us."

"Sorry, but I don't agree," argued Gerrit, the stress evident in his strained fractured voice. "I'm just not with you on that one, Jan. And... what about the guards identifying us?"

"They probably didn't see our faces with our hats pulled down over our eyes. My bet is they were too on edge to even look at us—"

"Don't be so sure of it," retorted Gerrit, annoyed with Jan's attempts at taking the high road when all he saw was a road blown to smithereens.

It was that night the foursome learned that names had been given. By whom and to whom no one was quite sure. It had been quickly whispered in a contact's ear and when later relayed to Cornelis parts were lost in translation. Enough remained to hear that Willem's name came up, in the context of someone questioning, "Where is he?"

Loose mouths blabbed.

Informers overheard.

The Nazis were curious as to why Willem disappeared the

day after the bombing.

Now he was a target with a bulls-eye on his back.

"Who snitched on you?" rhetorically asked Karl.

"Who knows?" responded Willem.

Jan had his suspicions.

## CHAPTER TWENTY-SEVEN

Were thoughts going through their minds, or were they unthinking frozen prey, like animals sensing a nearing predator? Were they so scared they didn't move? Didn't talk? Or were they conjuring up defensive reactions to protect themselves, like skunks spraying noxious chemicals, or cats making their hair stand on end so it appears larger, or do they play dead like opossums? Were their thoughts burned down to ashes like the files they destroyed, or the sad Jewish victims shoved into crematoriums? Would their immediate next step be the ovens at Auschwitz? Or would they be gifted time, to be transported, to arrive in Poland, stiff, filthy, starving, and half-dead to join the hundreds-of-thousands of others so unfortunate as to be stripped of all their worldly possessions, have their bodies and heads roughly shaved, leaving red-raw abrasions, then disinfected in preparation to becoming a slave? Would they be fitted with wooden clogs, if given any shoes and pajama-like rags? If this was to be their fate, how many days would they have, starting in the early morning while yet dark and freezing, clearing land, working on Nazi construction projects, or involved in other demeaning, demoralizing, backbreaking jobs, with a thirty-minute lunch break for a bowl of dirty water with, if lucky, a slice of carrot, a piece of turnip, or some cabbage? And if really lucky the same meal repeated for supper with an ounce of moldy bread. If fortunate enough not to be immediately killed how many days would they have becoming infested with lice and fleas that torture their bodies, driving some to madness? How many sleepless nights would they shiver under leaking roofs, losing a threadbare blanket to theft, or hearing the hacking of a pneumonia-ridden dorm mate? How many rapes would they witness? How many deaths would they have to watch, of a husband, wife, father, mother, brother, sister, child, friend, or some unknown guiltless victim, before the grim reaper came for them? Only to then turn to ash. Would it be better to die immediately? There were many questions, much to think about, nerves to rattle, with nothing to do about any of it but wait. Any attempts to stop thinking was near impossible. The waiting was hell.

The solemn quiet was broken by Gerrit when he put a hand on Karl's forearm and asked, "do you have any second thoughts?"

A long introspection and a glazed-over, faraway look came, before Karl pensively said, "there are lots of thoughts. That can't be helped. But do I regret what I've done, my activities? The answer isn't a simple yes or no. It's more, what choice did I have? In my case, being part-Jewish, as far as the Nazis are concerned, I was doomed anyway. As to joining the resistance, that I don't regret. I couldn't live with myself if I watched all this senseless destruction, ripping families apart, excavating lives—"

"Excavating…hmm," assuming it was a misspoken word; that Karl meant exiling, or perhaps evacuating, Gerrit interrupted.

Karl understood the puzzled look on Gerrit's face, the way his eyes squinted when his brow wrinkled. "That's how I see it," he went on to explain, "the overt and stealth ways to uncover Jews, through paperwork, through interrogations, through spies, you name it. They want to dig up all the Jews and exc—"

"Kill them," interrupted Willem, wondering what a Jew in hiding must feel like, the ones not yet dug up, as Karl so crudely put it. It was a fit example that made him clench his jaws. "Bastards! No-good, goddamn bastards!" He slammed a fist into the wall.

Jan grabbed hold of Willem's arm. "Relax… you'll draw attention—"

"I can't relax," he snapped back, "neither can you." Willem looked at Jan's fingernails, once well-groomed, that were now bitten to the quick, drawing blood. Scabs on his dry, dirty arms were picked raw. "Who're we kidding? And," Willem dug his thumb into his right thigh until it hurt, "about that question… any second thoughts? I've not a one! Only regret I have is I couldn't save more Jews. Damn those heartless murderers!"

"Shhh," Jan moved closer to Willem and put an arm around his shoulder. Feeling the heat coming off Willem's body, the taut muscles, he nestled into his neck and murmured, "we may still save more. Who really knows what may happen from here?" He half-believed what he had just said, somewhat relying on past events, times that what he thought was going to happen didn't match up with reality. Many discussions were had with Willem about entertaining ideas, especially worries, that don't come to fruition. How many times had they anticipated something that hadn't happened? It was just that now the odds were significantly against them. It was harder to entertain the slim chance that they'd make it out of that attic without Nazi interception. Shifting positions, Jan pressed tighter giving Willem a one-arm hug. "How about we talk new plans?"

Willem's defeated, limp hand found Jan's and gave it an appreciative pat.

"Plans?" appeased Gerrit. "What do you have in mind?"

"There are more files—"

Jan was interrupted by squeaking sounds coming from the ladder.

Cornelis pushed the attic hatch so hard it flew up, startling Willem. Heart pounding, he panicked when he saw saliva bubbling from Cornelis' wheezing mouth, his quickened breathing making it hard to get a word out.

Half of Cornelis' body was into the attic, "you have to leave," the words heaved from his lips. "They're coming!" There was no time for Cornelis to say more than, "we've been compromised."

There had not been time for discussion with his source, not a minute for Cornelis to recheck and verify. They had to rely on what he'd been told, in a hurry, what someone had risked his life to relay.

As Cornelis lowered his body, Jan pleaded, "can you tell us anything more? Where should we go?"

"I'm sorry men, I'm sorry," he descended further. "All I know is the Nazis found out this is a hiding place. I don't know if they suspect who I'm hiding." His arm reached up for the hatch, his head half above the floor, tears glistened in his eyes when he said, "Godspeed, my friends."

Willem, Jan, Gerrit, and Karl wasted no time gathering the small amount of clothing and leftover food, before dividing it up. Scrambling over each other, they decided to split up and do their best to find safe places with friends. There was no time to disagree. No time for Jan to cling to Willem; he knew their best chance to save themselves was to go it alone. On this point, he would not compromise. Nods concurring, they climbed down the ladder. Once outside the front door, they saw Cornelis helping his feeble mother into a horse-drawn wagon, leaving his truck behind. His best chance of escape was over back hills and forests to a friend's farm, as roads would be blockaded.

Willem embraced Gerrit, and bid him farewell with parting words, "thank you for everything. Be safe, my friend, be safe."

He took Karl in his arms and whispered, "thank you for keeping us sane, my friend. Thank you for all your good work. Stay safe."

To Jan, after kissing him tenderly on the lips, Willem looked into his misty blue eyes, ran his thumb over the dimple on his chin, and warmly smiled the words, "I love you, Jan. See you soon." He knew that filling his last words with hope was what Jan needed the most, to help sustain him through whatever came next. Their thanks and love for each other, was in their glistening, tender eyes and the few seconds more of their warm lingering touch.

Nothing further passed between them as they loosened their hold on each other, stepped back until they were at arms-length fingers touching, then let go. Willem stayed back a few seconds to watch his friends run in different directions. It gave him a small sense of satisfaction that no one would be left at Cornelis' farm when the Nazis arrived.

Willem ran across an open field with a slice of dried bread in his jacket pocket, holding a knotted bundle of clothes; an undershirt, shirt, and sweater. He headed in the direction of a forested area where he would find some protection from what was sure to be a cold night. Past a dairy farm, he came to a field of lime-green sprouts, the first signs of spring to emerge from sandy patches, yet too early for the colorful array of red, pink, yellow, and orange tulip blooms. Soon millions of blooming bulbs would bring magnificent floral displays. He breathed in the memory of his young years when times among the colorful fields brought peace.

His life had gone full-circle and once again, in nature, he needed to find harmonious solitude. He used to think, I am in this alone. This world. Back then the aloneness was a painful feeling of isolation. Now, after years of finding loving friendships and intimate relationships, he no longer felt alone. He ran with the might of the wind carrying him, a heart filled with love, a determination to endure. And if he didn't survive, he had no regrets.

He was out of breath when he arrived at a path leading to a thicket before an oak grove. Next to a pond, he found an old thick towering tree and slid down under its canopy of filled limbs. His muscles ached, his head hurt and he was enveloped in exhaustion, physical and mental. Having forgotten to wind his watch, it had stopped. The sun, at forty-five degrees off the horizon, told him it was nearing four in the afternoon. Fatigued from little sleep in months and even less whilst in the attic, he made peace with his situation and surrendered to his tiredness. Within minutes, covered in the clothing he had with him and dried leaves, he fell asleep on a pillow of rounded dirt.

Willem awoke in the middle of the night to a crisp, clear, starry-filled sky, his body shivering. Hugging his arms tightly around his chest to keep warm, his arms tingled and grew numb. So did his mind, until finally, it had quieted. All that existed, in that moment, was the feel of the soggy ground under his back, the chill settling into his bones, the spasms running through his muscles attempting to retain heat, the night-time sounds of the forest, and earthy smells given off by leaf mold and soil. His stomach tightened, complaining angrily, as he felt in his pocket for the dry piece of bread, he hadn't wanted to eat the day before. He savored it slowly, sucking on a corner to prolong the flavor on his tongue. When its texture turned mushy, he broke the piece off with his teeth and rolled it over his mouth to make it last.

Mentally calculating how many days it had been since the bombing, he figured it was April 1st. It seemed longer, as he planned out his day. The speed of time was an oddity he never understood. How the same sixty seconds changed, so much, depending on the circumstances of a situation was an anomaly. Watching someone choking for a minute seemed like a lifetime whereas the same minute involved in making love instantly evaporated. Then there were the moments without time, like the present, where things happened in one consecutive step after another. His next movement was preoccupied with what was his best bet for avoiding capture. The answer was to stay in wooded ground, away from cities and populated areas. Wondering how many co-conspirators had been betrayed and arrested, he knew the SS would be out in full force. It was best to head away from the westerly waterways heavily patrolled by the Germans. It was also imprudent to head east, which would take him smack-dab into Germany. His best option was to head in a southern direction, towards Belgium.

He didn't make it far before he heard a distant sound of barking dogs. Not exactly sure which direction it was coming from, he kept moving south. The sounds grew closer. The dogs must have picked up his scent. He had no choice but to stay put, to run meant the dogs would be let loose to maul him to death or the lesser evil he'd be shot in the back. He determined his best chance was surrender, so he stayed put.

Two growling German shepherds and a small army of Nazi soldiers surrounded him.

"On your knees," a tall-hefty soldier screamed.

"Your papers!" A small-framed Nazi with a rounded face and an upper-lip mustache that looked like Hitler's glared down on him. Shoving a gun to the back of his head, he viciously seethed, "don't try anything or it will be your last move!"

The loud voice vibrated in Willem's brain – he had no papers to show. Remembering, bring no identification with the night of the bombing, then it's harder to trace who we are, so he said, "I lost my papers."

"Your name!"

Willem hesitated until the soldier grabbed him by the hair at the back of his neck and jerked his head up.

"Your name!" Another refusal to answer and the soldier slammed a fist into Willem's cheek.

On the verge of losing consciousness, he mumbled, "Willem."

"Last name!"

Willem remained silent.

A whiplash jerk to his neck sent a sharp pain up to his eyes. "I will not ask again. The next movement of my hand will sever your spinal cord and leave you like a sack of potatoes, unable to move. The vultures will feast on you while you wallow in regret that you didn't answer."

Another hard pull from the hand holding his hair, Willem gave his full name.

With a joyous celebratory note, the short Nazi exclaimed, "we've got him! This is the very famous Willem Arondéus who thinks he can outsmart Hitler's army." Lifting his chin, he contemptuously pursed his lips when he smacked Willem's head with the back of his fist knocking him over. A foot to Willem's ribs and he raucously resounded, "Jew-lover!" over the cacophony of cheering Nazis, barking frantic dogs, and Willem's sighing moans.

On the ground, trying to catch his breath, the jeering-reproachful sounds from the mustached one convulsed through Willem's body. He took a beating to his head, back, legs, through questioning about who his co-conspirators were. Refusing to answer, they beat him unconscious. He awoke hours later on the cold, hard cement floor of a prison cell. It was a small, grim room, secured by a heavily-locked wooden door. A fissure of daylight came through a small barred window at the top of one wall. Graffiti covered the walls, an expanse of contrasting emotions – anger, desperation, contempt, and hope. Others scratched their marks onto the wall to establish validity that they had existed. Willem felt no need to add to the list of those held hostage, persecuted, and annihilated. He had left his mark in his paintings, in his novels, and in his notebook. He left more than his mark in his notebook; it was also an homage to those he loved, the people in his life who mattered and whose stories deserved a legacy.

Heavy footsteps approached the door to his cell, followed by the clinking of keys. "Up!" an older, tired-looking Nazi soldier addressed him.

Willem grabbed hold of the wall of graffiti to help himself to his aching feet. His legs quivered. He thought they'd give way as he trudged to the door and stood before the soldier. Willem looked at the wrinkled face, housing vacant eyes that were colder than the floor he'd just been on. He wondered, *how many victims did you abuse before you grew old and numb? Did you ever care?*

"Out," tired-looking, pointed a stiff finger to the hallway which Willem assumed was the direction to an interrogation room.

## CHAPTER TWENTY-EIGHT

Willem was marched, at gunpoint, down a flight of stairs, to a basement area, consisting of one long hallway with eight doors, four on each side. One, at the far end of the hall, was open, while the others were closed and bolted shut. The damp passage stank of urine and feces, the stench of fear left behind by unfortunate victims. The windowless hallway, with thick, poorly-painted, chipped concrete walls had a single hanging light poorly illuminating it.

Willem's left leg dragged behind his right, it was too pained and stiff from the beatings and sleeping on a hard floor. Irked by Willem's snail pace, the impatient soldier prodded him to, "move it!"

Attempting to move faster, Willem's left calf cramped-up. A painful spasmodic contraction spread up his thigh muscle to his hip. Unable to put weight on his left leg, he grabbed for the wall wondering if the beatings had caused permanent damage.

"I said move it! You lazy curse!" The tired Nazi suddenly woke up, his eyes darted vitriol, his lips tightened into a smug grin; it was the look of someone going for blood. His patience worn thin, as he kicked Willem in the leg he was favoring, sending him to the ground.

Bounding bootsteps ricocheted down the stairs. Two men appeared next to Willem's tormenter.

"Giving you trouble, Fritz?"

"Get him into that room." He pointed a stiff finger toward the open door.

Fritz? A quick flashing image of an earlier Fritz, the German soldier Willem had helped years ago, came to mind and just as fast drifted off as the two newcomers grabbed his arms and roughly dragged him to the room, adding to the aching bruises covering his back.

Experiencing what he had heard about for years, the horrific rumors of indecent, indignant, hateful acts because someone was born to look a certain way, Willem hated the psychopath at the top who gave orders. Adding to the insult, what in fact gave Hitler his power, were the inhumane servile sycophants that "yes sir'd" his every command, turning law and propriety upside down. Here it was, in Willem's face, casting off any small thread of doubt he may have had about how evil they were.

In the several minutes that Willem had been dragged to the room, he was on the verge of unconsciousness. Weak, dehydrated, no matter his condition, he knew, with certitude, that he would never break. Do what you want to my body but you will never have my soul. As pained as he felt, there was something inside him that held a strong resolve. Determined to never lose his humanity, it was then the fear of dying eased from his injured body. The ghosts of those subjected to injustices surrounded him with a protective cushion of empathy that he rested in. Like Jesus on the Cross, thy will be done. Guided by the light of compassion, he looked up at his persecutors.

Lifted up to sit on a thin, wobbly, wooden chair, with a small supporting back, he glanced around the blurry room filled with bright lights, painful to his eyes, to see a table and two chairs. In the far corner was a cabinet with one open drawer having a chain and strong rope dangling from it. Atop was a wooden contraption with a cutting lever on one side and a leather-belted crimp on the other. He hated to think what that was used for. Next to it was a small electric stove. He had heard about those electric stoves and how they were used to ignite hair. Attached to the upper walls were several rusted metal cleats, he was sure were used to restrain a person's wrists while being tortured. The last thing to catch his eye was a small table with metal pliers and some other tools he wasn't able to identify.

He had been left in the room, the chamber of torment, alone, slumped over, with his head on the table. Waiting for his interrogators, he must have passed out, for some time later he was suddenly awakened by the door opening.

A handsome man in a perfectly-tailored, striped suit entered, composedly closing the door behind him. Blue-eyed, straight neatly-cut blond hair, and a slightly curved nose, he was the vision of the perfect appearing Nordic Aryan. In one hand he held a bottle of something to drink, in the other a pack of Reemtsma cigarettes. He placed the bottle and cigarettes in front of Willem. "Daniël Göring," he said, holding out his hand in introduction. Allowing a smile to form on his lips, he added, "no relationship to our most prestigious commander-in-chief of the Luftwaffe," referring to Reichsmarschall Hermann Göring, head of the air-force.

Willem gingerly slid his hand across the table to meet Göring's.

Göring took a lighter out of his right breast pocket and made some comment about how he didn't indulge but by all means for Willem to go ahead. "I try to keep my breath free of tobacco… I never know when I will encounter the Führer."

The casual, intimidating name-dropping wasn't lost on Willem, neither was the irony of the cigarettes. Well-known to him was the Nazi's anti-tobacco program that condemned tobacco consumption. A German scientist's work that found a link between tobacco and lung cancer prompted Hitler to order the program. It was also not lost on Willem that Hermann Göring, who created the Gestapo, was a heavy smoker and the only intimate close to Hitler who openly smoked. It was scornful that cigarettes were freely used on prisoners as gifts of enticement. Some gift – lung cancer, thought Willem. He looked down at the clear liquid in the bottle then up to Göring.

"Go ahead," Göring calmly said. "It's water. You must be

thirsty."

Splattering water down the sides of his mouth onto his jacket, Willem took no time to inhale the drink.

The man across from him watched as if he had all the time in the world. Unlike the earlier soldiers, he exhibited diplomatic patience. All an act to get what he wanted. Names. Hearing Willem's stomach gurgle, Göring said in an unauthentic-sounding, honeyed voice, "forgive my ill manners, you must be hungry."

Göring's words were a little too pleasant. Had Willem not been in an SS interrogation room, they might have meant something but in this setting, nothing from this deceitful man was to be trusted. Nonetheless, he would eat and drink to try to keep his strength up, so he nodded yes.

Göring went to the door and ordered the guard to bring a sandwich. Back across from Willem, he motioned to the cigarettes, "feel free."

Willem, having enough difficulty breathing through his bruised ribs, left them on the table.

"Ah, you must be honoring our anti-tobacco campaign. A smart man. I heard you were an intelligent man. A fine artist and author. From a good family. Your father helped our cause," he stared at Willem for a response.

There was a response. Willem wanted to take the empty bottle and bash the man's skull. But he remained silent. No matter his anger, he would not cater to the charade of civility.

"Yes, your father's fuel business was a great asset for—"

A knock on the door interrupted him.

"Enter!" Göring commanded in a harsh tone that was more befitting to what Willem felt was the real nature of a brutal SS interrogator, under his pretending-to-be-a-friend mask.

A guard entered and put down a plate with an egg and cheese sandwich, before Willem.

"Bring more water," ordered Göring.

"Yes, sir."

Aware that salutes were missing, the formalities of Nazis' greetings were not present, food and drink were offered and the decorum displayed was a clear invitation to relax and Willem could understand how witnesses or suspects brought in would let their resistance down and talk. Too many were starving. Food had become more valuable than money. The Nazis knew all the buttons to push to achieve what they wanted.

Göring reached across the table and moved the plate closer to Willem. He pointed an aggressive finger at the food. "Eat." His mouth moved into a tight-lipped smile. "Enjoy." His squinted eyes betrayed the motion he forced onto lips.

How much loathing lives under that cloak of deceit? Watching Göring slide his right hand back, Willem did as he was told, quickly so as not to have the food ripped away.

Göring waited for Willem to finish, his look burning into Willem's chilled chest.

Looking down, as he finished the last of the food, Willem's eyes caught sight of Göring's hand, his manicured fingernails were pristine. *How much blood is on your hands?*

"So, Willem, you don't mind my calling you Willem?"

Willem sighed, responding with a head sweep. He saw no need to ignore the man, no reason to needlessly antagonize him. That would come, he was sure, when he failed to give answers.

"I would like to—"

The guard entered, interrupting Göring's next question, one that Willem was sure would dissolve the niceties. A look at his senior was all that came from the guard as he placed the pitcher of water and glass before Willem. The commanding oppressive air had turned too thick for words, the guard knew his place.

"Drink."

Willem complied, washing down the last of the crumbs.

Göring's demeanor changed, he pulled his shoulders back and intently focused on Willem's face. "You can make this very easy for yourself. I am a good friend to have. I trust you don't want to irritate me by not answering a few simple questions." Underneath the spurious facile tone was a threatening message.

Willem's strategy was to offer nothing. To respond evasively. To endure. He sucked in a deep breath.

"On the night of the bombing, where were you?" Göring leaned in.

There it was. Willem's mouth became a desert that the water before him would never quench. Adrenaline coursed through his body. Closing his eyes to cover what he was sure were dilated pupils, a stress reaction he didn't want Göring to see, he mumbled, "hmmm," as if trying to find an answer. He took another deep inhalation to calm his heart rate, scrunched his brow to look puzzled and opened his eyes when he curiously asked, "bombing?"

"This is the game you want to play?" Göring slammed an open palm on the table.

Willem's body jerked back.

"I will get answers!" He stared with the same cold, vacant eyes, as the older soldier who'd brought Willem to the room. "You can make this easy for yourself."

In an undertone, barely audible, Willem groaned, "surely you can understand that I have been beaten, knocked unconscious... my memory—"

"Then we will just have to work on your memory returning. I repeat once more, you can make this easy... or not, Willem Arondéus, which will it be?"

The viper had struck. The foreplay was over.

Willem rubbed his chin and conjuring up his best pleading expression, said, "I forgot the question."

"That is your answer! That is what you have to say! To me!" Göring's taut tone formed rippled ropes in his neck. Heading into an apoplectic rage, he screamed, "one last time and I warn you! The night of the bombing! Where were you!"

Willem's dry mouth made it impossible to swallow. He dared not reach for the water.

Taking the silence as a refusal to cooperate, Göring burst up and stormed out.

Willem sat there. And sat there. Alone in that torture dungeon for hours. The water was gone, his urine and feces were on the floor and he had nothing to clean himself with. Bruised and aching, stiff, with a body temperature running hot and cold, he lowered himself to the floor attempting to sleep. He listened to creaks and settling noises. Muffled activities from the floor above. The pitter-patter of what he was sure were rats made his skin itch. Exhausted, it was impossible to fall asleep.

During the next twenty-four hours in that basement room, Willem thought he'd go mad. Were the others safe? His thoughts went to Jan, the face he loved to hold and caress, his features were animated while in conversations and sultry during lovemaking. He also thought of Johanna, how steadfast a friend she had been through the years, a loyal partner to Freida. The others came and went through his mind; Gerrit, Sjoerd, Karl, and many others whose names had slipped his mind. The cheerful memories mutated to mourning admonitions about treacherous actions. We have been betrayed. Images haunted Willem, he feared the worst.

Within the next forty-eight hours, dehydration was beginning to set in, his urine turned dark and scant, constipated bowels wouldn't move and his lips cracked from a lack of moisture to keep the skin intact. His itching, dry eyes had trouble focusing on the opening door and the two plain-clothed men entering who dragged him to the chair. Weak and tired, he felt a tepid cup placed in his hand.

"Drink it," commanded one of the men with brown hair.

The other with a dirty-blond, straight, combed-back haircut, looked a little like Daniël Göring. Willem couldn't be sure.

Willem had trouble bringing the liquid to his mouth, spilling it down the sides of his lips onto his filthy shirt. One of the men grabbed hold of the cup and brought it to Willem's mouth, tilting it just enough for him to sip all the liquid. The sound of more water being poured told him they were rehydrating him for round two of whatever. Would they question him, or use some of the equipment in the room to assist him to want to talk? Their form of assistance was sure to bring more pain. Another few sips and the room looked less fuzzy. He waited while they moved about, clearly wanting him more alert, to stop moaning and start talking. The sound of a chain jangling, the click of an electrical appliance and unintelligible words were background noise to the coarse rhonchi coming from Willem's airway. More water and he coughed up a thick blob of greenish-brown phlegm.

A disgusted sounding voice exclaimed, "der Mistkerl!"

Willem had heard those words before, his brain translating them to dirty swine. Words for enemies of the almighty Führer and his enabling gang of murderers. More water and he no longer questioned what was being said, by the two thugs, their words were clear as a shard of glass. Finally, the questions came. Again, he deflected, until they, like Göring, lost patience. After that things moved fast. All he remembered days, maybe a week, later, was that he was chained by the wrists and left dangling from one of the cleats on the wall. Stretched, with his toes barely touching the floor, he was given water and stale bread to keep him alive. Alive, if that's what you could call it.

His thoughts were erratic and irrational, he had no idea how his hair became singed, or the tips of his fingers turned red and swollen. The isolation was disorienting. He thought he heard sounds, what he thought were familiar voices. He couldn't be sure. Certainty was no longer a luxury he possessed. He had no idea how he had landed back in his original prison cell, the one that he occupied before going to the basement. What he had endured had been wiped out of his addled mind, all except what he felt in his essence, that he had not revealed the names of his co-conspirators. His loyalty was confirmed when a junior Nazi underling brought him a meal.

"You should have told them what they wanted. They found out anyway." He left a tray of something that looked like mashed potatoes mixed with a little meat and a glass of milk. "Fool," the soldier said, heading out.

"Wait," whined Willem. "Please, what did you mean found out?"

The Nazi turned back and pathetically shook his head.

Willem thought he saw a trace of pity in his eyes.

# THE OLD GILT CLOCK

## CHAPTER TWENTY-NINE

Days turned into a murky grind, the only distinction separating the hours were light and dark, sunrise and moonlight. Time became warped as blooming tulips danced in spring and Willem thought he hallucinated when he smelled the vibrant fragrances of May on the uniform of a Nazi guard who brought him meals. Spring had been Willem's favorite time of year, a time for rejuvenation. Until now it had never been a cliff to fall off of but rather wings to alight on flowering limbs. This spring welcomed nothing but June, the month the trial had been set for.

An eerie premonition filled the cell Willem occupied and with it came familiar voices. They sounded so alive, plausibly real. *Have I been confined and brutalized into hallucinating?* Unsure what was actually happening from what his mind conjured up, he was sure he remembered the guard who brought him a meal mentioning, "they found out anyway." It plagued him. Desperate for an answer, he imagined what it could be and that's when he heard a voice. Johanna's to be exact, so clear and vivid, he was sure she must be trying to get through to him. It had happened before with her, when he'd had his attention on her, only to unexpectedly run into her. I was just thinking of you, to which she would respond in kind and they would joke about being twins. But now, there was no way he could anticipate running into her. Johanna's words grew dim as Willem's preoccupation with what the guard had said floated back into the forefront of his fevered mind, loud and clear, black, bold-printed thoughts on a Nazi symbol blindingly strobed before his eyes. He blinked hard to make it go away, to rid his vision of – "THEY FOUND OUT ANYWAY."

Willem pounded on his cell door and yelled through a miniscule opening by the bolt for a guard to come. He scratched his fingernails down to skin, banged a desperate foot against the door's casing and grew increasingly agitated. "What did you mean!?" He screamed himself hoarse, finally giving up his commotion at the door, pacing to fill the time. Drenched in sweat, he rubbed his forearm raw, drawing blood.

Finally, the arrival of the watery porridge, a slice of stale bread, and pale brown tea but the guard was new, hushed and refusing to so much as make eye-contact with Willem when he put the tray down.

Several times Willem tried to question the guard, "can you tell me if you know what the guard from the…" to no avail.

The guard was already out the door.

Willem had endured being punched, kicked, hung up, burned, sensory deprivation in a dark, rodent-infested room making him rub his skin raw but this, this was breaking him;

despairing that his friends too were in the same predicament. The repetitive thinking drove him catatonic, frozen stiff with worry about the decimation of those he loved. But a tiny defiant voice of sanity still resided in Willem's consciousness. *If you bastards have succeeded in capturing us, you will never have us, our loyalty, you will never rob us of our courage. Never!* His body had been beaten down, his mind electrocuted with deprivation and painful overstimulation and even though he felt like a living corpse, he was steadfast with purpose to hold on to his integrity no matter what. He rested in the sanctity of his belief that his friends felt the same.

Three days after the guard made that comment, the one Willem's waking hours wouldn't let him forget, he got his answer. The same underling who had dropped the bombshell earlier brought Willem his supper. Right away, he was different than all the other guards, making sad, lowered-lid eye contact like he was looking at a wounded bird. Not in the usual get-it-over-with hurry; this guard walked slowly, appearing deliberate, like the walk to view a casket at a funeral. His solemn countenance and manner gave Willem pause.

Putting the tray down on the flimsy mattress next to Willem, the guard took a tired breath. He quickly glanced back over his shoulder to the closed door, then turning back to Willem, his cheeks grew rosy like he was going to do or say something *"verboten"*. He bit his lower lip as if holding back what he seconds earlier looked like he wanted to let out.

Willem grabbed his arm. "Please… what did you mean… what you said—"

"Your friends are here. That's all I can say."

The muscles on Willem's chest pressed in, strangling the air out of him. His throat seized, preventing his vocal cords from making a sound. Struggling to get a breath in, to loosen the constriction, he tightened his hold on the guard. Barely able to utter a sound, he croaked, "how?"

The cold, bleak room turned frigid when the guard leaned in, right up to Willem's ear and whispered, "someone turned on you."

That slammed into Willem's gut like a shattering bullet spreading burning shards of metal through to his back. "The others?" pleaded Willem for more information about who else was imprisoned.

"That's all I know," hot breath filled Willem's ear. The guard stood back and in an audible voice said, "eat your food."

"Eat your food," repeated with breakfasts and suppers for an interminable amount of time. It was all anyone would utter to him. They wanted him fit for what would follow, the propaganda trial for the world to see. More deception.

Overall, Willem had lost close to two months. It was near the start of June when a new Nazi officer entered his cell, chin-lifted and eyes glaring contempt. His orotund voice, authoritatively informed Willem without any preamble, "you will stand trial for the bombing of the Municipal Office for Population Registration."

He concisely stated the crime. Message delivered, he left. Willem knew the underlying message was, you will not get away with subversion against the almighty Führer, you rotten pig of a Jew-lover.

A plain-clothed, sunken-figure-of-a-man was shown into Willem's cell. Overweight, rounded-face, balding, a particle of food was wedged between two brown, front teeth and his unhygienic breath stank. "Adriaan Janssen," held out a pudgy hand, nail-bitten to the quick, extending from a wrinkled-faded shirt cuff and added, "I'm your assigned attorney."

Willem didn't know whether to laugh or send him away, as he watched the man pull his striped wool, jacket sleeve over the display of what looked like a several-day worn and slept-in shirt. A caged animal, Willem had no choice but to hear him out.

Thankfully, though, it wasn't all for loss, for the man had an inkling of compassion, and it was from him that Willem once again heard, "an anonymous traitor turned you in."

And again, Willem asked the same question he'd asked the guard. "Others?" Having been told, "your friends are here," he wanted confirmation. To know exactly who.

"Sadly, yes."

"Can you tell me who?" asked Willem not wanting to unnecessarily divulge any names to a man he wasn't sure he could trust.

One by one, the attorney named the others charged with the bombing.

Willem hung his head, mumbling, "can you do anything to help them?"

"I haven't been assigned to them." Seeing the despair Willem had sunk into, he added, "I'm sorry but there's very little anyone can do," said the defeated-sounding attorney, who at least had the decency to be honest.

Willem wondered how this man came to be in the position he was in, as the more time he had with him the more Adriaan acted like he was also being held hostage. "You're Dutch?"

Adriaan quietly nodded. There was a thoughtful undertone to his resigned posturing, perhaps there had been too much familiarity with others who had been in Willem's circumstance. He exuded a regretful sadness when he spoke and with a simple nod of his head, when he chose not to use words, not to reveal too much, it was as if to say he wished he could do more, not just for the man in front of him but all the unjustly-treated, law-abiding citizens whom he had professionally dedicated his life to helping.

"You were a practicing attorney before the Nazis—"

"Yes," he understood what Willem wanted to know. "It's complicated," was all he would say.

Was he related to a Jew and oppressed into being a Nazi's whipping boy? Was he a Dutch citizen who had been exonerated of some sin against the invaders and this was his punishment? Willem had many questions entering his mind, the most important was *could this attorney be of benefit to me?* Willem was about to test that out when he asked, "can you get a message to the others?"

"I'm not allowed to see them. And—"

"You can't risk it?"

"Correct," Adriaan straightened his jacket and stood. Slumped shoulders and with a concerned frown on his lips, he said, "I can say this, Willem..." Putting a comforting hand on Willem's shoulder, "I will be honest with you," he apologetically spoke. "That's the best I can do," was all he said before taking his leave.

Flat on his back, on the hard, uncomfortable mattress, Willem stared at the ceiling, his thoughts shifting to what was up there beyond the top of his cell in the rooms and offices where decisions were being made. Who decided the names of those carted off in trains? Who decided the people to be shot? Or was there no plan other than to kill Jews, to rid the world of vermin, as they called them and anyone in the way of that mission? What a joke! They, the disgusting-rabid-saliva-drooling monsters, were the ones to be disposed of. Surely not Jewish people and surely not Willem's friends. Jan, Sjoerd, Frans, Karl, Johanna, Frieda, and the others, the names, whirled in his head. The days that followed, right up to the lock on his cell door turning, were blurred. In came a guard with clean clothing and a bucket of water with soap.

"Wash," he slammed down the bucket, spilling water onto Willem's legs.

The water was not clean, rather, rusty, appearing to be from what must have been an old, worn pipe. A dead-man walking deserved no more. Willem's attention went to the swirling water, a few soapy bubbles popped leaving a slimy film on the surface, like the sweat-soaked membrane on his shirt that was stiff and stank from remnants of broken-down body waste. The buttons, molded to the material, were hard for Willem's stiff fingers to undo.

The guard, refusing to offer any assistance, stood robotically, like a wax figure, with lines of repugnance carved on the creases of his downturned mouth.

Failing to get the top button loose, Willem pulled the material apart, ripping it off. The rest of his clothing came off without effort and he washed himself with the small dried out piece of soap left in the water. Given nothing to dry himself with he used his ripped shirt.

When the guard was satisfied that enough dirt and smell was gone from Willem's body, he pointed to the gray pants and beige shirt, he had dropped on the mattress. "Put those on." He had to make Willem presentable to be in court, which meant ridding him of observable filth and body odor.

Feeling the thick, cotton texture from the second-hand shirt, Willem wondered who the former owner was. Was it another resistance worker? An unfortunate Jew? What life lived in the shirt? What man ate meals with his family in the shirt? Tended to an ill child? Walked his dog? Did a hard day's work? Whoever it had been, no good had come to him. Certainly, no good would come to others who would wear it after Willem donned it on his march to the grave. Dressed and standing before the guard, the escort began.

Willem arrived in the courtroom and was seated next to

Adriaan. There had been no trial preparation. Nothing to indicate to Willem that anything but a Nazi kangaroo court was about to take place and this trial, if it could be called that, would be no different. Where are the others? Jan, where are you? Karl? Gerrit? Where are you all? Adriaan informed him to keep quiet; "I'll handle everything."

Noting a different attitude in his attorney, Willem was sure the perfunctory manner was how Adriaan had to present himself in front of prying eyes and ears. "Can I please ask—"

"Shhh," Adriaan instantly swished a hand in Willem's direction to quiet him. On a notepad before him, he wrote, "you will antagonize the court if you sit here talking. Pay attention and leave everything to me." As quickly as he passed the note, he pulled it back adding, "I'm sorry. My hands are tied."

Willem shook his head as Adriaan scratched over the last two sentences, ensuring no one else would see them. Pathetic. Understanding that this prelude was to be the way the preordained procedures would commence it was impossible for Willem to stay focused and to pay attention. It was preposterous, that in a city where law and legal representation were highly valued, where the Paris Peace Conference in 1919 proposed the international tribunal be, that Willem would not have his fair day in court. Regardless of his own personal treatment, his main concern was for the others. He knew what his inevitable outcome would be, perhaps there was hope for his friends.

The circus began with all the usual formalities, standing for the judge, entering the case for the record, and swearing in witnesses starting with the prosecution. He looked at his attorney knowing that any defense presented would serve no purpose, the whole debacle was a reprehensible display of wasted time.

Willem listened to the guards from the Municipal Office for Population Registration, one-by-one be sworn in and identify him as the perpetrator, answering the prosecutor's question, "how can you be so sure?"

Each singularly, when it was his turn on the stand, answered the same exact thing, by rote, as if their responses had been prepared in advance. "He was the one that gave the orders."

Again, the guards, one-at-a-time while on the stand, had been questioned to ensure there was no doubt, the guilty verdict was already evident on the jurors' contemptuously contorted faces. The judge and everyone in that sham courtroom enforced Hitler's will. The law be damned, it was no longer decisive in legal proceedings. Paying attention to this mockery of the legal system nauseated Willem. Why pay attention when it was only churning his gut and so he stopped watching and listening until it was his time on the stand.

In this hell Willem was in, the Bible in his hand felt out-of-place. No God of kindness or love could possibly exist in this court of Satan. Willem had one thing to say, the only thing he felt important and of value. "I take full responsibility for the bombing." It was his unspoken pleading attempt to generate leniency for his friends. If Hitler needed a head on a platter, let it be mine, determined Willem. His plea went unheeded. The others endured similar proceedings. Parodies of courtroom civility and etiquette were played out by arm-raising, heel-snapping puppets dancing to Hitler's tune for revenge. Despite Willem's protestations of guilt, the preordained façade found Willem and twelve of his co-conspirator saboteurs guilty. The verdict, clearly decided beforehand, sentenced Willem and the others to death by firing squad.

On June 18, 1943, Willem left the courthouse with shoulders held erect, forehead lifted, refusing to avert his eyes from the jeers, smiles, handshakes, and joviality over the sentencing to death of those whose only crime was to help save hundreds-of-thousands of Jews in the Netherlands. Escorted back to his prison cell to await his fate, a smile found its way to Willem's lips as he silently thanked Jan, Johanna, Sjoerd, Frieda, Gerrit, Karl, and the others who had helped with the bombing. He also gave thanks to the thousands of other resistance workers who worked tirelessly to help save the lives of Jews.

In the days that followed, Willem was sustained by thinking of those who had been saved. He thought of the magazine articles he'd written to recruit Dutch resistance workers, which amounted to a number close to 200,000 landlords and caretakers helping Jews. That, added to the 800,000 records that had been destroyed, accounted for over a million Jewish people being helped. There was no time for regret. There was simply only time to walk courageously up to the date set for his death: July 1, 1943.

The date he would rejoin Jan and the others and move on to what he hoped was a better place, a world without hatred, prejudice, and persecution.

That same decent guard, who showed him kindness earlier, was assigned to him. By the way the young man acted, Willem wondered if he'd somehow arranged, without asking, to be assigned to the block where Willem's cell was. Perhaps to display a piece of humanity back to the man who had worked for a higher good to help others.

"Mashed potatoes, ground meat, and milk," as he placed the tray down next to Willem. "The usual… but," the guard slid a hand into his pants pocket and pulled out half a chocolate bar letting it accidentally, with a wink, fall next to Willem.

Covering it with his hand, Willem's mouth softly curved up.

An understanding sadness clouded the guard's face, an expression Willem had seen before in those trapped into doing things they abhorred. A stiff, unnatural visor-of-pretense had been lifted and a child stood before Willem, a teenager forced into something beyond his control and acumen. He knew the obsequious demeanor the despot created. He wanted to reach for the guard, to speak what normal unaltered human beings say, those untainted by persuasive propaganda and unrelenting corrupt power. Although that conversation would never be had, between them was an unspoken recognition of the worth of a human being. Not because he is useful or can serve some means but because there is, in him, that light, however dim, that recognizes itself. In Willem, the guard saw humanity. In the guard, Willem saw compassion. Reminded of his precious gilt clock, Willem mumbled for the guard's ears, "thank you for doing some good."

Watching the door close, the chocolate growing soft in his hand, Willem knew he'd never see that guard again. He broke off a piece that had teeth marks on it, the part the guard must have eaten. It made the bar taste sweeter, what the guard had done. Chocolate was a scarcity, hard to come by. In this horrible setting, so was kindness. The kindness, more than the candy bar, was exactly what Willem needed as he waited out his last remaining hours on earth.

The night was filled with bad dreams Willem tried to rid from his mind for they only brought unwelcome emotions. The memories of his father's abuse, bullies' taunting, Nazis' hateful retribution needed to be purged, like pus from an abscess. Working their way out to the ether, the next batch of mental images were filled with love, laughter, poignancy, some bittersweet but none Willem would trade. His only wish, which wasn't a regret, was to see Jan and the others. To embrace them and give the oral thanks he had silently done a million times since leaving the farmhouse. It was not to be and so he lived his remaining time accepting what was. Things as they were, that he could do nothing about but embrace or resist.

On the eve before July 1st, his last night to breathe the fetid stench of prison, to visualize the scribblings of tormented souls going to their deaths, to hear the sounds of tiny rodent's feet,

Willem was surprisingly calm. Stepping into the unknown was something he was familiar with, what he'd learned to walk into without fear. He had his father to thank for entering an alcoholic's unpredictability into his early years. The vacillating moods depending on who Hendrik drank with, how his business dealings succeeded or not, taught Willem that nothing was certain, except change. Just like with his father, what Willem thought would be his experience those last few days of his life weren't at all what he had expected. He still had a smudge of chocolate on the palm of his hand, a reminder that kindness exists in places least expected.

Wide awake through that night, like an old battery running out of electrical juice, his mind quieted, while his senses remained vividly alive. A noise outside his cell and his heart sped, thoughtless rhythms pulsed through his arteries. Feeling the movement of his breathing, the gentle gurgling of his intestines, stimulation in his bladder that he needed to urinate, a cold pressure under his tailbone where something hard poked through the threadbare mattress, the roughness of his dry, cracked skin, the moisture of his tongue, he marveled at the endless inter-dependent elements that came together in homeostasis keeping him alive. Alive. An odd concept, he thought, for he could never imagine not existing. Perhaps in some form, ethereal or whatever, he would go on. Once again, embracing the big unknown, something shifted. An interest as to what was death really? Certainly, the fear of death is some inbred reaction to things he'd been told, a fright factor. Now, faced with its inevitability, drained of emotions that held the pain from his past, sustained by love, he felt not fear but rather curiosity.

The morning came and so did the guards to escort him to the field of fusillade, they laughingly called it. The ground where blood dripped, was what he knew it to be. The place where fright, tears, searing wounds, loss of consciousness, loss of life, loss of bowel and bladder function existed. It was a place where vultures circled above the bodies of lives that once meant something to a spouse, a child, a parent, a friend, a teacher, an entire community. Reduced to nothing in the eyes of corruption, their existence will continue through remaining relatives, those who knew them, and the stories passed down to and by strangers like that Russian gilt clock that found its way to Willem. They will be remembered. The Germans will never erase compassion carried on songs of love.

One guard on each side of Willem, it was a slow march to the firing squad. He was ready. He had seen his attorney and relayed his last words. Not being the only homosexual in this group of resistant crusaders, what he defiantly said was, "let it be known that homosexuals are not cowards."

All had been done. All had been said.

Standing on the dunes of Overveen, on the eastern fringe of the North Sea dunes, the weather changed from overcast to sunny. The last sight Willem would see before he died was ten Nazi soldiers wearing feldgrau wool uniforms. Like in his past, when noticing patterns and geometrical forms on material inspired his art, his eyes took in the pressed front pockets with scalloped flaps, creases that sided the five front buttons and the bottle-green color of the shoulder straps and collars. A dull ray from the sun bounced off their steel curved helmets. Positioned with their Gewehr 41 rifles aimed and ready to fire, they stood atop the lush green expanse and pointed their weapons at the man who stood tall and proudly lifted his head.

The command was given and shots were fired. More than were needed to mortally wound a heart and bring a body to its knees, fallen and forever immobilized. Willem's lifeless body slumped on the grassy mound his hand still smeared with an imperceptible spot of chocolate. Dew droplets merged with the dissipating heat of his body, evaporating into mist. A light breeze circled a few loose leaves.

On that July day, at the beginning of a new month in the Netherlands, as the sun drifted beyond the horizon, a breath of wind entered an empty apartment through a cracked space on a windowsill. A blackout curtain drifted against an old broken clock on the nearby desk and if anyone were present, they would have sworn that the stilled hands, on that broken-down timepiece, moved.

# EPILOGUE

Whether or not Willem found out before his death how the Nazis discovered his involvement in the bombing remains unknown. Here is what is known of what occurred a day or two before Cornelis told the foursome in his attic that they had been compromised by an informer.

Commotion in the first-floor entrance hallway of Willem's apartment building alerted the landlord trouble had arrived. A loud knock shook him out of the comfy chair he'd been relaxing in, a book he'd been reading fell to the floor. Behind the peephole stood an intimidating group of uniformed SS men beside a medium height, heavyset plain-clothed man with a dour expression. A nervous twitch ran up the landlord's left thigh.

The SS stormed up the stairs to Willem's apartment and waited while the confused, pale landlord struggled with the key in the lock. The sound of jangling metal preceded a snap, the landlord's hand was shaking so ferociously the key broke off, jamming the lock.

"Out of the way," a fist slugged the back of the landlord's head sending him into a dizzying whirl.

The medium-height, overweight man, in a gray-flannel striped suit, with uncharacteristic Nazi facial attributes by Aryan standards, sternly commanded, "kick it down." Focused eyes on his rounded face never left the action of the two SS kicking blows. Clearly not fast enough to his liking, his hairy eyebrows spread apart, his eyes became so large they obscured his forehead as he whipped out a gun from its holster. Shots were rapidly fired at the lock. When that didn't yield to further kicks, more bullets flew into the knob and door jamb, splintering wood.

When the Nazi in gray-flannel kicked the wooden fragments to clear the way, the landlord stumbled back and tiptoed down the stairs away from the ruckus. A large enough space was made for the seven men to move through and it didn't take long for the place to be torn apart. The bed was stripped down to a bare mattress. Drawers were rummaged through with items one-at-a-time emptied onto the floor. The armoire was opened with shirts and pants flung about. The bathroom and kitchen were ripped apart. Nothing was found. Over at the desk with pulled out drawers the fat Nazi saw a remaining object, an old, rusty, piece-of-junk clock, not worth plundering. Furious that they'd come up empty-handed, he ordered them out.

"Move it," ordered plain-clothes to a junior SS soldier who had bent down to remove something stuck in his boot.

As the junior Nazi finished pulling out a splinter of wood, he noticed a pointed scratch on the floor that matched the width and configuration of the metal bed frame leg. Sliding a hand under the bed, "Sir," he looked up at the rounded face, "nothing there."

Gray-flannel glared down at him. "Move the bed!"

Small fingernail scratches were seen on the edge of one of the boards.

Gray-flannel's protruded overabundant lower lip, drooled saliva when he forcibly commanded, "pry that up!"

There it was. They had hit pay dirt! Willem's notebook.

A broad smile crept onto senior's lips as he unblinkingly focused on the pages. Thumbing through the content of what Willem had written; the plans, the names, he went into fits of knee-slapping glee. "Look at this," he squealed to no one. The names of all involved! There is sure to be a promotion in this!"

That was how Willem's co-conspirators were found out. Although the person who backstabbed Willem and set in motion this epoch betrayal remains unknown, suspicions were cast at a particular person.

Ans van Dijk, a collaborator and black marketeer, had an acute sense of survival. At all costs. Where she got this from is hard to understand as her upbringing was not different from other loyal resistance workers. She was the daughter of Jewish parents. She was married once and divorced, after which she began a lesbian relationship with a woman named Miep. It was during this relationship with Miep that Ans achieved a strongly desired goal to open a millinery shop in Amsterdam. The timing was unfortunate, for soon the Nazis invaded and occupied the Netherlands and Ans lost her store; it was closed by the Nazis in 1941 as part of the seizure of Jewish property. Devastated that Jews weren't allowed to own businesses or even work in retail shops amidst other restrictions, her dream was further shattered when her partner fled to Switzerland without her.

Ans found ways to make a living, ways she didn't openly share with those she socialized with at Bet's café. But it didn't take much intelligence to notice that collaboration with the Nazis wasn't beneath her. Strange interludes, gestures, and facial expressions when in contact with Nazis lent to suspicions that she had been in communication with the SS and therefore could not be trusted. Jan knew this but when he confided in Willem, it was Willem's good nature that discounted it. After all, she was Jewish and a lesbian, not a reliable source for information. Jan tried to persuade Willem that was all the more reason for ass-kissing.

It was Bet's belief that Ans, hanging around her bar after the bombing and being present during the event that followed, when the bar was ravaged and a man killed, was suspicion enough. Ans had, in fact, said things to Bet at that time, in an undertone, that gave Bet a bellyache, "where is everyone? The place has been vacant since the bombing."

"Vacant?" replied Bet, "look around." She motioned to the people at tables and others at the bar.

"Where's Willem and lover boy? And that obnoxious Sjoerd?"

Obnoxious! Bet wanted to slap her and was it not for the entry of the Nazis, she might have. Instead, she fumed, look who's talking!

Distrust about Ans wasn't just from idle gossip, especially after seeing her across the street schmoozing with an SS officer. No, that was not just a coincidence. Sure enough, it was later discovered that during the planning of the bombing, Ans had been discreetly arrested by the Nazi intelligence service. Promise to work for the Nazis or be sent to a concentration camp, there really was no choice for the devious woman who was known to be cruel to her own kind. She harbored an angry attitude because of being treated unfairly in the past and didn't care who she took it out on as long as she didn't lose again. She promised. She was released. She went on to pretend to be a member of the resistance, even so much as to offer to help Jews hide and obtain false papers.

The cunning, conniving woman exposed over a hundred people, including her own brother and his family. Ultimately, she may have been responsible for the deaths of as many as 700 Jews, many who were sent to and died in concentration camps. Among her victims, it is suspected were Willem and the others who bombed the public registry office.

She wouldn't get away with it but unfortunately, it did take time for justice to catch up with her. Sadly, it wasn't during the war when she could have been stopped from doing more damage to innocent victims. After the war, she moved to The Hague. It was there she was arrested and charged with 23 counts of treason. Brought before the special court in Amsterdam, she confessed on all counts and pleaded for leniency explaining that, "I only did it out of self-preservation." Sentenced to death, it was appealed and upheld by the appeals court. Her last-ditch effort, requesting a royal pardon, was also denied.

On January 14, 1948, Ans van Dijk was executed before a firing squad. On the eve of her execution, she was baptized by a Roman Catholic priest.

POST NOTE:

Nearby to where Willem was executed, the Erebegraafplaats Bloemendaal (honorary cemetery) is now a sacred Dutch memorial place. None of the graves were originally located there. The cemetery is the final resting place for victims who were executed in multiple places in the Dunes. There, among the list of notable graves, is Willem Arondéus.

In 1945, after the liberation of the Netherlands, the Arondéus family was awarded a posthumous medal by the Dutch government in Willem's honor. In 1984, he was awarded the Resistance Memorial Cross. Additionally, in 1986, Yad Vashem, Israel's official memorial to victims of the Holocaust, recognized Willem as Righteous Among the Nations.

# THE OLD GILT CLOCK

## AUTHOR'S BIO

Paulette Mahurin is an international, Amazon best-selling literary fiction and historical fiction novelist. She lives with her husband Terry and two dogs, Max and Bella, in Ventura County, California. She grew up in West Los Angeles and attended UCLA, where she received a Master's Degree in Science.